A River of Lost Souls

J.C. Cooksey

To Mom, thank you for sharing your cultura and stories with me, especially the scary ones. Every woman I write will echo your strength

CHAPTER ONE
Empty

Three cups of coffee and two bowls of Count Chocula cereal did little to further Isabel's progress. She stared at the blinking cursor that hovered over a blank page. Her laptop never seemed so judgmental. She slammed it shut and guzzled the rest of the chocolate flavored milk from her bowl.

I just need a little inspiration.

Isabel flopped on her sofa and turned on the television.

"The News is always bad. Let's see what terrible thing happened today." Isabel said as she changed the channel to the local news broadcast.

The President was making an address. Isabel scoffed and quickly changed the channel.

"Maybe I'll have better luck with a true crime show?"

Her fingers hovered over the dial, but she hesitated. True crime and murder investigations only fueled her paranoia, leading to incessantly checking locks and windows. She was desperate to find inspiration for her next novel, but not at the cost of her sanity.

Utterly defeated, Isabel resolved to watching *Evil Dead II*. At the midpoint in the film, when Ash Williams was severing his possessed hand, Isabel's phone rang.

"Oh, shit!" Isabel said as she nearly leapt off the couch. Her heart raced in her chest as she looked down at her phone. The number was unknown, but the area code was from her hometown.

"Hello?"

"Estella's dead."

The voice on the other end was cold and familiar. His breath was heavy, and his words hit Isabel like a truck. The rest of his remarks were an inaudible jumble Isabel would only decipher after he had hung up. She blankly stared at the phone, waiting for his words to make sense.

Aunt Estella died?

There were no tears or screams of agonizing loss, just a sinking sensation and a black void that spread from Isabel's chest through her entire body. She opened the blinds and stared out the window. People were walking their dogs and cars drove by as if it were a normal day.

How can the world keep moving, she's gone?

She stared out the window for what seemed like hours watching as the world continued to function without Estella in it.

Eventually, Isabel wandered to her closet to begin preparations for her return home. The majority of her wardrobe was black, which was beneficial for occasions like funerals. She stood in her walk-in closet and searched for something appropriate. Black dresses hung neatly on the rack. For years, she had endured ceaseless teasing about her color preference, often being asked, "Who died?"

If she were asked that question today, she wouldn't be able to issue a snarky retort, but would be compelled to say that the last of her family died today.

"Fuck, this shouldn't be this hard. Just pick one," Isabel said, as she ran her hand across varying shades of black.

Unable to choose, she closed her eyes and said, "Eeny, meeny, miny, moe."

She retrieved a black lace dress from the rack and proceeded to toss a few band t-shirts and jeans into her suitcase.

With the methodical dexterity of an automaton, she went through the motions of packing and arranging the flight home. All the while she tried to summon a happy memory of her aunt. The happiest days of her childhood were spent with Estella, but she was unable to conjure any recollection. She couldn't recall a single moment. There was a blank space in her mind where Estella had once been and in its place a cold, empty sensation took root, a sinking hollow ache. She was emotionally numb, which she imagined would be as close as she would come to being undead. Hours fell off the clock, and she hadn't screamed, cried, or had a breakdown. The day continued to pass in a cold haze. As Isabel prepared for bed, she tried again to remember her aunt. There was nothing of Estella left to draw comfort from, not even memory. Isabel drifted off to an uneasy sleep, void of rest.

Cold sweat trickled down her forehead; the nightmare had taken hold. Legs flailing, she tossed and turned in bed. The nightmare was a familiar one that hadn't haunted her dreams in years. It always started and ended the exact same way. She was forced to relive the most terrifying day of her childhood: the day she almost died.

Panic, pain, and fear were cast in vivid detail. Though her waking mind successfully repressed those thoughts, nightmares would not abide what the waking mind would rather forget. The subconscious mind filters anxiety through dreams, plunging the dreamer back to the root of their deepest fears. Isabel was no exception as she was cast back into the river where she had almost drowned.

The river adjacent to her childhood home was unwieldy as it cut past the rocky and brush-laden shoreline. The afternoon sun rested in a cloudless sky. The diffused rays of light cast against the rippling current gave the river a rhythmic appearance, one that belied the dangers lurking beneath. She was helplessly pulled beneath the surface of the water. The powerful current relentlessly thrashed her small body like a ragdoll as it carried her further and further from home.

Isabel struggled to keep her head above the silt-filled waters as the current dragged her downstream, the darkness beneath the surface only adding to her terror. The water was frigid, and Isabel's muscles struggled to continue fighting against the powerful current. The awareness of certain death was overwhelming as the feeling began to leave her extremities. Unable to speak or scream, the only thoughts she could grasp were the words "Help, Help!" which repeated in her mind over and over again as if it were a silent prayer.

Enveloped by the darkness, sinking further beneath the surface, her lungs burned, and her muscles failed. The last bubbles of air floated to the surface; death was certain. Hands gripped her wrists and pulled her up. She was miraculously rescued from the water and carried to the shore. Her savior laid her on the sandy bank. Her vision became fuzzy; blackness filled her periphery.

Consciousness faded as her rescuer's pale, bony fingers wiped the water from her face. She coughed and gasped for air. Her ears buzzed, but she could hear a soft voice call to her.

Isabel.

She woke up in a tangle of sheets and sweat. Her first panicked thought was that she was on the riverbank. She could still feel the touch of the cold, bony fingers across her cheek. She incoherently scanned the room for her rescuer. She shook her head trying to clear the nightmare fog and surveyed the familiar sight of her bedroom. The darkened room seemed surprisingly alien, as dark shadows cast unfamiliar shapes across the walls.

"You gotta be fucking kidding me. Really?"

Isabel looked back to the notebook resting on her bedside table. On the recommendation of her agent, she kept a dream notebook or more specifically a nightmare notebook. Recently, her nightmares were fuel for writing concepts and she often resorted to pillaging her dreams for story content. She turned away from the notebook, deciding to leave that particular nightmare alone. Painfully aware that her recent writing was garbage, Isabel scolded herself for her lack of innovation.

Nightmares in writing could be considered lazy or cliché, just leave it alone. Besides, this one was a little too personal.

She stared off into the darkness. The only source of light in the room, the dull red glow of her alarm clock; 4:00 a.m.

"Ugh, it's too early."

She considered flopping back down in bed and trying to force herself back to sleep. Her flight wasn't until later in the afternoon, and this was a rare occasion when she could sleep in. The pillow was hot and moist from perspiration. She flipped it over and laid flat on her back.

The night was cold and dry. The Santa Ana winds blew in through the open window, the white curtains billowed. They resembled ghosts, dancing with the shadows in the room. They rustled loudly, but the cool breeze was too appealing to close the window. She forced her eyes shut.

Go back to sleep; it was just a nightmare.

But it wasn't just a nightmare. It was a memory which had been long since suppressed.

"Why after all this time?"

The bitter taste of frustration stung the back of Isabel's throat as she considered the question. The emergence of her long-forgotten trauma must have been due to Estella's death. After all, the near drowning had taken place at the river located near Estella's farmhouse. After her parents' murder-suicide, Estella raised her. Before drifting off to sleep, Isabel had tried to conjure a memory of Estella. It seemed cruel that the fist memory of Estella to return was a traumatic one.

Prior to receiving the news of her death, she rarely thought about her aunt. Those memories were a mix of joy and sadness which she refused to revisit. She didn't feel pain or anything else, there was simply a void where emotion should have been. She knew that when the empty feeling in her chest faded, so would the emotional numbness. Eventually, everything would come rushing back in a horrible barrage of memory and loss. Isabel wasn't sure she could handle it. The reality of Estella's death could shatter her; she might go insane. She didn't know when the feeling would return, but she welcomed the emptiness, for now.

The nightmare might have been a manifestation of the emotions she was repressing.

Grief must be stirring up old memories.

Isabel had purposely avoided thinking about her near drowning. Until tonight, she had successfully avoided any recollection of the incident.

She was saved, but her rescuer remained unknown to this day. Estella suggested that Isabel had swam to shore since she was found alone after the incident. Isabel insisted that she had been rescued, but she relented after Estella had her assessed by a psychiatrist to make sure she wasn't displaying symptoms of schizophrenia. At the time she didn't know what the word meant, only that it was the name of her mother's disease and the reason why her mother heard voices and had visions. Her mother's mental instability was suspected as the reason for the disillusion of her parent's marriage. Her father became abusive to her mother and eventually murdered her before turning the gun on himself. This was the shadow that continued to follow Isabel.

The very utterance of the word "schizophrenia" made Isabel's heart pound. She feared it almost as much as drowning. The prospect of developing the disorder filled her with dread, and often resulted in a panic attack. She never wanted to be like her parents.

The anxiety of inheriting her parent's dysfunction and disorders was constant. Isabel had numerous panic attacks in her early teens and Estella would often try to ease her worry. Estella told her that knowledge was the greatest

7

enemy of fear. She armed herself with information about her mother's condition. She researched the symptoms and statistical information. Her wealth of knowledge lessened the stigma. She drew solace in knowing as much as she could. She often recited facts to herself when considering the prospect of inheriting the disease.

In moments when she was paralyzed with fear about becoming like her mother or father, Isabel would go through her mental checklist. The first and most important fact was that children with mentally ill parents did not always inherit their parents' disorders. Her father's violence was not her own, even if she recognized his anger in her. She vowed never to follow his path of verbal abuse. She hated contending with her parent's label of victim and abuser, it was a terrible inheritance.

In recent years, thoughts about her father were exiled. She refused any memory of him as if it was poison. Her reminiscence of her Mom and worries about her condition were few and far between. The nightmare was drudging up all kinds of terrible fears. She forced down a flood of recollections, banishing her mother and father. Her Mom had become nothing more than a boogeyman representing her fear, while her father represented the wreckage of the past.

Following each instance of the nightmare, she was left thinking about her rescuer. Isabel knew she had been saved; it wasn't a delusion. The question of her rescuer's identity often tormented her, but not in a very long time. She rarely looked back and tried not to think about her past. It was too dark and full of sadness.

Repression wasn't healthy, but it was a lifeboat.

Going back to sleep was impossible. Opening her eyes, she stared at the shadows on the walls and resigned herself to getting up. She tried to shake off the barrage of unhappy memories and clumsily rolled out of bed.

Isabel walked down the dark hallway to the bathroom. Maybe a few splashes of water across her face would be enough to calm her nerves.

She absently turned on the faucet. It vibrated, a strange sound emanating deep from within the pipes. Nothing came out. She leaned close to faucet and tapped it with the back of her hand. It rattled as thick, dark liquid sprayed into the sink, splattering the white porcelain with black sludge.

"Gross."

She jumped back. Her hand slid down the adjacent wall to find the light switch. Harsh florescent light filled the room. As her eyes adjusted to the light, she stared at the mess in the basin.

A cold sweat permeated her skin. The sludge resembled the murky waters beneath the river in her nightmare. Fear gave way to annoyance as the muck slid down the drain. It was just her luck to have some terrible plumbing disaster strike hours before she had to leave town.

"Shit! What's this going to cost to fix?"

Frustrated by the sight, she looked into the mirror, inspecting her reflection, hoping none of the liquid sloshed on her. Her dark hair was a bushy mess, disheveled and swirling wildly around her shoulders. She exhaled as she poked at the soft flesh under her eyes. Her brown eyes were deep set with dark circles surrounding them. Her skin was washed out in the harsh bathroom light.

"Geeze, I look like a reject from *House of Wax*."

9

She was sleep deprived and the stress of the day was wearing her down. Thankfully, none of the mysterious sludge had made its way out of the sink. Isabel stared at the draining muck.

What is going on?

Isabel glanced up at the mirror and gasped as she caught sight of a silhouetted figure walking towards the living room. She spun around; no one was there. Beyond the hallway, the living room was outside the reach of the glaring bathroom light. There were no signs of movement; the room remained eerily still. She stepped into the hallway. Her feet squished against wet carpet.

"What the hell is happening?"

She lifted her leg, inspecting the bottom of her foot. Black sludge dripped from her heel. Disgusted, she stood on her tiptoes trying to avoid spreading the mess. She reached a floor lamp, pulling the chord. Soft light flooded the living room. She inspected the water damage. Several footprints stretched along the carpet, leading to the front door. Her heart pounded in her chest as cold sweat trickled down the back of her neck. There was someone in the house. The shadowy reflection must have been an intruder. She clinched her fists, as a rush of adrenaline pulsed through her body.

"Isabel."

Her name carried on a whisper as the cold breeze ran through the house.

She stopped dead in her tracks. The front door burst open with a gust of wind. The handle slammed into the wall, chipping off a large piece of drywall. She jumped with a shriek. The Santa Ana winds pounded against the open door, blowing in dust and dead leaves. She clamored to the open door, grabbing the handle as her name echoed in the wind.

"Isabel."

Her knees buckled, and her heartbeat thundered in ears. She slammed the door shut, pushing hard against the resistance of the wind. She turned back to the living room, the wet footprints smudged and streaked, as if being wiped up by an invisible force. The footprint swirled in a circular pattern and vanished. The floor was dry and clean, it looked as though the footprints were never there.

"Oh god, am I losing my mind?"

Isabel took several slow breaths, trying to ebb the steady flow of worry that flooded her thoughts. Her heart pounded in her chest. Calming breaths did little to settle her unease. She needed to get out there before anything else happened, even if it meant sitting in the airport for hours.

There was no debate, no inner impulse to stay. She ran back to her room, changed her clothes, and proceeded to grab her suitcases. Thankful for the foresight to pack her bags earlier that day, she didn't bother to look back as she left.

CHAPTER TWO
Haunted

Isabel sat in the airport with her nose buried in a book. She was reading the final paragraph of Shirley Jackson's *The Haunting of Hill House*. The paperback book was old and well-worn from repeated readings. The cover curled; pages were dogeared and smudged with coffee or chocolate stains. It was one of her favorite books. She committed to reading it once a year since Junior high. In each reading, she discovered something about storytelling or herself. She relished losing herself in a horror story. There was a certain catharsis in getting lost in a tale of darkness, which was different from the all too real darkness she had experienced throughout her life.

As she closed the book. The scent of cooking beef from Habit Burger tempted her. The glowing sign beckoned to her from across the airport lounge, but the fear of inflight onion breath kept her seated. She may be odd and socially awkward, but she wasn't the kind of creep to impose her digestive issues on her fellow passengers. When she was stressed, she craved garbage food: pizza, burgers, and sweets.

"Oh god, sweets. I'd kill for a Cadbury Cream Egg!"

Disappointed, she sighed. It was too early in the year; Easter was months away. Maybe a De La Rosa mazapan candy would do the trick. She loved their crumbly texture and nutty flavor. It reminded her of happier days from her childhood. Every Friday after work her dad would bring her a little De La Rosa candy. She scanned the glowing shop signs, doubtful that she would be able to acquire such a candy at the airport.

Sé fuerte.

She harnessed her willpower. She was not going to give into emotional eating, and she didn't need the additional stress of digestive upset from overindulging in sweets. She placed the book in her bag and rifled through her purse in search of a granola bar.

Her phone toppled out her bag and fell to the floor. Without checking for texts or missed calls, she shoved it back. She refused to get lost in social media, and she didn't want to receive condolences or strained sympathy texts from her agent or editor. Unable to find a suitable snack, she picked up her ticket and watched people as they passed her. Some hastily shuffled around while others embraced in sentimental goodbyes to their families.

Though she enjoyed observing peoples' behavior, a twinge of jealously followed when watching family interactions. She hated herself for being jealous of the benign happiness of strangers. Isabel stared blankly out the windows facing the tarmac, she fidgeted with her ticket as her mind wandered.

"There is no such thing as ghosts. The phantom figure in the apartment was just a manifestation of grief," Isabel told herself.

There are always reasonable explanations for strange occurrences.

She developed her love of horror early on, when her father would read her *Goosebumps* books or *Scary Stories to Tell in The Dark.* As a kid, she watched the Drive-In Movie Massacre show on Channel Ten every Saturday night. The show featured the old classic black and white movie monsters which were her favorite. The horror host Devina, the demon mistress of monsters, introduced Isabel to some of her favorite movies. She idolized Devina, dressing as her for Halloween for three years in a row. Aunt Estella, recreated Devina's costume for Isabel, but omitted the plunging neckline. When Isabel protested the alteration, Estella stated that the changes were nonnegotiable for an eight-year-old

There was a time she wanted to believe in ghosts and monsters, but those hopes faded with age and were later dismissed as nothing more than magical thinking. Cynicism and life experience proved monsters and ghosts were relegated to myths and legends. Ghosts were a metaphor for unresolved issues, and hauntings occurred in a delusional mind. Werewolves and vampires were analogies for aberrant behaviors. Beneath the veneer of civilization there were monsters, but not the kind that sprouted hair and howled at the moon. Real monsters had human faces. Her idea of monsters consisted of murderers, rapists, and sometimes politicians. She had experienced more than her share of horror and terror, but none of it was perpetrated by a ghost or ghoul.

She stared out the large window, without looking at anything in particular. A shadow reflection streaked across the window. Lurching forward in her chair, she looked back. A row of people sat with their faces buried in their phones. A couple kissed before departing. No one else saw the figure. It vanished. Her thoughts crashed into one another like a tidal wave, obliterating everything in its path.

Her chest tightened; she clutched her ticket. She couldn't take a deep breath. Cold sweat ran down her back. She gulped for air and dug her nails into the fabric of the arm rest. There was no relief, and no stopping the surge of panic. The panic attack echoed drowning, desperate to take a breath. She tried to lean back but couldn't move, gasping for air as if breaking through the surface of the river from her nightmare. It lasted only a few seconds, but it felt like an eternity.

Trembling, she opened her eyes. A few people looked up from their phones, watching her attack with mild interest. She took a slow breath as she straightened her crumpled ticket. Having a panic attack in public was a worst fear, realized. She looked around. People averted their gaze, returning to their phones.

Fuck, that was embarrassing. Please, pay no attention to the lady quietly losing her mind in the airport.

She gulped down the embarrassment and tried to collect her thoughts. She couldn't breakdown. There was still so much pain ahead of her. She needed to keep it together, at least through Estella's funeral. She was seeing things, hearing voices, and now having panic attacks, but she couldn't afford to have the mental breakdown she deserved. She would visit Dr. Duvall once the funeral was over to discuss the disembodied voices and hallucinations of shadowy figures.

Dr. Duvall would help; she was a constant source of reason and logic. But Isabel didn't want to speak with her just yet. She had to go to Estella's funeral, it was her last chance to say goodbye.

She had been under the care of her psychiatrist since she was in her early twenties. Isabel had been monitored by several doctors and had been evaluated numerous times over the years. She was eventually diagnosed with anxiety and depression. Prior to Estella's death, Isabel had never experienced hallucinations or heard disembodied voices.

The stress of her death broke me and now I'm going insane.

The funeral was tomorrow, and she had to return home for the first time in over eleven years. True dread lurked in the unanswered question about Estella's death. Isabel and Estella were estranged for years. No happy family reunion awaited her, only death and that river.

Following the death of her parents, Isabel lived with Estella at her ranch in a small town in the southwest. Like so many rural farming communities, it was a monument to a forgotten past. Relics of the Old West and sites of famous battles were venerated and marked a certain pride in a history of blood and war. Alongside contemporary shops and restaurants, historic structures that survived the damage of time lined Main Street. With varying degrees of kitsch and camp, the past lived alongside the everyday.

She used to love that place; it was her closest approximation of home. Prior to the death of her parents, Estella would always take Isabel out on the town. She took her to all the best shops and ended the visit with a trip to Lovett's Ice Cream Parlor. Two scoops of mint and chip ice cream and all was right with the world. Worries about her parents faded and she was free to be a kid.

In the year leading up to her parents' death, she was sent to stay with Estella on numerous occasions when her parents' fights became more explosive and frequent. Her father, Alberto would call on Estella on a weekly basis

As Isabel grew older, Alberto was having a harder time concealing the severity of Marisol's illness and his abuse of her. Isabel had vague recollections of seeing bruises on her mother's arms and face, but she didn't understand what was happening at the time. The most erratic of Marisol's behavior occurred when she was experiencing positive symptoms; she heard voices and hallucinated. This was when her their fighting got the worse. Her father would rage and scream at her Mom. During those times Isabel would hide in her room and pretend it wasn't happening. Marisol also had bouts of catatonia during the negative stage of symptoms which were the hardest on Isabel. Her mother's distance and silence were unbearable, while her father would just ignore her mother. At least with the positive symptoms, Marisol was still able to interact with her, despite her fragmented and rambling speech.

Alberto wanted to spare Isabel the sight of what he called Marisol's decline, at least that's what he told Estella. In all honesty, the older Isabel got the more she looked like her mother, and she knew her father hated that. She was sent to stay with Estella for longer periods of time. She had a good relationship with her aunt, and after moving in, the two became even closer. Estella was a warm and loving woman. She offered calm, stability, and safety. She was one of those rare people who always tried to see the best in others.

When Isabel complained to Estella about her fears about becoming like her parents, Estella said, "Your Mom was just very ill. Your father was not equipped to handle it,

17

and he turned into someone capable of the worst. There was good in her heart and whatever good that was in her, she passed on to you. You are different than both of them."

Estella was always gracious and rarely made discouraging remarks about others without provocation. Isabel admittedly did not share this trait. She often saw the worst in people; she figured that was what made her well-suited to write in the horror genre. Her ability to see the darkness of others and her early understanding of death, made her a particularly successful writer.

The past was a treasonous mix of pain and sadness with a few golden moments sprinkled in-between. Many of the happiest moments of her youth were with Estella. Their estrangement tainted even her joyful memories with the sting of regret and disappointment.

The dam of emotional numbness began to crack; tears streamed down her face. Unbridled anxiety flowed through her as she thought of attending Estella's funeral. Isabel had always hoped for an eventual reconciliation. She prayed for the day when Estella would call, and she could come home. That call never came, and now, it never would.

Hot tears stung her cheeks and streamed down her chin, splattering her ticket. She bowed her head, letting her hair fall in front of her face, and wept silently. She hoped to avoid making a spectacle of herself for the second time.

How many times can someone get away with having a meltdown in the airport before security is called?

She took slow measured breaths, trying to regain her composure. Deep breathing did little to quell the anxiety of returning home, and she was soon lost in the maze of memory and regret.

Estella's marriage to Joe was the cause of their estrangement. Their courtship and engagement were brief, and Estella often said that Joe swept her off her feet. After Isabel left for college, Estella had been left virtually alone to run the ranch with the exception of a few staff members. Loneliness got the best of her, and she settled for Joe.

Joe was large, about six foot two and was still quite formidable for a man in his mid-fifties. He had salt and pepper hair, which he slicked back with stale-smelling pomade. He had a smoker's gristly laugh and yellow teeth from years of chain smoking. Joe used his daunting size to his advantage. An aura of intimidation and aggression surrounded him. On more than one occasion, Estella bailed him out of jail due to a barroom brawl. He had been a drifter prior to working as a ranch hand for Estella for about two years prior to the start of their relationship. He was known for freeloading off a few local widows, until they caught on to his racket and promptly kicked him to the curb.

It was not only Joe's imposing physical appearance that made Isabel uneasy but a general restless, dissatisfaction that pervaded his company. Joe was always on the lookout for something bigger and better. During many drunken tirades, Isabel would hear about his latest get rich quick scheme. His endeavors always fell flat, and Estella would have to contain the financial fallout of his harebrained plans.

Isabel shared her concerns about Joe with Estella, but her aunt wanted to give him the benefit of the doubt.

"He's a good man who's trying his best. *No lo entiendes*." Estella said.

"*Entiendo todo*," Isabel said, in frustration.

Estella only spoke Spanglish when she was rattled or wanted to emphasize a point. When Estella spoke to her in Spanish out of frustration, Isabel would always reply in kind.

"*No me digas qué pensar, Isa.*"

"I'm not telling you what to think." Isabel said.

"It doesn't matter if you think he's no good, I know he's a good man. *No lo entiendes.*"

Estella repeated that refrain so often, Isabel wondered if she was trying to convince herself. She kept a close eye on Joe whenever she returned home from college, although he was generally on his best behavior when she was home. On a few occasions, she saw bruises on Estella's arms. Estella would explain them away as the hazards of farm life. The tension between Isabel and Joe grew.

One evening, Joe staggered home from the bar in a drunken stupor. He was in a sour mood and looking for a fight. Isabel returned home early from her semester break and had gone upstairs to wash up before supper. She returned to the kitchen in time to see Joe punch Estella in the face, knocking her into the table and toppling to the floor.

She sprinted across the kitchen and grabbed his arm before he could strike Estella again. He pushed hard against her, and she shoved him, knocking him back several steps. Isabel worked on the farm since her preteens; she was strong and capable. She landed a right cross directly to Joe's nose. Blood spurted and he stumbled, landing in a chair by the kitchen table.

She ran to the living room and grabbed the shotgun from the fireplace mantel. Estella swayed back and forth as she tried to stand up. She braced herself against the fallen kitchen table and called out to Isabel.

"Isa, please stop!"

Joe's eyes watered as he sat slumped in his chair. He cursed and wiped away blood from his nose and chin. He focused on Isabel, who was now standing in the kitchen pointing a shotgun in his face. His dull gray eyes reflected a darkness that Isabel knew all too well.

"If you ever touch her again, I'll kill you!"

Estella shuddered, waving her hands around wildly, pleading with her to put down the shotgun. She recalled the bruises on Estella's arms and her many excuses. Her body shook with fury at the thought of all the pain Joe had inflicted upon Estella while she was away. She had never felt this kind of anger. Her blood boiled and adrenaline coursed through her. Heat flushed from her chest to the top of her head. She wanted to kill him. Every ounce of her being wanted to pull the trigger.

I've got to stop him. He hurt Estella, so many times and got away with it.

Joe looked past the barrel of the gun into Isabel's eyes. The blood running from his nose dripped into his mouth and he spat the blood on to her shoes.

"Little girl, you don't know who you are fucking with. Put down the gun and get outta my house."

"Please stop, don't do this Isa!" Estella sobbed and pleaded for Isabel to put down the shotgun. Her words fell on deaf ears and Isabel remained motionless.

She glanced at Estella. Her swollen cheek was causing her eye to shut. Her aunt's expression of terror filled her with a rage.

"Crazy little bitch just like your mommy or maybe more like your daddy, a killer. What you gonna do? Shoot me? I'm unarmed and haven't laid a hand on you. You attacked me, I'm bleedin' all over the place."

He wiped blood and snot from his nose as he glared at Isabel. Blood dribbled down his chin and landed on his sweat stained shirt. She shifted the barrel of the shotgun to point directly between his eyes.

"You're a dead man." Isabel said. She meant it; she was going to kill him for hurting Estella.

"Don't do this, put the gun down *mija*, please don't. You're better than this. Be better than this." Estella said.

Estella's final plea got through to Isabel and she glanced at her broken and weeping aunt. It was the desperation and fear in Estella voice that gave Isabel pause.

Seizing on the moment, Joe raised his hands and said, "I'll leave! I'll leave right now!"

He rose slowly from the chair and headed for the door; all the while Isabel followed his movements with the shotgun. The door slammed behind him, shaking the door frame and rattling the wall in his wake. She quickly put down the shotgun, turning to care for Estella.

"I never want to see you do anything like that ever again. For a moment, I thought I was looking at Alberto. You looked crazed, just like your mother and full of rage just like your father. I thought you were going to kill him. If I hadn't begged you to stop, would you have shot him? What would your father say if he saw you like this?"

Estella's words were pointed, striking Isabel in the heart. She was afraid to answer. Her hands trembled as she helped Estella into a chair. There was no denying that she had lost control and, in that moment, she could have killed Joe. She stared at her blood-spattered shoes.

Joe deserved far worse than what he got.

Estella insisted she could handle herself and that Isabel had crossed a line. Isabel grabbed a steak from the fridge and placed it on Estella's cheek. She knelt on the floor examining Estella's injuries. She looked into Estella's eyes. They revealed a startling truth. Estella feared isolation and loneliness above all else. Her deepest shame was completely exposed, laid bare for Isabel.

"You've made the situation so much worse." Estella said.

"I saw him knock you to the ground! How is that okay?"

"I can't be alone, not now. You have your own life to live and Joe cares for me. You don't understand, I need him."

"I love you, Estella. You are all I've got left. I don't want to lose you to some drunken asshole. You don't need him."

Estella wept, holding her face in her hands. Unwilling to respond to Isabel.

She was defeated by fatigue, the exhilaration from the fight was fading fast, leaving only the solemn resignation that Estella was in denial. She pleaded with Estella to leave Joe. But Estella persisted in her justifications for his behavior.

"He loves me and takes good care of me."

The arguments were exhaustive; neither relented. Two days of shouting and tears reached its climax when Joe returned home. Joe delivered flowers and a groveling apology to Estella. She readily accepted both. He even knelt down and wept, promising he would never harm her again. Isabel listened through the walls to his simpering apology with apt outrage.

"I promise that I'll quit drinking and I'll never lay another hand on you again. But you act different when Isabel is around. You change, you forget all about me. She needs to go; we need time to ourselves. I want to take care of you. You don't want her sticking around, having to care for you, do you? You really think she can handle it?"

Estella shushed Joe before he could continue any further.

"You're right honey. I need you. Please trust that I'll do what's best for everyone."

Happily, Joe left to retrieve his belonging from the old motel by the side of the highway. The hotel serviced truckers passing through and prostitutes. As soon as the door shut behind him, Isabel hurried downstairs to confront Estella.

"Why are you taking him back? Do you really think he's going to stop? He could have killed you!"

Estella touched the side of Isabel's face.

"Since your uncle died, I've been alone. I am tired of waking up alone and I'm afraid of dying alone. Loneliness can drive you to accept and settle for things you never thought you would. Joe can be kind and loving. He takes care of me. It's too late to start over."

"I can't sit back and watch him abuse you,"

"Then you should leave. *Deberías irte de aqui.*" Estella said.

Joe returned to the ranch for good later that afternoon. Isabel packed her bags for school and prepared to leave the farmhouse. Joe puffed his chest and snorted as she passed him on her way out the front door. The smug expression of triumph on his face was sickening. Tears welled in her eyes when she looked back at Estella. Standing in the hallway, her aunt looked weary, cast in the darkness of Joe's shadow. He loomed over her as she watched Isabel walk out the door. Her long, silver hair and simple blue dress caught the breeze, and for the first time in Isabel's recollection, Estella appeared frail.

The admiration of childhood faded into bitter disillusion. Estella was a fallible woman, who chose an abusive husband out of fear and loneliness. She paused for a moment, staring at her, desperately trying to summon a plea or goodbye. Estella averted her gaze staring at the floor. A lump swelled in Isabel's throat, her mouth was dry, and the words died before they could pass her lips. She turned away from Estella and left the farmhouse without saying a word. It was the last time Isabel saw her.

"Flight 237 is now boarding."

The boarding call repeated, echoing over the loud speaker and pulling Isabel back to the present with a jolt. The voice on the speaker was so abrupt, she nearly jumped out of her skin. She held in a nervous laugh and thought of the retro cartoons that featured the black scaredy cat. The cat always appeared the same; with an arched back and hissing as it clung to the ceiling, spooked by every innocuous loud sound. The speaker cracked with an eardrum bursting pang and her stomach lurched. She took several slow breaths, collected her belongings, and prepared to board.

CHAPTER THREE
The Return

The flight home went by quickly, and she made it to the ranch by sunset. She stood before the farmhouse, staring at the empty porch. Estella used to wait there for her every time she returned home.

The house looked the same. The wooden deck slanted to the ground, the white paint on the walls chipped in the same weather-worn patterns. Wind chimes clanged against one another as a cold breeze blew past. The cold air and the emptiness of the house made the familiar scene, alien and unnatural.

I thought it was just a cliché, but Wolfe was right. You can never go home again.

She willed herself forward and walked up the two creaky front steps.

Home is less about a place than the people who occupy it. When those people are gone, what is left? Everyday objects that held little importance before were now imbued with memory, significant only to those who shared space and time surrounded by them. A clock was a simple clock, but if it belonged to your beloved grandmother, then it had significance. When those we love are gone, their homes and worldly possessions become reliquaries and their belongings become objects of sacred importance.

How many objects in the farmhouse would now hold sacred value? Was sacred value instilled, simply because it had belonged to Estella? Would the electric mixer hold the same significance as the afghan Estella knitted?

She didn't know. She couldn't make that determination until she entered the farmhouse.

Isabel walked to the front door and gripped the knob. The prospect of opening the door, filled her with anxiety. She was paralyzed by the thought of entering the farmhouse void of Estella's comforting presence. The house was filled with souvenirs from Estella's life. Little reminders of her were scattered here and there. Estella collected tchotchkes and antiques with regularity.

She couldn't fault Estella for her collecting habit. Isabel was terribly sentimental. She kept seemingly inconsequential mementos. She still had a VHS tape of *Evil Dead II*, her favorite movie, and she had a desk drawer full of rejection letters for her first manuscript. She was far from a hoarder, but her apartment was admittedly cluttered with meaningful objects. Isabel must have inherited Estella's sentimentality.

The little things mattered the most to Estella. She cherished a macaroni necklace Isabel made for her in first grade. She regularly wore the necklace until at Isabel's behest, she retired the necklace to her jewelry box. The sight of the necklace filled Isabel with a strange sense of pride. She jiggled the door handle as she wondered if Estella had kept the macaroni necklace. It would be nearly impossible to banish nostalgia and reminiscence. She would have to push those urges down if she was going to get through the next few days.

Isabel looked up at the windows, half expecting to see Estella's ghost waving down at her. She bit down hard on the inside of her cheek, chiding herself for being morose and self-indulgent. She shouldn't be thinking about specters and ghosts.

What will this place be like without her?

She didn't believe in ghosts, but she was sure that an empty building that once housed a happy family, would undoubtedly be filled with the ghosts of memory. Grasping the doorknob, she still couldn't compel herself forward.

I can't stay out her all night, can I?

"*Sé fuerte*. Stop dicking around and just open the goddamn door." Isabel muttered.

She steadied herself, taking a deep breath. She turned the knob but lacked the resolve to push the door open. She rolled her eyes and returned her gaze to the doorknob.

"Just open the damn door."

Cicadas buzzed in the high grass that surrounded the farmhouse. The soothing familiar hum reminded her of happier days. Her happiness lived in the shadow of pain and disappointment. Each moment of joy was soured by an equally heartbreaking memory. Acid rose in her throat, and she swallowed down the frustration.

"Isabel."

She flinched as the ghostly voice called her name. She clenched her jaw and goosebumps erupted on the back of her neck. This was the same voice she heard calling her name in her apartment from last night.

Auditory hallucinations are a symptom of schizophrenia.

"You are going to drive yourself crazy. It's okay; move past this. It's an expression of grief and guilt. I can do this," Isabel said with wavering confidence.

She took a quivering breath, trying to stem the tide of memory. Regret was a sharp pang, settling deep in her stomach. She stood in front of the door, unable to open it. Her fingers clutched the doorknob, unwilling to make a second attempt at turning the handle. Her eyes filled with tears, blurring her vision. Her hand was incapable of doing anything more than clasping the door handle. The silence of the moment was shattered by a familiar voice.

"Who's there?"

Breathless, she spun around. Diego Gomez, her high school sweetheart. He had grown up on the neighboring ranch and was a part of her happiest memories of home, although their breakup gave the memories a bitter-sweet air. Growing up, she had few friends. The terrible details of her parents' death loomed over her, followed her around like a ghost, taking the form of whispers, taunts, and accusations on the lips of cruel school children. Diego was the exception; he offered only friendship and kindness. He railed against those that publicly mocked Isabel, often getting into fights defending her. From elementary school through high school, Diego was her closest friend. In high school, their relationship evolved into the sweetest kind of love: first love.

Diego was tall and handsome with full black hair. His dark brown eyes exuded a certain kindness. His skin was darker and tanned. He had little more than a five o'clock shadow but his scruffy appearance only added to his handsome features. A wide smile broke across his face as he realized who she was.

"Isa!" Diego said.

He ran up the steps to greet her. Isabel wheezed as he hugged her hard, squeezing the air from her chest.

"Joe asked me to keep an eye on the place. He said he would be away a couple of days while he tried to settle Estella's estate. He didn't mention you'd be coming here. We don't get a lot of visitors coming down the back road, so I thought I'd check things out."

Realizing they were still embracing, Diego awkwardly let her go. They both stood in momentary silence before she gave a weak smile. She was happy to see Diego and she welcomed getting out of her own head.

"Joe said I could stay here while he was gone."

"I'm sorry to see you under these circumstances, but I'm glad you're back. Honestly, I wasn't sure you'd ever come home,"

"It's no secret that Estella and I weren't on speaking terms, but I loved her. I always thought that maybe Joe would die, and we could patch things up."

"I am so sorry about Estella."

Isabel nodded and wrapped her arms around herself. He looked the same yet different. In the years she had been gone, he had grown up and matured. He had slight wrinkles when he smiled at her, yet he still seemed to exude the charm and kindness of his youth.

Inviting Diego in for a cup of coffee would make it easier to enter the farmhouse.

The cold breeze prickled against her skin. It was getting colder and dark. The wind chimes clanged together and swung haphazardly in the breeze. The wind was picking up speed. She would have to enter eventually. With Diego here, at least she didn't have to enter alone. She gestured her head and without looking, reached out and opened the door. She stood back, allowing Diego to enter ahead of her.

With the ease of familiarity, she flicked the light switch. The living room filled with a warm glow from two old floor lamps. She scanned the room as the ghosts of years past flowed through her mind. The farmhouse seemed colder, emptier. All that was left of Estella was memories, and Isabel's last recollection of her was heartbreaking. She longed for the emotional numbness to return. She wished she could avoid the hollow ache of Estella's absence or the emptiness of the farmhouse. She was all too aware of the stillness; the silence was intolerable. She needed to say something, anything to break the silence.

"Would you like a cup of coffee?"

"Yes, please."

"Do you still take it with lots of cream and sugar?"

"Yes."

"At least somethings never change." Isabel said.

Diego nodded with a smirk, as they walked through the living room and into the kitchen. She busied herself prepping the coffeemaker. Diego grabbed the creamer from the fridge before sitting down at the small breakfast table. Isabel was acutely aware of the strangeness of their familiarity and how easily their old routine returned. After many late nights of going to concerts or B-movies, they would return to the farmhouse and have a cup of coffee. B-movie nights at the Starlight Drive-In theater were her favorite. They saw all the classic monster movies and slasher flicks, while making out.

Those were good times.

"Is the Starlight Drive-In still open?" Isabel said.

"Yup, it's still going. A few years back they updated the screen to a digital projector."

"Wow, digital projection. Times really have changed, but I'm glad it's still here."

"Not all the changes to the Drive-In have been for the better. I have to warn you. They changed from Red Vines to Twizzlers."

Isabel scoffed in mock outrage, "How dare they."

They both chuckled and silence fell between them. She turned back to the coffee pot, tapping her finger on the counter as she waited to think of something else to say.

When all else fails, pleasantries will do just fine in lieu of awkward silence.

"So, how have you been, how's life on the farm?"

"It's been good. Since I took over operations after Dad died, we've seen exponential growth. We are all about sustainable farming now."

Isabel smiled, "Still trying to save the world, huh?"

Diego always had a mind for sustainable farming and the desire to influence change in the industry. While they were dating, he would constantly share his frustration with his father's old-fashioned way of working. It was clear that he had remained focused and forward thinking. In that moment she was impressed that his optimistic and caring nature had not diminished with the passage of time. So many people give up and give into the traditional way of doing things, but Diego had a vision and he fought for it.

"How's the writing going? You know, my Mom still reads all your books. I've been so busy with the work; I'm about one or two books behind."

"You actually read my books?"

Nervously Diego chuckled, scratching the back of his head, "Well yeah, Isa, I love your horror stories. I've always enjoyed your very vivid imagination."

"Honestly the last book wasn't that good, you aren't missing anything. So, how's Erica?"

"We split up about two years ago, so I'm not really sure how Erica is doing these days."

Diego rubbed his thumb along the side of his ring finger. She winced and stopped herself from unloading a torrent of apologies.

"Oh fuck, I'm sorry."

"Don't be sorry; it's fine."

Unsure of how to respond, she turned back to watch the slow drip of the coffee, filling the pot.

I should have checked in on the folks at home through social media but looking in on their lives from a distance hurt too much and only served to drudge up painful memories.

"Well now that I've got the uncomfortable conversation rolling, I need to ask you a few questions."

Diego sat up straight in his chair and said, "Okay Isa, shoot."

"How did Estella die?"

"What? No one told you. Joe didn't give you any information?"

He stared at her with an expression of what she assumed was a mixture of confusion or sympathy.

33

It was shameful to not know the answer to such a seemingly basic question.

A lump swelled in her throat, she took a slight breath, speaking in a somewhat smaller voice, "Joe called and said that Estella had died. Her funeral was set for tomorrow. He had some business to take care of in the city and I could stay at the farmhouse while he was away. That's it. He hung up before I could ask any questions and he hasn't returned any of my calls."

Filled with a toxic mix of shame and guilt, she couldn't look up and see the expression on his face.

I shouldn't have to ask this of anyone.

Isabel choked down tears. Swallowing hard, she gulped and said, "I'm surprised he even bothered to call."

Silent, Diego rubbed the back of his neck. The coffee machine beeped, the low tone disrupting the sensitive moment. She walked over to the machine and poured two cups of coffee and placed them on the kitchen table. She sat down; her eyes focused on the flowery pattern of the tablecloth. She spent many mornings tracing the outline of yellow and pink flowers with her fingers as she ate breakfast with Estella. If she closed her eyes and inhaled, she could almost smell the sweet scent of pancakes cooking on the cast iron skillet. Every Sunday, the house was awash with the pleasant aroma of frying bacon and pancakes. Estella would form the pancakes in various animal and dinosaur shapes. Her adept culinary skills were on full display as she flipped Minnie Mouse shaped pancakes in the air. Isabel's gaze drifted to the stove. The cast iron skillet sat on top of the front burner grate.

There's the first object of sacred value.

A sharp twinge of pain shot through her, every item in the farmhouse, every piece of furniture contained some memory of Estella. Some of the memories were warm and brought comfort, while others tore into her chest, leaving a cavernous space in their wake. The image of the toppled table and blood-spattered tablecloth from the night of Joe's attack on Estella, flashed before her eyes. But the desire to know what caused Estella's death forced Isabel's thoughts to the present. Diego rubbed his thumb along the lip of his mug as she sat, waiting for him to speak. Diego thanked her for the coffee. Mustering her patience, she nodded and waited for him to continue.

"Joe told us what happened after Estella's body had been found."

Isabel choked on her coffee, "What do you mean her body was found?"

Her body had to be found, what did that even mean? Where did she go? How long had she been missing? What the fuck happened to her?

Questions slammed together in her mind, blurring in a confounding mess.

"Joe came by Mom's house and spoke with Mom and me. He told us that he got home from Debbie's bar and Estella was missing. He searched the property for her. A few hours later he found her body floating in the river. She had apparently committed suicide."

"Suicide?"

Diego's words hit Isabel like a truck, utterly obliterating her. Her chest felt heavy, it was hard to take a deep breath. There was no way Estella would commit suicide, not after what happened to Isabel's parents.

She would never kill herself.

"What do you mean, she committed suicide?"

"Joe said Estella was terribly depressed after her cancer spread. He was adamant that Estella didn't want to go through all the trauma of surgery and chemo again."

"She had cancer?"

Diego looked at Isabel perplexed, "I thought she told you? She was diagnosed prior to your big fight. I remember that she talked to Mom about it. I thought you knew?"

"I didn't know she was sick, she never told me that she had cancer. You really think I would have left if I had known?"

"I'm so sorry, Isa, she never told me that she was keeping her diagnosis from you."

Isabel slid her hands across her face. Her head felt heavy in her hands, and she slumped forward resting her elbows on the table. The weight of his words was crushing. Of all the ways in which Estella could meet her end, suicide never seemed like a possibility. There are ways of ending life that are humane, done with the help of physicians, but drowning. Committing suicide in that manner was a horrible way to die. Isabel knew what it felt like to drown, it was agony.

Estella's last moments were filled with agony.

Her imagination conjured terrible images of a frail and sick Estella, wading into the shallows of the river and sinking below the surface. For fear of seeing anymore gruesome imaginings of Estella's demise, she opened her eyes.

"Maybe she didn't want you to see her like that? Every time she would go into remission the cancer would come back. It seemed like a never-ending battle. She would retreat from everyone, even Mom would go weeks without seeing or speaking to her."

Isabel couldn't speak. It was as if the world was shattering around her, creating a terrible pounding sound that splintered through her every thought, or maybe the pounding was the sound of her heartbreaking. The pounding was ceaseless and echoed through her entire body.

"Joe said that Estella talked about suicide after the last recurrence, but he insisted that he didn't think she would actually go through with it."

Isabel began taking labored breaths, she clinched down on the coffee mug. Her hands trembled as she slammed the mug on the table. Hot coffee splattered on the tablecloth. Without thinking, she began wiping it up.

"No, this must be some kind of mistake. She would never commit suicide. It must have been some sort of accident."

"I'm sorry Isa. Joe said she wasn't acting like herself in the days leading up to her death. He said she was hearing voices. Maybe she wasn't in her right mind?"

"He said she was hearing voices?"

"Yes, he said she kept hearing voices call her name. He said he worried that the cancer was affecting her thinking."

"Fuck." Isabel said as she sat back in her chair.

She fidgeted with the napkin as she tried to make sense of everything. She sat in silence for several moments.

Suicide.

The word rang hollow in her ears.

Estella was hearing voices. Sweet fucking Christ, is all my family doomed to go crazy?

Diego walked around the table to hug her. His arms wrapped around her. His hug was unexpected. She leaned into him.

He rubbed her back as he whispered, "I'm so sorry, Isa."

His touch was familiar and tender. It had been so long since she had been held; she needed it. Keeping people at arm's length was exhausting, and she missed being hugged by someone who knew her, someone who cared. She let herself weep uncontrollably into his chest, He held her tight, anchoring her to the reality of the situation.

From the time they were children he had always been there for her, fending off bullies and comforting her. He would wrap his arms around her when she would talk about her parents or when she would express fears. He was always there for her when the inevitable flood of tears would begin. She held him tighter. She had gone far too long without an emotional anchor. She felt as if she had been adrift at sea and finally come home to familiar shores.

"I'm so sorry. If you want, I can stay on the couch tonight. If you don't want to be alone?"

She was tempted to have him stay, but she feared she may cry into his chest for the entirety of the night if he indulged her.

No. I need to be alone to sort things out. I want time to think, cry, or breakdown without an audience.

"No, I am okay. I think I need some time to process everything but thank you."

Isabel walked him to the door.

"I'm glad it was you who told me how Estella died. I don't think I could have handled the news from anyone else. Thank you for being honest with me."

"Anything you need, I'm here for you Isa,"

Isabel closed the door behind Diego, resting her head against the door frame.

CHAPTER FOUR
Records and Old Photographs

Suicide.

That fucking word haunted her. Her mother's death was called a murder-suicide. She ran down the list of deaths in her unstable and tragic family history; Dad killed mom, then killed himself. Estella wasn't immune to their family tragedy either. And now there was another woman to place the blame on, Isabel's mother had been blamed for her father's actions. His actions were not so subtly justified and condoned by those who dismissed her mom as nothing more than a crazy woman. And now Estella would be gossiped about in the same way. The long fight with cancer must have broken her. She may not have been schizophrenic, like her sister but she developed suicidal thoughts and was hearing voices.

If I had been here, would that have made a difference? She didn't deserve to die that way. Drowning was painful, she didn't deserve to die in pain.

The wind outside stirred, knocking against the door. Isabel walked to the window and pulled back the lace curtain. She forgot how dark it gets so far from the city with no streetlights, blaring neon signs, or passing cars to light the night. It was pitch black except for the glimmer of moonlight illuminating the tips of the tall grass that blew in the breeze. The grass rippled like waves over a stormy sea. There was no one around for miles; she was alone. Completely alone. She became acutely aware of the stillness which filled the farmhouse. The wind outside whipped against the windows, humming and echoing across the walls. The clattering winds created a sense of dread.

She set her mind to washing the dishes, hoping the menial task would offer a momentary diversion from the existential dread of the day. She walked through the living room, entering the kitchen. Darkness loomed outside the kitchen windows. She was relieved she couldn't see the river. She wasn't ready to see it yet. Estella died in that river, and she almost drowned in it. The current carried nothing but pain and loss. The river was the physical manifestation of her deepest fears.

"This would be a perfect setting for one of my books."

Isolation and darkness where hallmarks of the horror genre. All good ghost stories took place in the middle of nowhere or a looming castle far in the mountains. She looked around, the farmhouse wasn't nearly as spooky as a Gothic mansion, but it was full of the ghosts of old memories. There was a time when Isabel thought it was impossible for anything bad to happen here. The farmhouse was a sanctuary, offering stability and safety. She looked around the empty kitchen. Punctuated by an unnerving silence, the farmhouse felt cold and empty. She shook her head trying to break her focus on the eerie stillness of the room.

"Yup, definitely a good setting for a book."

Talking to herself did little break her unease. She turned to the table to retrieve the cups. She placed one of the mugs in the in the sink and turned on the faucet. The pipes hummed. The entire sink rattled, shaking the counter, rattling the cup.

Oh god, Not again.

Trembling she shut her eyes. Gripping the mug tight, every muscle in her body tensed.

This can't be happening again.

The pipes bellowed as black muck spurted from the faucet. The black sludge was the same as last night. The faucet continued to shake violently; the black water seeped down the drain. The liquid was viscous and wreaked of old river water. The sound echoed in her head, pounding and drowning everything out. She couldn't think she couldn't breathe. She dropped the mug in the sink, shattering in the basin.

"Oh, please stop, I can't take this!"

With a thunderous rattle, the water turned to a clear trickle. She slowly approached the sink. The remnants of the sludge pooled in the basin and retreated down the drain. She shut off the faucet and abandoned the broken cups in the sink.

None of this made sense, why was this happening? Was there more to these voices and visions than just stress or grief? Was it possible to be haunted by phantasms of the past?

She ran down the list of strange occurrences. Last night the black sludge appeared in the sink, then the figure in the mirror and footprints on the carpet appeared and disappeared.

Oh god, the shadow appeared after the sludge.

Her core temperature dropped, and she shook uncontrollably at the thought that the shadow figure was standing behind her now. Unwilling to turn around, her eyes met her own reflection in the glass of the kitchen window. There was no shadowy figure standing behind her. Relieved, she looked down, no wet footprints on the floor.

She exhaled deeply and rubbed the side of her temples. Desperate to create distance between herself and the remaining sludge in the sink, she entered the living room. The stillness inside the farmhouse combined with the blustering wind outside, was intolerable. She jumped as the shutters smacked against the window frames.

And she heard it.

"Isabel."

She froze. This can't be happening. She turned toward the door, waiting for it to slam open. Nothing happened. The wind echoed outside and the farmhouse remained still.

"I can't go crazy just yet. I need to hold onto some of my marbles, at least until after the funeral."

She walked to the old record player in the corner of the living room. She sat on the floor with her legs crossed like she had so many times as a child, ready to pick out a record. She touched them with a mix of admiration and a rush of nostalgia. Her fingers intuitively found her favorite Johnny Cash album. She lovingly pulled the album from the shelf. Carefully she removed the record, placed it on the turntable, and set the needle down.

Johnny Cash's velvet deep voice and guitar rang out. Estella would play Johnny Cash records whenever she had a point to make. Estella would play Johnny's cover of "Won't Back Down" to remind Isabel to be strong and to never give into despair. Estella had been an integral part of creating the soundtrack of Isabel's life.

What song would Estella have picked for this moment?

The record skipped and for a moment the vocals intertwined into a deep booming jumble of sound. With a crack, the song "Ain't No Grave" began to play. The haunting melody reverberated off the walls and echoed through her chest, fracturing the wall of emotional numbness that had kept her from breaking down. Tears streamed down her face as Johnny's mournful lyrics echoed through the farmhouse. Isabel closed her eyes, lost in lyrics. She sat completely still; her chest rose and fell with each strum of the guitar. As the final strum faded, she sat listening to the record spin. Music offered no peace or reprieve from grief. The lyrics spoke directly to her pain. With tender reverence, she turned off the record player and put the record back in the sleeve. She kissed the cover and returned it to its place on the shelf. She stood up and her knees cracked with a startling pop.

"Ouch, that's not as easy as it used to be."

She walked around the cozy sitting room, touching an old afghan that hung over the wooden rocking chair. She ran her hand along the worn, floral crochet pattern. Estella had made the blanket back in the seventies, well before Isabel was born. It always hung off the back of the old rocking chair. During chilly winter nights, Estella would wrap herself and Isabel in the afghan. It was oversized and covered both, with room to spare.

The chair creaked and rocked slowly as she lifted the blanket. She held it close to her chest. The familiar weight and warmth offered the tenderest of recollections. On one rainy day, Estella transformed the afghan into the door of a living room fort made from every blanket in the linen closet to banish boredom. They spent the entire day playing games among the piles of pillows and blankets.

She wrapped it around herself and sat in the rocking chair. It creaked louder than she remembered. Many happy hours passed with Estella in the chair, slowly rocking back and forth as she told Isabel folktales and ghost stories.

Ghost stories.

Isabel went straight for the dusty bookshelf across the room and slid her fingers along the numerous books to find one of her childhood favorites, *Latin American Folktales and Ghost Stories*, a glossary of ghost stories and legends from Mexico and the American Southwest. She caressed the worn leather spine. Gently, Isabel pulled the book from the shelf, running her fingers over the inlayed gold lettering.

She opened the book and was hit with the musty scent of old paper, pleasant and enticing. Years of exposure to the dry farmhouse conditions made the pages crisp and slightly discolored. She scanned the table of contents.

"The burden eater, page 138."

She didn't remember that particular legend. She flipped to its page. Emulating story time with Estella, she began to read aloud. If reading did not bring her comfort, at least the sound of her voice would break the silence and distract her from the solitude.

"A burden eater is an individual, often female of Aztec origin, that has the ability to remove the pain and misery of others through a ritual act and a kiss. Not much is known about the ritual other than it is often performed before death so that peace is achieved in the final moments of life. It is unknown if the burden eaters' kiss removes sin or simply removes misery. The Catholic church has disavowed the use of burden eaters and they are forced to live and work in secret. Living on the fringes of society and offering help to those in search of peace and reprieve from a lifetime of sadness. burden eaters are supernatural beings but are considered to work in the service of the light, rather than categorized as creatures of darkness."

Isabel considered what it would feel like to be free of burdens. She wondered if burden eaters could banish the ghosts of the past and truly free a soul from torment. She'd lived so long with the burdens of her past, she could hardly fathom what life was like without them. The legend of the burden eater was a refreshing notion, considering that most of the book was filled with nightmarish monsters, casting women in the roles of the villainous creatures and tempters of men.

"Huh, I could really use a burden eater right about now." She chuckled and sat down in the old rocking chair, she continued to read through the book, coming to a story titled La Llorona, the Weeping Woman.

"In life, the weeping woman was a beautiful wife and mother. She lived in a small rural village with her husband and two small children. Shortly after she gave birth, her husband lost interest in family life; he frequented brothels and had elicit affairs with several women. His philandry was made public after he impregnated one of his mistresses. Outraged, she could no longer suffer the indignity and, in a fit of insanity, drowned her children in an act of revenge. When she realized her actions, she committed suicide by drowning in the river.

"According to legend, the devil turned her away at the gates of hell. As punishment for her brutal crimes, she was condemned to be a bride of darkness, forever searching rivers and waterways for her children. She is often seen wearing a tattered veil and white dress, alluding to her curse as a bride of darkness. The appearance of this apparition heralds' darkness and death. Her spirit is summoned to waterways that are marked by tragedy and death. Sightings of the weeping woman have been recorded throughout Mexico and the Southwestern United States. She stalks the water's edge calling the names of her desired victims and luring them to the river.

"The legend of La Llorona is connected with the myth of the Aztec goddess Cihuacōātl, the weeping goddess that wanders from village to village in search of her lost son. She is depicted with a skeletal face and serpent belt. She stalks crossroads and rivers. Under a moonless sky, she steals children sleeping from their beds. She drowns the children in the river, sacrificing them in hopes of retrieving her son. The appearance of Cihuacōātl is known as an omen of death or impending war. La Llorona is considered to be a modern incarnation of Cihuacōātl mythos.

"A warning for readers, do not answer the call of the weeping woman. If you hear her calling your name, she has marked you for death and will haunt you until she lures you to a watery grave."

Isabel's voice trailed off in a quiver as she finished the macabre passage.

She closed the book, quickly putting it back on the shelf.

That's enough of that. No more ghost stories for the night.

She shuffled around the room. As a child, she was fascinated by the legend of La Llorona. The connection between the story of La Llorona and her life circumstance was lost on a young Isabel. She chalked it up to youthful ignorance that she failed to correlate her father's actions with the tale of the weeping woman. Upon rereading the legend with the comprehension of a disillusioned adult, the similarities were apparent. She wondered why there were no such legends about fathers like this? No evil fathers, just wicked and cruel mothers. Mothers get the rawest deal and are always the bad guy. Look at Norma Bates, blamed for the insanity of her son and Isabel's own mother was the same. Her father's actions were always met with a little caveat that included the fact that he broke due to her Mother's insanity.

The story of La Llorona hit too close to home, a crazy mother killed by the person who was supposed to love and protect her, held no intrigue or fascination for her. After all, she lived it. To further cement her connection to the legend, the story ended with suicide by drowning, exactly how Estella's story ended. Her skin prickled as it erupted with goosebumps and her heart pounded in her chest as she waited to see if the disembodied voice would call to her once again. The wind continued to pound against the creaky shudders but there was no voice calling her name in the distance.

Isabel rubbed the back of her neck.

"It's just a stupid legend. No one likes a scaredy cat, pull it together!"

She scolded herself. Isabel longed for the naivete of her youth. She loved that book and bonded with Estella over ghost stories and legends. After her parent's died, she developed a grim fascination with death. Estella channeled Isabel's dark interests into literature and storytelling.

The nature of storytelling changed for Isabel when Estella had a bout of the flu. Isabel read to Estella while she recuperated in bed. She evoked Estella's animated tones and mannerisms. Estella enjoyed the role reversal so much that she told Isabel to read her a story each night. Once Isabel had finished reading all the books in the house, Estella asked her to start making up stories of her own.

Unsurprisingly, Isabel's early stories were filled with monsters and ghosts. She often ripped her plots directly from the writings of Poe and Lovecraft. The strange tales she created in her youth brought her joy, and she wasn't about to let grief sour those memories.

Those memories were golden, I need them now, more than ever. I have to try to hold on to the memory of that innocence.

She ran her hand across the collection of books. The shelves were filled with titles by Edgar Allan Poe, Shirley Jackson, H.P Lovecraft, Stephen King, and Ray Bradbury. There was a large space on the third shelf where it looked as if an entire row of books had been removed. She stared down and wondered what had occupied that space. Her thoughts drifted back to Estella's impressive collection of horror and science fiction books.

"I can't believe Estella used to read all these creepy books to me. No wonder I'm such a weirdo." Isabel said, an echo of pride rang in her voice.

She flopped on the sofa and sat in silence. A deep sense of bitterness rose in her chest as she noticed that the photograph of her and Estella, that sat above the mantel was replaced with a picture of Joe and Estella. She stood up and pulled the picture from the wall. Joe was bloated and glassy eyed. Estella looked thin and pale in the photo, similar to the last time Isabel saw her. Her smile was strained, forced. When Estella really smiled, she beamed. Her whole face would light up. She looked away from the picture, unable to stand the sight of Joe.

Was it the cancer or was it Joe's abuse that broke her, which of these monsters destroyed her true smile?

As she reached up to put the picture back, she noticed a patched hole in the wall which had been covered by the picture. The patch was roughly the size of a fist. She looked around the room disgusted to find that the walls were filled with pictures of Joe. Her heart sank as she realized there were no photographs of her in the house. The walls were once lined with photographs of Isabel and Estella, but now they were replaced by pictures of Joe's various fishing and hunting trips. The pictures of Isabel chronicled her growth and milestones, but they were gone. Estella and Joe had removed all evidence of her life at the farmhouse. There was no indication she had ever been there. She had been erased, or worse, forgotten. All images of her had been banished, no doubt at Joe's behest.

"That motherfucker."

Her hands shook as she held the frame. For a moment, she was tempted to smash it, but she composed herself and returned the picture to the wall above the mantel. Anger was an easier emotion to handle than sadness. Anger was cold and hard; it obscured the lingering ache of loss. Her anger and hate were fully focused on Joe.

She stared at the picture, focusing on Estella's weary smile. She wondered if she should she be angry with Estella. Joe was a clear-cut villain, but Estella surely bores some responsibility for the way their relationship disintegrated. She bit down on the inside of her cheek. As she attempted to decipher her feelings toward Estella, a bitter taste rose in the back of her mouth.

This must be what resentment tastes like.

Her hate for Joe was old and well-nourished but her feelings for Estella were confounding. She wasn't sure if she was angry at Estella, but she hated that Estella hid her cancer diagnosis and sent her away.

"I could have helped her. Why didn't she let me help?"

The questions seared in her mind, burning through every thought. Her head throbbed as a rush of regret pounded against her skull. She rubbed the bridge of her nose, trying to steam the pulsating pain of a headache. She wished she could go back in time. She would have stayed, would have sent Joe away and taken care of Estella.

She looked at the picture of Estella on the mantel and said, "I should have fought harder to stay. I never should have left you. I'm so sorry."

Regret was a burning ache that took root at the base of her chest and tightened like a vice around her ribs. She hated Joe for abusing Estella, and she hated herself for leaving. Exhaustion tugged at her, but Diego's words rang in her ears.

Suicide.

The word repeated, tormenting and further exhausting her. She rubbed her temples, but it did little to relieve the pulsing of her pounding headache. Estella suffered from headaches and allergies; the upstairs bathroom was always well stocked with headache medicine.

Ibuprofen then sleep. I can deal with the rest tomorrow.

She got up and climbed the creaky stairs. She stopped at the landing and hit the switch for the hall lights. Given last night's encounter, she had no interest in walking through the hallway in total darkness. Antique tulip sconces lined the walls. The lights hummed and flickered, casting strange shadows over deer heads, antlers, and pictures of Joe and Estella. As she reached the first sconce, she tapped the light with her finger and to her immediate relief, it stopped flickering. A steady glow of yellow light illuminated the hall. Her ease was short-lived as with each step the lights continued to flash. The wiring in the house was old and each step vibrated from floor to wall.

"Just an old house with old wiring, nothing creepy or out of the ordinary about that."

Her words failed to detract from unnerving shadows, cast by the inconsistent strobe of the lights. Despite herself, she kept a steady pace as she made her way to the bathroom. Without fully entering, she extended her hand into the darkened bathroom. She held her breath as her finger found the light switch. She feared some monstrous hand would emerge from the darkness and pull her in. With the flick of her wrist, light filled the bathroom, there were no monsters hiding inside.

"Ghost stories have got my imagination running wild. God, I'm such a chicken shit."

The fluorescent glow of the bathroom light revealed the same blue flowery wallpaper pattern that she remembered from her youth. She reached the mirrored medicine cabinet and audited her appearance. Her eyes were red, puffy, and she had smudged her black eyeliner and mascara while crying.

"I'm a mess."

She turned on the water. Thankfully, there was no rumbling or black liquid spewing from the pipes. She splashed cold water on her face, it was soothing as the hot tears were washed away. She soaked a pink washcloth under the running water and placed it on the back of her neck. The cool water soothed the tense muscles and reminded her of her purpose for braving the creepy hallway She opened the medicine cabinet to retrieve the ibuprofen.

"Oh, shit!"

The cabinet was filled with at least a dozen different pill bottles. All the bottles were prescribed to Estella. A few of the medications treated nausea, but most were pain medications. She stopped searching through the maze of bottles when she found the ibuprofen. As she reached for it, several bottles fell into the sink. She placed the ibuprofen on the counter and retrieved the fallen medications. She froze when she recognized a large dosage of a Benzodiazepine, commonly referred to as benzos. Benzodiazepines are prescribed to treat severe anxiety. Isabel had been prescribed the medication in the past. Instead of easing her anxieties they made her all but catatonic. She didn't eat or write; all she did was sleep. Those pills were oblivion in a bottle.

She shook the pill bottle. Taking one pill would remove her pain, at least temporarily. She wouldn't have to think or feel. She could be dead to the world. After taking benzos for a few months, she had what addicts call a moment of clarity. Her life was in disarray, and she resolved to never fall into that void again. She opened the bottle and rolled a pill into her palm. To take that pill would be a betrayal to herself.

"*Sé fuerte*, I'm not going to give in, there's no easy way out of grief. What I'm feeling is terrible but feeling like a zombie is worse."

Emboldened by her desire to accept the pain, she emptied the bottle into the toilet and flushed the pills.

Adios temptation.

She walked to the sink and popped two Ibuprofen in her mouth. She stared at the collection of pill bottles. A cold sweat permeated her skin as she thought of Estella's suffering.

Poor Aunty. She must have been in so much pain and under extreme stress, to have had to take all those meds.

The combination of the medications must have put Estella into a groggy, zombielike state. She stared at the collection of bottles, certain there was no way that Estella was of clear mind while taking those medications. A sickening question sliced through her thoughts and pounded against her skull.

Did Estella commit suicide in a drug addled state and was that why she was hearing voices?

She slammed the medicine cabinet shut, her stomach churned like a washing machine, gone haywire during an electrical storm. She gripped the sink to steady herself. The room around her started to blur, instinctively she closed her eyes, breathing through the nausea. She couldn't stand to be in the bathroom any longer and walked back into hall, her eyes filled with tears. Crying would only make her headache worse. The revelations of the day were numerous and exhausting, the possibility that in a drug intoxicated haze, Estella killed herself was too dreadful to further consider.

She pushed the tormenting questions away; she would deal with them tomorrow. After a few hours of sleep, she might have some undiscovered insight into Estella's state of mind. She was tired and craved the comfort of her old bedroom. She walked down hallway, less concerned about the flickering lights than the prospect of keeping her thoughts in check for the entirety of the night.

The warm glow from the tulip sconce, revealed another patched hole in the wall. She balled up her fist and placed it over the patch. Her fist was small compared to the hole. It was clear that he had punched numerous holes in the walls, but who repaired them? She couldn't fathom Joe calmly fixing the drywall after he smashed his fist into it. Estella must have done the repairs, she always cleaned up his messes and covered for him. She looked at the photos and hunting trophies that lined the hallway. She was tempted to peek behind each frame, but the flickering lights strained her tired eyes. Desperate for the comfort of her old room she rested her head against the door.

All signs of her existence had been removed from the common areas of the house. She was fairly certain that Joe would have forced Estella to get rid of every last item belonging to her. She tapped the doorknob with her thumb and wondered what was the likelihood that her room remained unaltered.

Holding her breath, she opened the door, half expecting to see the room filled with buck skins and empty beer cans.

Wow.

The room was not only unchanged, but it was obvious that it had been regularly dusted and well kept. It was a monument to her youth. Everything was in place, except the closet door was slightly ajar. She approached the door and stared into the sliver of darkness.

If I were in a horror movie a monster would pop out of the closet. Right about now.

The disembodied voice that punctuated her eeriest of moments, came to mind and she shivered.

"Stop freaking yourself out!"

She rubbed the goosebumps on the back of her arm. She hated jump scares, but they were pervasive in contemporary horror films. Closets were the perfect settings for jump scares. She hesitated, almost expected it in real life. Smirking she shook her head and tried to shut the door, but it wouldn't budge. Something was pushing past the door frame. Her heartbeat sounded in her ears as she opened the door.

Thankfully, there was no boogeyman or literal skeletons hiding in the closet. Old coats and her high school Letterman jacket hung on the rack. A large box, overflowing with framed pictures and books occupied the floor of the closet. She bent down and assessed the contents of the box. The book covers were familiar; they were hers. Estella had collected Isabel's entire body of written works. She opened the book titled *Darkness Awakening*. It was her first novel. Many pages were dogeared and small stains of coffee or chocolate were peppered throughout the pages.

Well, that explains the empty shelf.

Putting the book back in the pile, she turned her attention to the pictures in the bottom of the box. Carefully, she picked up one of the damaged frames. The photo was intact despite the broken glass. It was the photo of Estella and Isabel that once hung above the mantel.

Joe had launched his fist through the glass frame, but she didn't throw the picture away. She kept the photo and everything else. That probably had Joe seething.

She looked through the rest of the pictures. Estella kept every picture of Isabel, and they were neatly packed away for safe keeping. She looked around the room filled with surprise.

How many hits did she take to keep my room intact?

Heat rose from her neck to the top of her head. The vein on the side of her temple pulsed as her blood pressure spiked. There was little solace in the knowledge that Estella prevailed in keeping Isabel's room as it was. She put the picture back in the box. Gently, she slid the box to the back of the closet and closed the door. Monsters in the closet or not, there was no way she could sleep with the closet door open. Her thoughts of Joe faded as she shuffled around the room, taking in the nostalgia.

Posters of Joy Division, Ramones, and Black Flag lined the walls. Ticket stubs from shows and concerts were taped to her vanity mirror. Her Glo Worm rested at the foot of the bed. She turned on her desk lamp and sat at her writing table. Stacks of writing journals rested on the desk. Flipping through a few College-Ruled Notebooks, she read a few pages with mild curiosity.

An old picture fell out of the notebook and landed on the She-Ra latch-hook rug. She bent down to pick it up, holding it close to the desk lamp. The edges of the photo were bent and yellow with age, but the subjects in the picture were crisp and clear. It was the last photo of her parents, taken a few months before they died. As she stared at the image of her them, memories surfaced.

This picture was taken on a good day.

To escape the summer heat, her family had gone to the beach. The photo was taken in front of green, foamy waves. Alberto was young. He had a mop of black hair and his tan skin shone in the summer sun. He appeared to be in his early thirties. Hesitantly, she shifted her gaze to the image of her mother. Marisol looked different than Isabel remembered.

On the rare occasion, when she thought of mom, she envisioned her as an Ophelia like waif from Hamlet. Isabel imagined Marisol roaming around the house in a bathrobe with disheveled black hair. That wasn't the image of the woman in the photo, Marisol appeared happy and healthy. Her eyes were clear and bright. She was on her medication and doing well. There were no bruises on her arms or signs of the abuse that was happening. In the photo it was clear it that she gone a long time without positive or negative episodes and had a temporary reprieve from her Alberto's fists.

The first recollection was pleasant, what followed wasn't. She ran from the waves and made sandcastles with Alberto. Marisol watched and laughed as her large, brimmed hat blew away in the breeze. Isabel and Alberto chased after it and Isabel managed to catch the hat just before it blew into the ocean. With pride, she presented the sand covered hat to Marisol. The happiness of the memory faded as darker recollections tugged at Isabel.

The good days didn't last long after that.

Marisol would sporadically stop taking her medication. Each time she abandoned her medication regiment, she detached further from reality. Alberto would then start drinking more and the fights escalated.

"Look at that smile; we had no idea what would happen."

Her eyes drifted back and forth between Alberto and Marisol. An icy realization hit her with startling force. Staring at a picture her family was like looking at the photo of a stranger. Regarding her sparse recollections of parents, Isabel held fast to the notion of keeping what is dead and gone, buried. She buried Marisol and Alberto's memory deep inside, to a place only accessible in nightmares, appearing as a phantom of embodying all of her fears.

Isabel was exhausted and emotionally drained, unable to fight the rising tide of memories. Anger rose in her chest and stung the back of her throat. She glared at the picture.

How can someone so crazy seem so normal and happy?

Her parents' blissfully unaware smiles stood in stark contrast to their horrible end. She had lived longer without her parents than with them. Tonight, all her old ghosts were making appearances.

Her earliest memory of her mother was witnessing Marisol talk to people that weren't there. During positive episodes of her condition, Marisol experienced apocalyptic disillusions. Her mother was obsessed with the end of the world and insisted the darkness was speaking to her.

Mom was a real piece of work and Dad was a monster. They destroyed my childhood.

Isabel wished she could extract all that remained of Marisol and flush her, like she did to the benzos. While benzodiazepines offered escape into the void, Marisol was the void. The clearest of her memories, smashed through the haze of time and avoidance. Isabel closed her eyes preparing for the worst. There was no escaping the darkest parts of her history.

What Isabel remembered with frightening clarity was the sound of her mother's screams. Within a blink of an eye, Isabel was a scared kid listening to piercing shrieks echo through the house as Marisol argued with one of her hallucinations. Covering her ears from the shrill screeching, Isabel ran to her room and hid in the closet. Pounding footsteps rumbled up the stairs behind her.

The bedroom door burst open. It smacked against the wall shook the door frame. Marisol called out to Isabel, her voice quivering with a forced calm.

"Where are you?"

Isabel trembled and covered her mouth to stop from yelling. From the slats in the closet door, she saw the disheveled figure of Marisol enter the room. Isabel's toy box had been knocked over as her mother tore apart the room searching for her. Crashing boxes and clatter of glass breaking overshadowed her mother's incoherent shouts.

Isabel's face stung from the force of her hands clamping around her mouth. Her yelps were muffled but audible enough for Marisol to hear. Marisol tilted her head in the direction of the closet and slowly turned. She peered down at Isabel through the slats. The closet door slid open. Marisol shoved aside the clothing on the racks and grabbed her. She squeezed Isabel's shoulders with a vice grip. She tried to wriggle free, but Marisol dug her nails in.

"I need to save you. The darkness is coming for us. It will overtake the world! Your father is lost to the darkness now. I can't save us, but I can save you."

Marisol's eyes were wide. Her pupils were so dilated that her eyes were black. Isabel cried and screamed. It was the first time she recalled being afraid of her mother.

Following that afternoon, Marisol's behavior became increasingly aggressive. Isabel was too afraid to tell Alberto about the incident in the closet. She buried the image of her mother's black eyes and crazy ramblings. She had almost managed to forget about that terrible day, but Marisol's instability escalated, and Juan's rage exploded.

A week later, Marisol took Isabel out of school early. They drove around for hours aimlessly as she weaved in and out of traffic, rambling to herself. At one-point Isabel was sure she was going to run the car off the road.

Marisol wailed, "No, I won't let you take her. Darkness, no, please. You can't have my baby!"

She considered leaping out of the car to get away from Marisol, but fear forced her to stay put.

Mustering all her wits, Isabel pleaded with Marisol, "What about daddy? We should go home to protect him from the darkness."

"You're right, *mija*, I need to protect all of us from the darkness."

Marisol pulled over and got out of the car. She paced back and forth in front of the car for several minutes before returning to the driver's seat.

She turned back to Isabel and said, "I know how protect us from the darkness. Let's go home."

As the car pulled in the driveway, Alberto ran to meet them. He yanked Isabel out of the car, hugging her and demanded she go inside. She watched from the living room window as her parents argued. Alberto yelled and Marisol mumbled under her breath. He grabbed Marisol's arm and dragged her into the living room.

"I called the police. I was worried you were in a wreck. You can't run off like that Marisol!"

"I needed to drive and clear my head. I needed to come up with a plan to stop the darkness."

"You're off your medication. You're not thinking straight, there is no darkness. The world isn't ending. You are fucking crazy!"

Undeterred Marisol continued, "Beto, I am not off my meds. I see everything so clearly. I realize now that I can't stop the darkness, but I came up with a plan. I will save Isabel."

He screamed and grabbed her by the shoulders and shook her several times. She resisted and he slapped her, knocking Marisol to the ground. Isabel stood in the living room, frozen as she watched her father beat her mother. She didn't scream or cry she just stood there watching as her world changed forever after that. It was terribly unnerving to see her the violence her father and mother hid. Alberto walked past Isabel and into the kitchen, he slammed the liquor cabinet door open, almost ripping it off the hinges.

"You are going to stay with Aunty Estella for a little while." Marisol whispered to Isabel.

Relief filled Isabel at the thought of leaving. She was happy to run from her parent's darkness. Seeing her father hit her disoriented mother was too much for her to handle. After Alberto left to the liquor store to buy more beer, Marisol called Estella. Estella drove the four-hour trip to Estella's ranch in silence. Isabel assumed she was afraid to ask her about the events of the day. She was relieved she didn't ask, unsure of what she would say. Isabel knew that what she was experiencing was well beyond her comprehension. Periodically, she caught sight of Estella staring back at her from the rear-view mirror. She was unable to decipher whether her expression was of worry, fear, or confusion.

Dad killed Mom two days later.

Mustering her every last ounce of self-control, she forced away the memory of her that day. The taste of bile rose in the back of her throat. Guilt had a caustic aftertaste.

For years she blamed herself for her mother's death. Believing that if she had told Estella about witnessing her father hit her mother, she could have stopped him. The sting of old regret was nauseating and although she no longer blamed herself for what happened, she wished she had spoken with her Estella.

Hindsight was cruel. Isabel's stomach lurched in tumbling knots. Another wave of acid stung the back of her throat. She swallowed hard, trying to force down the memories. For a moment, she thought she might vomit. The more information she remembered, the worse she felt. She asked Estella once if she knew that her father was hitting her mom. Estella just said that Marisol hid it well, and Beto seemed kind and charming.

The past is a minefield.

As a child, Isabel knew the basic information about her parents' death, but it wasn't until many years later that she discovered the graphic details. In her teens, she searched news reports about Alberto and Marisol on the internet. Fearing Estella would discover Isabel's search for information, she headed to the local library. The building had always been a haven of knowledge and seclusion. As she read article after article, the devastating details were worse than she could have imagined. Alberto had stolen the neighbor's handgun and shot Marisol in their bedroom while she slept. The article suggested that, unable to cope with Marisol's condition, he a had a psychotic break. He shot holes into Isabel's empty bed. The words "The darkness is coming," was scribbled on the wall in Marisol's blood. Alberto then laid down in bed next to Marisol and shot himself.

Isabel never saw the destruction left in the wake of Alberto's murder-suicide. She never returned home after their death, and only vaguely recalled the funeral services. While researching, Isabel came across a photo of the writing on the wall and images of the crime scene. It was suggested that her father had incorporated his mother's delusions into his own and that's why he left the message about the darkness. Isabel vomited in the waste basket at the library and never again looked up information about her parents.

Pulled from the void, Isabel placed the photo on the table. She wished she could bury the pain of her past beyond her recollection. Estella made it easy for Isabel to forget about her parents. There were no pictures of Marisol or Alberto in the farmhouse, or so she thought. Estella removed all photos of her sister, and they rarely discussed life before Isabel lived on the ranch.

Having a better understanding of mental illness did little to ease Isabel's anger over her father's actions. She hated that she recognized herself in their faces. She resembled Marisol, but she had Alberto's eyes. She hated that her family was reduced to just another domestic violence statistic. She shoved the picture back in the notebook. She needed rest and to leave the ghosts of her past behind for the night.

She hoped that succumbing to the oblivion of sleep would offer temporary peace from an emotionally perilous day. She walked over to her bed and sat down. Retrieving her Glo Worm from the foot of the bed, she cuddled it as she tumbled on top of her comforter. The pillow was sunken and lumpy. She sat up, there was a head shaped indentation in the center of the pillow.

"Who had been sleeping here?"

She laid back down, the scent of Estella's rose water night cream was all over the pillow.

"Why was she sleeping here?"

It didn't matter. She was grateful to smell her scent again; it was the closest she would ever get to being in her presence. This was the last comfort Estella would bring her. She inhaled deeply, taking in the gentle, clean aroma. The sweet rose scent was beyond comforting and she closed her eyes, letting herself drift into the limbo of sleep.

CHAPTER FIVE
Nightmare Revelation

She was drowning. Isabel desperately gasped for air as the black water engulfed her and then she was pulled from the river. Carried to shore, her small body was placed on the ground. The cold hands of her rescuer touched her face. Their fingers were dripping wet and bony. She had never known the identity of her rescuer. Resisting the growing darkness of unconsciousness, she opened her eyes, and her vision slowly adjusted to the light. The blurred figure came into focus, revealing a gaunt woman in a white dress. She lifted her torn veil; this was no ordinary woman.

"La Llorona!"

The weeping woman nodded and continued to stare at Isabel. La Llorona was ashen white with purple veins that rippled like tree roots beneath her skin. Dark circles surrounded her ghostly blue eyes, and midnight black hair swirled around her shoulders, cascading down her back. La Llorona's tattered dress clung to her slim, almost skeletal figure. The weeping woman stared at her, but there was no malice in her expression. Her countenance was akin to the interest of a cat observing a wounded bird, before pouncing on it. Isabel gasped as she waited for the phantom to strike.

La Llorona raised her skeletal hand in a reprimanding motion and said, "Isabel, you must stay away from the river. It is dangerous. Stay away."

The soft voice was familiar, it was the voice that had been calling her name since Estella's death. The weeping woman turned back to the water. As if pulled by an invisible force, the ghostly figure of La Llorona walked backwards. The weeping woman's eyes never left Isabel's as she sank into the blackness of the river. La Llorona descended further and further in, the water reaching her glowing eyes, then she vanished.

Isabel woke from her nightmare. Gasping for air she realized she wasn't in bed. Her eyes darted left then right. She was standing inches away from the reeds which lined the river's edge. Her legs were stiff and unsteady. Her toes dug into the sandy riverbank. If she had woken up a moment later, she would have waded into the shallows.

"What the fuck am I doing out here?"

Fog rolled off the water and seeped into the woods behind the river. Groggy and confused, she stared at the dark river. She was standing where she had been rescued by La Llorona. The cold sting of morning air chapped her exposed skin. Low fog swirled around her ankles. Her teeth chattered and she trembled. She wrapped her arms around herself and took several panic-stricken breaths. Her exhalation disappeared as wisps in the air. The soft pink light of dawn reflected in the rippling current, giving the water a crimson hue.

Would La Llorona surface from the depths of the river?

Was she drawn back to that place by her nightmare, or did the weeping woman call to her? Unwilling to stay and find out, Isabel stumbled back as she took several unsteady steps. With comfortable distance between herself and the river, she turned and ran back to the farmhouse. Slamming the door behind her, she wiped away cold tears. Attempting to take a deep breath, her muscles tightened. She slid down the door, falling with a thud on the kitchen floor. Her heart pounded in her chest. The rapid beat of her heart echoed the pounding of current against the rocks.

Drowning in a panic attack, she collapsed on the floor, gasping for air. Chills ran through her entire body. Her vision blurred and she passed out.

Isabel opened her eyes. Her head was throbbing, and her chest was tight. For a moment she was confused as to why she was on the floor. Recollection seeped in with the sunlight that trickled through the windows. She went over the list of recent terror inducing events.

"I was sleepwalking, ran to the house, then I must have passed out during the panic attack."

Saying it out loud didn't make her feel any better. The warm light of day flowed through the windows and stretched across the kitchen. Her chest was sore, she rubbed her side, hoping it would ease the tightness.

Her arms trembled as she pulled herself from the floor. There was a sharp pang in the bottom of her right foot when she moved. She slumped back down and lifted her foot, a small shard of glass stuck in her heel. Counting to three, she winced and pulled it out. Her feet were filthy, covered in a mess of mud and blood. She had several small cuts on her feet and legs. She must have cut herself while sleepwalking.

Oh fuck, sleepwalking. That's new. Wait, no it wasn't, I've done this before. I used to sleepwalk.

She hadn't experienced sleepwalking since she was a little girl. In the months after she moved in with Estella, Isabel had several incidents. On a few occasions, she walked out of the farmhouse and through the backyard. Estella always found her before she reached the river. Estella was concerned and sought the guidance of a physician.

The doctor said it was an expression of trauma and that the nightly disturbances would cease in time. Estella reinforced the locks on the kitchen door and put in a security gate. Eventually, the sleepwalking stopped and became just another vague memory.

"I can't deal with this!"

She needed to wash away the awful night and clean her wounded foot. A hot steam-bath was the solution. Limping down the hall and up the stairs to the bathroom, she was careful not to look out the windows, for fear of seeing La Llorona standing at the river's edge.

The steam rose from the hot water, and she took a deep breath to calm her nerves. She pulled off her pajamas, still wet from the morning dew, and stepped into the old clawfoot tub. Her muscles ached, and a large knot had taken up residence between her shoulder-blades. The hot water soothed her cold skin and sore muscles. She examined the bottom of her injured foot. The cut was deep but wouldn't require stitches.

Walking in heels later today would be fun.

Placing a washcloth over her eyes, she rested her head against the edge of the tub. Letting her arms slump at her sides, she exhaled deeply. The tension and stiffness eased with each breath.

She loved the clawfoot tub. In childhood it was the scene of epic pirate battles and rubber duck races. Following track practice in high school, the tub was filled with ice to help with muscle recovery. She preferred the former to the latter. Ice baths were brutal, but they served their purpose. The tub was a sanctuary, offering recuperation and rejuvenation. She was safe there and she could rest. Listening to soothing repetitive sound of the water slowly dripping from the faucet, she let the tension flow from her body and into the water. The warmth and steam enveloped her. The mundane comfort of the moment was not taken for granted. For the first time since Isabel received the news of Estella's death, she was calm. Blissful unconsciousness beckoned to her.

Being haunted by a specter of her own making was wearing her down. The addition of La Llorona to her nightmare must have come from reading the excerpt about the weeping woman in the book the previous evening. Her overactive imagination was influencing her subconscious.

There was a rational explanation for every strange occurrence, even if it meant I've lost my mind.

She recalled an article about sleepwalking as a symptom of sleep deprivation and stress. She hadn't experienced a decent night's sleep in days and the death of a family member is one of the top five most stressful life events. The lack of sleep and Estella's death were the perfect recipe for sleepwalking and panic attacks. Still, she doubted her examination of the strange encounters.

What about the shadow figure and the disembodied voice?

The visions of the figure and the voice could be manifestations of loss, or worse yet Estella's death triggered disassociation or hallucinations. Either way, she needed to make an appointment with Dr. Duvall. Once she was back home and away from all the memories of her childhood, she would be able to reflect upon the strange occurrences and perhaps gain some clarity.

She could deal with losing her mind after Estella's funeral. She tried to focus on the peace of the moment. The water was warm and calming.

"Take a break and just breathe."

Satisfied with her reasoning, she listened to the soothing rhythm of the gentle dripping of the water from the faucet. The steam rose around her, and she let her mind drift.

The droplets created ripples across the surface of the water. The ripples became large and turbulent, rushing around her as if pulled by a current. The walls of the tub vanished, and she was pulled beneath the surface. Opening her eyes, she was submerged in the blackness of the river. Adrenaline forced her into action, and she swam for the surface. The water was frigid, stinging her skin.

Breaking the surface of the water, she gasped. The choppy current splashed around her. As she tried to swim to the bank a hand grabbed her by the hair and pushed her underwater. She struggled, frantically clawing at the hands pinning her down. Digging her nails in, she managed to break their grip. Her head bobbed to the surface.

Spitting water, she screamed at the horrific sight in front of her. Beyond the reeds at the edge of the riverbank, two small children, a boy and a girl, lay lifeless. Gasping for air, she clamored to the bank, collapsing in the reeds on the shore. Her muscles were weak and failed to pull her any father. A hand grabbed her dress and pulled her back into the shallows. Trying to free herself, she turned toward her attacker. He was a tall, wide framed man. She was helpless as he pulled her closer to him. She kicked and punched him, but he fended off her attack with ease. Swatting away her punches, he grabbed her by the neck. She choked and coughed as his hands clamped around her throat. He glared down at her, his eyes were wide, and bloodshot.

He kissed her coldly, without affection and said, "Goodbye, *bonita*. It's time for you to join the children."

He pushed her head under the rushing water. She tried to scream but there was no air, cold water filled her mouth and nose. The silt-filled water burned in her throat and seeped into her lungs. A last rush of adrenaline pulsed through her. She trashed around but was unable to break him iron grip. Her strength waned as the frigid water filled her lungs. The last remaining bubbles of air escaped her nose and rose from the black water to the surface where the blurry image of the man stared down at her. She began to involuntarily twitch.

This was what dying feels like.

There was no light, no hope. There was only the blackness of the river. Her lifeless body floated, and her face broke through the surface.

Isabel sprang from the tub and fell to the floor. Her wet body smacked hard against the linoleum tiles. Her arms flailed as she tried to pull herself up. She slipped and slid, as she scrambled across the bathroom floor. Huddling against the farthest wall from the tub, she shook uncontrollably. Rocking back and forth, she screamed and cried.

"What the fuck is happening to me?"

Isabel was running out of rationalizations. The thin veneer of rationality was decimated. There was no other conclusion. She was just like her Mom.

"I'm a fucking basket-case."

The revelation brought no comfort. She huddled in the corner, crying as she replayed each horrible scene from the tub nightmare. The vision seemed so real, but her mother also thought her delusions were real.

She experienced death in the dream. Trembling and unable to banish the image of the two small children lying dead on the shore, she collapsed into a sobbing mess. Isabel wept until her eyes burned, and there were no more tears left to cry. After almost an hour, she was able to pull herself from the bathroom floor.

"It was just a nightmare, I'm not haunted; there's no such thing as ghosts. I'll get help when I get home."

***

Isabel slowly descended the stairs to leave for the funeral. Each step was strained, her legs wobbled as pain shot through her injured foot. She was unsteady. Her nerves hadn't completely recovered from the recent panic attacks. She gripped the wall as she walked.

"I'll get through today, and I'll deal with going crazy after."

She didn't want to be like Marisol and refuse medical care. She pushed down the thoughts of her mother in order to focus on the situation at hand. Getting through the day was going to be a challenge. Unsure if she was up for the task, she was determined to do her best. Her game face was set by the time she reached the living room. Isabel glanced at the kitchen floor as she entered and found a muddy trail of footprints. Isabel pinched the bridge of her nose, frustrated that she had forgotten about the mud she had tracked in from her sleepwalking adventure.

"Ugh, I made a hell of a mess."

She was emotionally exhausted and mentally spent. With a robotic resignation to the task ahead, she meandered to the hall closet to grab a mop and bucket. She opened the door and pulled the hanging cord, turning on the light. The bulb swung and flickered. Unable to see the top shelf, she stood on her tiptoes and reached up. Searching for the bucket, her hand slid across the cool metal of Estella's old revolver. It had been removed from its case, resting abandoned on the shelf.

That's weird.

Estella's gun was always safely locked away. Given the way her parents died, Isabel was weary of guns. Estella could not abide fear in Isabel She set up a shooting range in the backyard for Isabel to practice. They shot cans and old plastic Cool-Whip containers off the fence posts. After firing, Estella would often grumble about the revolver.

"This old thing kicks like a mule."

Isabel was understandably reluctant; she hated the thundering crack of the gun firing.

"*Se fuerte*, you need to face fear head on, you can't go around it. The only way past it is through it." Estella said, before each firing session.

Estella would reassuringly stand behind Isabel, as she prepared to shoot her preferred target: tomato soup cans. The gun was heavy in her hands and her wrists shook as she took aim. Estella would gently put her hand on Isabel's shoulder and remind her of the rules. Her voice was calm and steady, imbuing Isabel with encouragement.

"Your wrist and your arms should be aligned, lock your wrist and breathe through the shot. Don't be afraid of the recoil. Just focus on your target."

Reassured by Estella's instructions, Isabel usually hit her mark.

"You're a dead-eye kiddo. Annie Oakley would be proud."

On more than a few occasions, Isabel would express her reservations.

"I'm fine shooting soup cans, but I don't think I could shoot anything that was living."

"You'll probably never need to use it, but all the same it's good to know. You are not your daddy and I know you don't have that kind of violence in you. I wish you trusted yourself more. Look at how well you did today."

Estella's patience eventually paid off and in time Isabel no longer flinched at the crack of gun fire. She handled the gun with cool adeptness, her fear banished. Although she reveled in Estella's praise, she still couldn't imagine using the gun for self-defense. As if she was reliving a stranger's memories, the innocence of those days seemed remote. The distance to her former self was oddly similar to the sensation of the tub nightmare, like she was experiencing the recollection of someone else entirely.

As a kid, she was happy to blow numerous tin cans to kingdom come. She wrongly thought she would never be able to point a weapon at a person.

Maybe that's why Estella was so terrified during my fight with Joe?

Isabel had been reluctant to use weapons, but when Estella was attacked, she was ready and willing to use the rifle. She was ready to kill with the skillset Estella had taught her. She wondered if that night caused Estella to regret teaching her how to handle weapons. Isabel was surprised by her actions during the fight with Joe. The result of that day left a stain on her soul and made her question her moral boundaries. Worried she would walk Alberto's path Isabel went to anger management and never owned a gun, and she hadn't touched a weapon since pointing the rifle at Joe.

She picked up the revolver and pulled the cylinder latch, to find it was fully loaded. This raised numerous questions, but she was running out of time if she wanted to clean up the footprints and make it to the funeral before the service started. Saving the questions for future consideration, she put the revolver back on the shelf, found the bucket, and grabbed the mop.

As she mopped up the muddy footprints, she couldn't help but notice that they resembled the wet footprints in her apartment. They were the same mixture of wet, black muck and stretched across the floor in the same pattern.

Were the footprints a premonition of today?

A chill ran down her spine and goosebumps erupted on the back of her neck and arms. It was just an eerie coincidence she told herself. She didn't believe in premonitions. Even if she subscribed to the notion of precognition, what was the point of a vision about muddy footprints? What otherworldly insight could be gleaned from such a glimpse into the future? The notion of visions of a muddy mess irritated her. I'm being stupid and superstitious.

The mucky black footprints, smudged and swirled, disappeared under the mop. The footprints in her apartment vanished in the same swirling pattern. Annoyed, she plunged the mop into the bucket and forcefully scrubbed away the last of the footprints. The floor was finally clean, as if the footprints were never there. They vanished just like the footprints in her apartment, but the footprints in the farmhouse required significantly more physical effort.

Disappearing foots prints required zero clean up, but I'd rather mop up real footprints any day.

She wiped the perspiration from her forehead, adjusted her hair and headed out the door.

CHAPTER SIX
Walking with a Ghost

The Graveyard was one of the oldest in the Southwest, with many graves dating prior to the Mexican Revolution of 1810 and the American Civil War. Mourners would have to pass many decrepit graves before they entered the modern graveyard and mortuary. Standing gravestones, crosses, and statues lined the uneven hillside. Many of the grave markers were in a sad state of disrepair. Gnarled, seemingly ancient mesquite trees lined the perimeter. It was still early spring, and the chill of winter had not completely left the air. Isabel pulled up the collar of her coat to shield herself against the blustery wind. Tree branches clattered in the breeze. The rustling branches echoed against headstones, creating an other-worldly chorus.

Absently, she grazed the tops of old stone crosses with the tips of her fingers as she walked by, looking at a few of the dates and names on the older headstones. A strong gust of wind knocked the large, brimmed black hat off her head. The wind propelled the hat with surprising speed as it rolled between headstones. She cursed under her breath, chasing after it until the hat hit the base of a statue. Panting, she reached for the hat, dusting off the leaves and debris before placing it on her head. The annoyance of the moment faded as her injured foot throbbed. She slid off her heel to examine her bandaged foot. A shadow obscured the sunlight in front of her and she looked up at the statue. Without shifting her gaze, she slid her shoe back on and stepped back cautiously, to fully take in the statue looming over her.

She focused on the statue's wings, then followed the angular pattern of the drapery, examining the stunning details. It was the angel of death. The wings were large and almost entirely wrapped around two figures of children. The reaper was depicted as a cloaked, beautiful woman with a calm expression and deep-set eyes. She was tall, obscuring the sun from her view. She noted that the statue looked very old and was missing part of its nose. The stone drapery around the angel's feet were weather-worn and chipped. Isabel inspected the inscription on the gravestone.

In memory of Jose and Amelia, children taken from their loving father.

Isabel noted the ages of the children, Jose was six years old and his sister, Amelia, was four. Isabel read the dates of their deaths, February 17th, 1819. She shivered as the skin on her arms erupted in goose flesh. The date was two hundred years to the day of Estella's death.

Her back stiffened; she couldn't shake the feeling that the reaper's eyes were following her every movement. Her index finger traced the outlines of the chiseled names of each child. Isabel's mind drifted back to her nightmare from earlier that morning. She looked up at the statue, her eyes resting on the two children. The sculptural designs of the children were purposely nondescript, and yet they were reminiscent of the children lying dead on the side of the riverbank in the nightmare. She shuddered and quickly pulled her hand away from the statue.

Stepping back, she blinked hard several times in attempt to clear the image of the children from her mind. She turned away, continuing her path to the funeral service. Isabel shivered as the wind tickled the back of her neck. The eyes of the stone reaper followed her as she passed numerous crumbling tombstones. Admittedly, too afraid to turn back and look at the reaper, she kept it in her peripheral vision until it was out of sight. The graveyard contained over a century of loss and sadness.

As she passed the part of the cemetery designated for children, she considered what kind of loving god would allow so many to perish. Isabel's faith in an almighty deity of good had been tarnished by years of loss and evidence to the contrary. On a good day, when asked if she believed in God, she would say that if God did exist, she imagined that He or She wasn't very active in the day to day lives of humanity. Although raised Catholic, she determined that God might have created the universe then left us to our own devices. Those whom Isabel engaged in theological discussions often stated that her worldview was jaded. Isabel wholeheartedly disagreed. Her existential examination of faith demonstrated a certain gratitude for creation without demanding much else from God. There was a small part of her that hoped that maybe there was nothing beyond this life. The peace of silence and non-existence might be a kindness, to be forever cognoscente of each terrible moment and memory seemed cruel.

She stared at the small cherub statures as she passed and thought even those most innocent children were not immune to the cruel vicissitudes of life. She forced her gaze straight ahead, determined not to look back until she had passed through the children's section. Her thoughts drifted back to the tub nightmare. Images of the dead children on the shore seared in her memory.

"Was I at the grave of the children from my nightmare?"

She chided herself for indulging her irrational fears. She was sleep deprived and, in a stress-addled state, making connections where there were none. She wished she believed in ghosts. Phantoms, and specters could have been a convenient scapegoat for the strange happenings

There was a reasonable explanation, and she had read about it, in an article discussing the Diathesis Stress Model. The model characterized the development of schizophrenia later in life as a combination of genetic vulnerability and environmental stressors. There was no doubt, considering her current circumstances that she fit the model.

When the funeral was over and she returned home, Isabel would get evaluated, take the proper steps, and seek treatment. Exhausted, she didn't want to think about her trauma anymore. In the past few days, she had her fill of self-analysis and paranoia. She repeated Estella's mantra for fear, a means to ward-off getting lost in the labyrinth of her own panic.

"*Se fuerte*. You need to face what you fear head on; you can't go around it. The only way to get past it is through it."

She whispered the words over and over again until she saw a woman in a black dress placing flowers at a grave. Isabel bit down on her lip to keep from repeating her mantra a final time.

As she approached, the woman dusted off her dress and stood.

"Bird, is that you?" Isabel said.

Birdie Rodriguez had lost a significant amount weight in her twenties, but her cheeks were still plump, which made her look like a Disney princess. She was curvy and lovely. Her long black dress caught the breeze, giving her an ethereal air.

"Yeah, it's me. I was just visiting with Dad before heading to Estella's service."

Isabel walked around the gravestone to Birdie. It was newer, about fourteen years old. She stared at the inscription.

Manuel Ernesto Rodriguez, Loving husband and father.

The date of his death was April 19, 2005. Isabel remembered attending Mr. Rodriguez's funeral. Estella insisted they go and show support for the Rodriguez family. Isabel was reluctant to go to his service because Manuel committed suicide. He hanged himself after his farm and home were foreclosed. Isabel worried attending the funeral would trigger some repressed memories of Marisol. At that time, she had successfully buried almost all recollection of her mother after researching the details of her death. She feared seeing the sad faces of the Rodriguez children would bring those memories back from the dead.

It was a sad day, and she sympathized with his family but didn't reflect on her loss. Instead, she recognized the expressions of misery on Birdie and Manny's faces. She understood their pain all too well. She wanted to offer sincere condolences to them. Manny Junior was in high school and a fellow classmate. He was quirky, kind, and he never judged Isabel by her family history.

During most of junior high and the early part of high school, Isabel didn't particularly like Birdie, but sympathy for her loss outweighed hostility. Birdie was an upperclassman and one of Isabel's childhood tormentors.

Birdie would shout in a sing-song voice, "Your Daddy was a psycho killer, and your mommy was a loon!"

They had several schoolyard fights. Isabel broke Birdie's nose in middle school, even though Birdie towered over her and outweighed Isabel by twenty pounds. Birdie was a cruel bully, until her dad died. It seemed to Isabel that Birdie was too heartbroken to take delight in hardship of others after that. She stopped teasing Isabel and ceased to even acknowledge her presence in school. Birdie's abject avoidance confounded her. She braced herself for an insult every time Birdie passed her in the halls, but she would walk by in a daze with hardly an upward glance.

Although the circumstance of Manuel's suicide was different from Marisol's, it was met with the same level of stigma and scorn. Birdie was taunted and ostracized by the same tormentors who harassed Isabel. Manny ignored the negativity, but Birdie internalized it. Isabel knew how awful it felt to be judged for the misguided actions of a parent. She took no satisfaction in witnessing Birdie's pain; she wouldn't wish that kind of hurt on anyone. Walking to school each day with the anxiety of being the subject of gossip and bullying was gut-wrenching. It filled Isabel with a constant anger and a pit in her stomach. She knew that Birdie was living with that same pit, gnawing away at her sense of self. In that state of mind, adrenaline was always pumping, and you never knew if it was a fight or run kind of day.

Their relationship changed one rainy afternoon; Isabel stumbled over Birdie crying on the floor of the girl's bathroom in the English building. Compelled to offer comfort, Isabel knelt down and rubbed her back, like Estella used to when she would cry. Birdie barely registered her presence. She shrunk away from Isabel's touch and looked up.

"Oh, it's you." Birdie said.

"Are you okay?"

"No, I'm not fucking okay. Adeline Reynolds asked me if I was going to kill myself just like my Dad. What is wrong with people?"

Isabel bit down on her lip and shook her head. Birdie's mouth fell open. It was obvious that self-awareness had struck Birdie like a bolt of lightning. She stared at Isabel and broke down into a blubbering heap of tears and running mascara.

"Shit, I was so horrible to you. I'm sorry. I'm so goddamn sorry. I was so awful to you."

Isabel walked to the adjacent bathroom stall, pulled off a few sheets of toilet paper and handed them to Birdie.

"Here take this; you look like Alice Cooper." Isabel said.

"Oh, thanks." Birdie said as she dabbed at her eyes with the toilet paper.

"It will be okay; you just need to calm down. You can't let them know they got to you. Don't let them see you break. Be strong."

Birdie grabbed Isabel in a smothering hug, pulling her down on the floor. After that day, they became friends with a unique understanding of one another. She wished that Manuel's death was the last disaster to befall the Rodriguez family, but her hopes were soon dashed. The Rodriguez name became small-town famous a few years later. The tragedies that rocked their household was enough for them to be considered cursed by many superstitious members of the community. Their name became associated with misfortune. Stigma clung to their name in whispers and suspicious glances. Small towns love their labels like the town drunk, the esteemed families, and the kids from the wrong side of the tracks. Every town has their share of infamous families, those marked by tragedy and loss. The Rodriguez family was the most recent in memory, until now.

When Manny Junior returned from the Afghan War, he suffered from post-traumatic stress disorder. He spent a few months getting treatment in an inpatient facility. Manny was out of treatment after six months. Although his condition improved, he was met with ignorance and unease. He was the topic of discussion for the entire town.

He worked hard to maintain a sense of routine and stability but was unable quell people's misconceptions about post-traumatic stress disorder. Despite his progress he was considered damaged. Constantly monitored or scrutinized, he couldn't go to the grocery store without a procession of whispers following behind him. Locals watched and waited for him to explode. Unable to tolerate the gossip and rumors, he moved to another town. Two years later, he was living happily with his wife and daughter on their farm. Manny had outrun small-town infamy and found peace.

Birdie stayed in town; she endured the gossip with her head held high. Isabel respected Birdie's courage. She hadn't faced the town yet and wasn't sure if she was capable of keeping Birdie's level of composure and grace. Isabel's family history was much darker than the

Rodriguez's. Murder and multiple suicides were now their legacy.

Insanity is the banner of the Martin Del Campos family.

Birdie reached out and hugged Isabel, forcing her thoughts to the present. Birdie rubbed Isabel's back before letting go.

"I'm so sorry about Estella."

"Me too." Isabel said.

"How have you been? Your life looks pretty exciting on Facebook with all the traveling and book tours."

"It's been good, How's nursing?"

"Work is, you know, work. There's really not much to report. Small town hospitals don't get much action. We get a few overdoses and there's been a bit of a measles outbreak because of the anti-vaxers, but other than that, it's a pretty good gig."

Isabel nodded pleasantly.

"I saw on Facebook, Wyatt's birthday party looked great. He's getting so big."

"He had such a good birthday and thank you for sending the Duplo blocks. Wyatt loved them. I was going to send you a thank you note but you know, the best intentions of a busy mom often go nowhere."

"No worries, Bird. I'm happy to send your kiddos gifts, especially since I've never been back her home to properly visit with them.

"It's okay, hon. I understand why you haven't been back. I can't believe Wyatt is four and Lilly is almost eight. You'll have to come by and see the kids while you're home. We should have dinner before you leave."

"I'd love to, thanks."

Birdie was the only person from Isabel's past that she kept in contact with, even if at times, it was only sparse interactions on social media. The burning sting of shame rose in her stomach as she acknowledged her intentional distance from Birdie. She muted Birdie's photos and content on social media a few times over the years. It was hard to see images of home in the background of Birdie's life. She enjoyed interacting with Birdie through periodic texts and holiday cards. She stared at her lovely friend and realized how much she missed her.

"It's good to see you Bird, I missed you."

"I missed you too, honey. It's sad to see you back home like this, but I'm glad you're here."

They looked out past the top of the hill. A large crowd congregated near the side of the courtyard, farthest from the chapel, signaling Estella's service would soon commence. Isabel sighed.

"I'm not sure I'm ready for this?" Isabel said, as she looked at the crowd.

"You'll get through it. The worst part is the gossip that follows, but hey you get to leave town after this."

"I'm so sorry that you had to deal with all of that following everything with your Dad and Manny."

"The gossip about Dad and Manny has actually died down quite a bit. Believe it or not, things have been better over the last few years, but I had to take certain steps to appease the more superstitious members of the community."

"What do you mean, did they make you sacrifice a chicken?"

"*Chingona*! No, but I did have to have a Brujo come from Mexico to get rid of the *mala suerte*."

"How did he get rid of your bad luck?"

"He came to my home with a bunch of palo santo, candles, herbs, and eggs, then he said a bunch of prayers. And poof, no more *mala suerte*. The ritual seemed to help with the stigma, but people still talk."

"Maybe I should go visit the brujo."

"You should girl, you definitely have the *mala suerte*."

"*Lo seas*. How bad is the gossip about Estella?"

"It's a small-town Isa, people don't have a lot to talk about. Estella's death was big news. You know how people are."

Isabel nodded and said, "I hate to think that suicide is what people will forever associate Estella with. She was so much more than the circumstances of her death. She deserved better."

Birdie stood silent, she stared at the surrounding headstones.

"Look at this place. How old are some of these graves?"

She didn't give Isabel a chance to reply. Her eyes filled with tears and she said, "We are surrounded by history and tragedy. Our lives are built on top of the deaths of others. How many dead bodies are we standing on?"

Birdie wiped away her tears, kissed her hand and touched her father's gravestone. She turned to face the expanse of graves that rested on the hillside, leading to the valley below.

"You're right Birdie, this whole country is one giant graveyard. This land never forgets. This area is full of ghosts with living, breathing memories. It will never let us forget the tragedies that befell our families. I can't forget and neither can you. I feel like our pain is inescapable and worse yet, it's seen as spectacle," Isabel said.

"So, what if our families have become cautionary tales? We're more than our history. We are surrounded by death on a daily basis, but we don't think about it much. Estella was more than her death. She'll live on in your memory and you can choose which of those memories you relieve when you think of her. The opinions of other's really don't matter much, it's the moments you had with her that matter most. Please try to remember that, especially today." Birdie said.

"I'll try to keep that in mind but aren't you sick of being haunted by the past. I've been here less than two days and it's driving me insane."

"I think I'm just used to it." Birdie said.

There was solace in knowing that Birdie understood what she was going through. Birdie was a good friend, a real friend, and that was rare. Isabel had friends, but they only knew parts of her history. She neglected to tell people about her parents or her estrangement with Estella. She talked about her childhood and home in vagaries or not at all. Her agent and publicist worked hard to keep details about her parents out of social media. She hid so much of herself away, that it was nice to be around a friend who knew all about her past and didn't judge her for it. She was sure Birdie felt the same.

"Are you going to the memorial service after the funeral? I heard that Joe is hosting it at Debbie's bar?"

"No, Debbie and Estella didn't get along. I can't believe Debbie agreed to have the memorial service at her bar."

"If you're not going, neither am I. Honestly, I don't think I could handle seeing all the confederate flags and photos from Debbie's pageant days on the walls. Plus, the Women's Auxiliary wanted to host their own memorial since they agreed that Debbie's bar wasn't a suitable location for a memorial service. Would you like to go there instead?"

"Are they hosting it at the bingo hall?"

"Yes, Norma Crane made ten different kinds of pies, all in Estella's honor."

"Estella loved bingo and pie. That feels like a great way to honor her memory. Anyway, I think Joe wanted Estella's service at Debbie's because he knew I wouldn't go, plus he could get plastered at his favorite bar."

"Debbie hates anyone with brown skin that wasn't the result of a spray tan. You know there are some pretty terrible rumors about her floating around." Birdie said.

"Oh, I'm sure there are." Isabel said, as she rolled her eyes.

"Debbie was never charged, but she was suspected of being part of a white nationalist group that was accused of poisoning water containers, which were left in the desert for migrants."

"That's fucking evil!" Isabel said.

"Do you think she'll come to Estella's funeral service?" Birdie said.

"God, I hope not."

They looked out to the crowd of mourners who began taking their seats.

"You ready to go face some old ghosts?" Birdie said.

"As ready as I'll ever be."

Birdie grabbed Isabel's hand and said, "Don't let them see you break, be strong."

Isabel nodded and they walked through the small grass courtyard, where the service was to begin. The white casket was surrounded by colorful flower arrangements, flanked by multiple rows of folding chairs. It seemed as if everyone from the town had come to the funeral.

"Looks like the whole town came." Isabel said.

"You sound surprised; everyone loved Estella." Birdie said, earnestly.

Birdie found a seat in the backrow, giving Isabel an encouraging nod as she walked through the crowd to the front. Isabel took a deep breath to steady herself. Her return home would likely be the topic of discussion for Bingo night at the community hall, hosted by the Women's Auxiliary.

In a small town, gossip spreads like wildfire. Locals might not have known all the details of Isabel and Estella's falling out, but they knew enough. She expected idle chitchat. It comes with the territory, but there were more than a few community members that treated her with contempt. They saw her as an outsider, unwelcome, unstable, and possibly dangerous.

Estella worked hard to remove the stain of Marisol's actions, but Estella's suicide would undoubtedly undo all her efforts. Now, Estella's death would be met with whispers and gossip. The family history of tragedy would be pondered and discussed throughout the town.

How many of them were here for the spectacle? Oh god, we're just like the Rodriguez family, now seen as cursed or crazy. Suicide, insanity, or murder. Take your pick folks, none of those options are inaccurate.

Isabel received some notoriety and success in her career and hoped that would equal stability to those who viewed her as nothing more than the posterchild for family dysfunction. She held fast to the aspiration that through writing, her name would become associated with fiction and her passion for written word. Her efforts were in vain; she would never be fully accepted, not now, perhaps not ever. Estella's suicide would confirm their suspicions about her family, and they would now look to her with bated breath, waiting for insanity or violence to present itself.

Guilt rose up in her chest, making it hard to take a deep breath. She stared at the casket, Estella would have hated to see her standing at the edge of the procession, watching alone as a fearful outsider. She had always been able to detect the darkness in people, but that was not appropriate for today. Estella deserved better. She would not want Isabel to think about the town in that way. She would try and channel Estella's positive nature.

Sure, there are people here in search of gossip, but fuck 'em.

Isabel reminded herself, not all of the townspeople think that way. Estella was a well-respected, active member of the community. There are good and kind people here, who are mourning her loss. The sheer size of the crowd speaks to that. Their expressions are grim. No one is here, delighted by the notion of fresh gossip. Estella deserved Isabel's best today. She resolved to cast aside her socially awkward nature and fight the urge to isolate and withdraw. Determined to conduct herself the way Estella would, with comfort and heartfelt words of caring, she would be gracious and social. She would remind those that cast sideways glances at her, that Estella raised her right.

She smiled, shook hands, and thanked everyone for their condolences and support. She looked around the crowd to see if Joe had arrived. Her jaw clenched and her stomach churned as she saw him approaching, following behind the last remaining community members. She turned away from Joe's approach and continued to thank fellow mourners and former family friends. The seemingly endless stream of townsfolk tested her will to remain present. She longed to escape into her imagination. Although displays of false social niceties made Isabel uncomfortable in her own skin, she was reminded of her promise to conduct herself accordingly.

Diego waded through the large crowd to greet Isabel, but was quickly pushed aside by his mother, Rosa. She reached out and grabbed Isabel, embracing her with surprising strength. Rosa was a truly sweet woman. She was short and stout, but her figure only lent to the comforting and kind air of her company. Her deep-set smile lines and wrinkles around her eyes were instantly endearing.

Rosa released her and took Isabel's hands into hers. Rosa's hands were course due to years of farm life.

"I am so sorry for your loss. Estella was my best friend. I will miss her for the rest of my life." Rosa said as large tears rolled down her plump cheeks. She brushed away the tears from her face, dabbing at her cheeks with an old handkerchief.

"It is good to see you after all these years. We have really missed you." Rosa said, as she tilted her head in Diego's direction.

It was no secret that Rosa had hoped that they would have ended up together. After their breakup, Rosa expressed guilt over the demise of their relationship. Rosa told Isabel that she believed they split up because Diego had to stay and help with the farm, unable to go off to college. She blamed herself for the distance that grew between them, which ultimately ended their relationship.

Likewise, she harbored no ill will toward Rosa. She never blamed Rosa for the fate of her relationship with Diego. Isabel attributed their eventual split to life circumstance and distance of which there was no one to blame.

Diego was staring at his mother with abject embarrassment.

"Come on Mom, let me help you to your seat."

Diego was flushed as he turned back to Isabel. He hugged her but it was oddly formal and still not like his normal hug. His movements were rigid and overly stiff, he seemed to be aware of his mother's hopeful gaze.

"I'm so sorry about Estella, I'm so sorry for everything." Diego said.

The chaplain exited the rear of the chapel, and the congregation quickly found their seats. Isabel sat in the front row next to Diego and Rosa. They were soon joined by Joe, who sat three seats away from her. Joe looked at Isabel, giving her a blank stare without any sign of recognition or acknowledgment. Did he recognize her? With a spark of hostility, Joe rose from his chair and walked over to Isabel. In an instinctive, almost defensive motion, Isabel stood to meet Joe head on.

"I didn't recognize you. Looks like you've grown up some. Considering the girl, you once were, I can only imagine what a piece of work you've grown up to be." Joe said.

"The years haven't been kind to you." Isabel said.

Their eye's locked, neither one looked away, and a heavy silence filled the air around them. Joe issued a heavy exhalation before returning to his seat. Isabel clenched her jaw as the scent of putrid liquor surrounded them like a cloud. She bit down on the inside of her cheek to keep from screaming at him. Simmering, she sat down.

Diego took Isabel's hand, and her eyes met his. He gave her a slight nod and she steadied herself, taking a calming breath. She sat, calmly holding Diego's hand, without further interaction with Joe. For the entirety of the service, Isabel pushed her away her emotions. She was utterly numb, and she welcomed it. The cold, emptiness was tolerable; it was a shield, protecting her from a tidal wave of pain, The chaplain's words rang hollow in her ears. She took no comfort or solace in them. Approaching storm clouds loomed over the casket. Eventually the sun disappeared behind dark clouds, and the service ended.

Isabel rose from her chair as the crowd began to disperse. Birdie was the first to approach. Her eyes and nose were bright red from crying. She dabbed her eyes and hugged Isabel hard.

"You made it through the funeral; stay strong. Today is almost over." Birdie said, in a whisper.

"Thanks Bird."

"I'll meet you at the bingo hall?" Birdie said.

"See you there soon, I just have to finish up here, then I'll be on my way."

"I'm going to hold you to your promise to come to dinner, I'll make Albondigas for you." Birdie said.

"That sounds great. I haven't had a good bowl of Albondigas is years. How about dinner tomorrow?"

Birdie smiled and said, "Tomorrow night then. The kids are gonna be so happy to see you."

"I can't wait." Isabel said. She meant it.

Birdie walked away, still rubbing her cheeks and nose. Keeping to her resolution, Isabel shook hands and received farewells. As she exchanged niceties, she noticed a mop of bleach-blonde hair out of the corner of her eye.

"Aw, fuck. What the hell is she doing here?"

It was Debbie, the infamous town gossip, owner of her namesake bar and operator of the blog, God Save White America. Debbie hated Estella. There was no doubt in Isabel's mind that Debbie was there for the spectacle and to gather fresh gossip. Her presence was clearly a test of Isabel's resolve to conduct herself the way Estella would.

The woman was vile. She pushed Estella's good nature to the limit. When Isabel was a teen during a Fourth of July event, Debbie drunkenly accused Estella of being an illegal and a land thief. Isabel thought Estella might punch her, but Estella just shook her head and walked away. Later, while watching the fireworks, Isabel questioned Estella about the altercation.

"You were born here, and the family has owned the farm since before the area was part of the United states. Why didn't you say anything or beat her to a pulp?"

Estella was calm and collected and smirked when Isabel mentioned beating Debbie to a pulp. She playfully tilted her head to the side as if considering Isabel's question and leaned back in her lawn chair.

"*Ella es estupida.*" Estella said, as she stared up at the fireworks that filled the sky with splashes of colorful light.

"Aw, aunty, Debbie is much worse than stupid."

Her cheeks were flushed, and she clenched her jaw as she spoke. Her use of Spanish meant she was rattled by Debbie's ignorant remarks. The fireworks illuminated Estella's face in beautiful shades of rainbow colors as she spoke.

"She thinks that anyone with brown skin is beneath her. She wants me to hit her so I can confirm her belief that we are violent and dangerous. There's just no reasoning with a person like that. You have to rise above that kind of hate, otherwise you'll drown in it with them. *Sé fuerte*, even when they challenge your sense of self."

Estella always found teachable moments. Isabel admired her composure, even if she wasn't sure she would do the same in that situation.

Isabel tried to freeze the image of Estella's calm demeanor in her mind as Debbie stumbled through the crowd. Over a decade of heavy drinking had done untold damage to her appearance. She was short and skeletal thin. Her bottle-bleached hair washed out her pale and wrinkled face. Her sunken eye sockets were highlighted by a caustic green eyeshadow.

Isabel focused on Debbie's mouth, since her glassy eyes refused to meet hers. Debbie's lips were heavily wrinkled from years of smoking. Her pink lipstick did little to soften her weathered appearance. Her cheap, musky perfume assaulted Isabel's nose. It was pungent and did little to camouflage her liquor sweats.

In her youth, Debbie was considered a town beauty. Her 1969 Dairy Pageant Crown was prominently displayed in her bar along with photos of her glory days.

Was it all the drinking or the hate that stole her beauty? I guess the two aren't mutually exclusive, but her kind of hate was corrosive.

With the amount of time Joe spent at her bar, Isabel wondered if he and Debbie had an affair. They had plenty in common, both were drunks with a nasty streak, but Debbie didn't have the cash or the esteem he desired.

Debbie leaned in closer than Isabel was comfortable with, the aroma of alcohol and breath mints was almost too much. She licked her lips before speaking.

Sé fuerte.

"It's just so sad that you lost your aunt in such a terrible way. Suicide, who woulda thought." Isabel nodded and started to turn away from Debbie, but she cleared her throat and continued. "I'm sure it's gonna be hard to say goodbye to the ranch after Joe sells it."

"What do you mean?" Isabel said.

Isabel was completely caught off guard by Debbie's crass comment. Why on God's green earth would she ever think it was appropriate to discuss such an indelicate matter, moments after Estella's funeral?

Estella's words rang in her ears, "That woman is a damn fool."

Isabel's hands clenched and her wrists shook. She wanted to smash her fist right though Debbie's husk of a face. Estella wasn't even in the ground yet and Joe had already planned out his future which included selling the ranch. Worse yet, she was hearing the news from Debbie the only person she hated as much as Joe.

Debbie was unperturbed by Isabel's reaction. She turned to the coffin, swayed and turned back to Isabel, "Well Joey was saying that he was gonna sell the ranch, once he collects the inheritance."

"When did he say that?" Isabel said, stammering.

"Joey said the ranch had too many bad memories, you know with Estella having cancer and now this suicide thing. I thought it was gonna be the cancer that killed her, not suicide. I guess she didn't wanna be a burden anymore."

Isabel's mouth fell open, stunned, she stared at Debbie.

"Oh, don't look so shocked! A lot has changed since you've been gone. Your aunt was very difficult. Joey would come into the bar complaining about all the trouble Estella was giving him. She put him through so much and you were gone. He was the only one who took care of her. You can't really blame him for wanting to sell the ranch and make a fresh start," Debbie said, matter-of-factly.

Isabel took an exasperated breath and glared at Debbie. She was obviously drunk and unaffected by the somber tone of the exiting mourners. The imprudence of her comments completely eluded her. There was a malevolent glint in Debbie's eyes as she spoke, and it was clear that she was attempting to antagonize Isabel. For a moment, Isabel said nothing in response to Debbie. Instead, she just stared at her in abject disgust. Estella would walk away, but Isabel wasn't her. She might not allow herself to strike Debbie but refused to allow the conversation to progress any further.

"Get the hell away from me, right now!" Isabel said, seething and shaking with anger.

Debbie began to mumble incoherently.

"Not another fucking word, just go!" Isabel said.

Without comment or retort, Debbie diverted her gaze and stumbled away. Isabel's eye twitched as she watched Debbie sulk towards Joe. He had been watching their interaction from afar. Joe greeted Debbie with an affectionate hug. They stood close together, speaking in low voices. Debbie's arm movements were exaggerated as she began to cry and gesture toward Isabel. Joe nodded and hugged Debbie again.

Oh, fuck this bitch, I can't believe she ran crying to Joe.

Joe said loudly, "You pay no attention to Isabel. She's crazy like the rest of her family. Now don't fret about a thing. You go ahead and I'll see ya back at the bar."

He gave Debbie a wink and pat on the shoulder as she slumped away unsteadily. He turned his cold gaze to Isabel and approached.

Isabel chose to watch the mourners disappear in the distance rather than acknowledge Joe's hulking figure. She knew he wasn't approaching her to have a heart to heart. He looked like he wanted to rip her head off.

Joe's dry lips curled back, and he sneered as he whispered, "Well, I hope you're fucking happy."

"What's that supposed mean? If you're asking if I'm happy for telling off Debbie, then yes, I am. She's a vile bitch and I could have said much worse."

"I'm not talking about Debbie." Joe said.

"I have no idea what you're talking about. You're drunk. Maybe you should sleep it off before you make a scene."

"You're such an arrogant, entitled little shit. You never gave me a chance. You always looked down on me like I wasn't good enough for Estella.

"You weren't good enough for Estella. I saw right through you from the start."

"I took care of her!" Joe said.

"You mooched off her, you drank, you terrorized and beat her!"

In a low growl Joe said, "I know you hate me. Don't worry, I absolutely hate you too. After all this time I can't fucking believe she's leaving me with nothing and giving you everything!"

She bit down on the inside of her cheek, not wanting to reveal her shock. While she would never trust anything Joe had to say, his anger and resentment was genuine. Isabel was perplexed, but stubborn enough to digest this revelation without revealing her surprise. He didn't deserve the small victory he would bestow himself for leaving her speechless.

He leaned in closer and said, "I don't know how you did it, but I'll tell you what little girl, I'm going to fight this with everything I've got. I'll make sure you don't get a penny of what is rightfully mine!"

Unflinching Isabel stood fast, and Joe seized on Isabel's momentary silence.

"I took care of Estella for years. I stayed with her through cancer. Even after her hair started falling out in clumps. You shoulda seen her. She was like a rickety skeleton, but I stayed. I cleaned up her vomit and shit. You weren't there. She didn't wanna to tell you she was sick because she knew you couldn't handle it. I was there for her when no one else was. No other man wanted her; I gave her what she needed. I'm owed."

His words were awful, but partially true. Isabel wasn't there for Estella. Tears welled in her eyes as she imagined Estella sick and frail with only Joe to care for her. Her stomach sank, twisting in knots.

Did Estella believe I couldn't handle her cancer diagnosis?

This was not the time to consider such information. Joe would relish bringing her to tears, and she would never give him the satisfaction. Steadying herself she took a step closer.

"Listen you disgusting, drunk bastard this is Estella's funeral. You will not make a scene here. I know all about the plans you had for the ranch. If Estella left everything to me, then that means it's never going to happen. You want to fight for Estella's estate in court? Go ahead. I am sure the court will treat a wife-beating drunk fairly."

Isabel glared into his dull red eyes. There was a pause, and for a second, she was sure Joe would strike her. His face was red and bloated. His nostrils flared and the vein in his forehead throbbed and pulsed. He snorted in derision before tilting his head and cracking his neck.

He quickly turned away from Isabel, almost knocking into Estella's casket as he made his exit. What was left of the funeral procession watched the scene with expressions of staunch disapproval, shaking their heads and gasping as

Joe left. She him disappear among the statuary and tombstones.

Isabel stood, unable to move in a solemn kind of shock. She closed her eyes and exhaled. Her palms stung and pain traveled through her hands. Her wrist throbbed as she opened her fist to see that she had dug her nails in. Bloody indentations of nail marks etched across the soft flesh of her palm. She rubbed her hands together to try to ease the discomfort and steady her nerves.

Her mind swam with terrible possibilities. Isabel was unaware that Estella had left her everything. Joe and Estella's relationship must have been troubled if she chose to omit Joe from her will. This would explain why Estella was sleeping in her old bedroom. Sleeping in separate rooms was a hallmark of marital discord. Far worse, it might explain why Estella's revolver had been removed from the locked case and loaded.

Was Estella worried she would need to protect herself, was she afraid of Joe?

His temper had obviously worsened over the years, the patched holes in the walls were evidence enough of that.

Not for the first time, she questioned the circumstances surrounding Estella's death. Could Joe have been involved?

Did he encourage her to commit suicide, or could he have done something worse?

Her head throbbed; she pinched the bridge of her nose. There was too much to consider.

She wanted someone to blame. She wanted someone to hate, and Joe would be outstanding in that capacity. If she could focus her anger on him, then maybe she wouldn't hate herself for leaving.

What if she was jumping to conclusions or what if this was paranoia

The specter of doubt hung over her as she questioned the clarity of her reasoning.

"I can't think about this now." Isabel whispered to herself.

The groundskeepers would lower the casket soon and she needed to say goodbye. She picked up a Calla Lily from an arrangement that sat adjacent to Estella's casket. Looking down at the flower, she noticed several drops of blood had dripped from her palm and onto the pedals.

The crimson stain spread, expanding across the surface of the flower. The color reminded her of the red clay on the riverbank from her nightmare. Images of the dead children on the shore sliced through her mind in a rush of agonizing recollection. She dropped the flower and cupped her face in her hands. She rocked back and forth, trying to focus on the present.

"Just hold it together a little while longer, Estella deserves a goodbye."

Isabel wiped her hands across her coat, removing the last of the blood from her palms and walked to the floral arrangement to retrieve a fresh Calla Lily. She returned to the folding chair and tried to conjure the right words to say goodbye to her last remaining relative. She watched the leaves blow in the breeze as the rest of the mourners slowly departed. Lonely gravestones lined the hillside. The farms below stretched for miles. As far as the eye could see, rows of pecan trees rustled and bent in the wind.

She was alone. She shuddered and held her breath, worried she might once again hear the ghostly voice of La

Llorona call her name or experience some horrible waking nightmare.

She focused on Estella's casket to avoid indulging in fear. She stood, ready to say her final goodbye. Gently, she placed the single white Calla Lily on the top of the casket.

Isabel leaned down and whispered, "I am so sorry, Aunty. I wish I could have been there for you. I would have taken care of you. I wish you had let me help you. You didn't have to face cancer alone, and you didn't have to die like this."

She thought about Estella's death as she choked back tears. The questions were staggering, but Isabel didn't know where to begin. She felt unsteady and lost, like she had when she was young. She wished she could talk to Estella and ask for her advice, but those days were gone. Heat rose from her chest and traveled through her entire body as her anger gave way to determination. She resolved to discover the truth behind Estella's death. This kind of self-determination was new to Isabel. Her life was built upon the notion of burying the past and getting as far away from pain as possible. It felt unnatural to her, but she was determined.

"I swear, I will find out the truth. I love you, Estella."

Isabel slid her hand away from the casket and turned to walk through the cemetery. She strolled slowly among the tombstones, not paying any particular attention to her surroundings or where she was going. Her eyes barely left the ground. Her cheeks and eyelids burned as the cold wind chapped her tear-streaked face. A world without Estella in it seemed colder and darker. She approached the cemetery gate, where Diego and Rosa were waiting for her.

"I saw you talking to Joe, I take it the conversation didn't go well?" Diego said.

Isabel nodded, "It was bad."

"We are heading to the bingo hall for Estella's memorial service, are you going?" Diego said.

"Yeah, I'm headed there now. Birdie told me that Norma Crane made a bunch of pies, I need pie and maybe a drink."

"Do you want to get something to drink after the memorial?" Diego said.

"That sounds great; I'll meet you at the bingo hall."

CHAPTER SEVEN
Remembering the Dead

The bingo hall had been the epicenter for local festivities since the USO held dances during World War II. High school formals, club related social gatherings, and movie nights were prominently listed on the hall's calendar of events.

The main hall was used for larger events, but there were a number of smaller rooms reserved for intimate gatherings. Although the exterior of the building was old, the facility had been updated to accommodate new interests and technology. Some of the smaller rooms had been modified as studio art spaces and the largest included podcasting equipment. The vague scent of popcorn wafted in the air from last night's showing of Hitchcock's Vertigo.

The ladies-room with its caustic orange vinyl counter-tops and acid trip floral wallpaper was exactly as Isabel remembered. She let the cool water from the faucet run on her still sore palms. She cupped it in her hands and let the water spill over her fingers. Still buzzing with anger, she ground her teeth as Joe's words rang in her ears. Her eyeliner had smudged at the corner of her eye. She wept through the entire drive to the bingo hall.

"What a disaster. I need to pull it together if I'm going to face the crowd."

She turned off the faucet and adjusted her make-up. The bathroom door swung open hitting the wall. The door-catch rattled, startling Isabel. Birdie unceremoniously entered and smiled.

"Thought I might find you in here. How are you holding up? Lost your mind yet?" Birdie said.

"Hanging by the skin of my teeth. I think I lost my mind a few days ago so at this point sanity is kind of a lost cause." Isabel said, as she adeptly reapplied her eyeliner.

"The funeral service was very nice, and you should see the spread in the bingo hall. It's amazing. You're in the right place if you want to eat your feelings."

"Good, my plan was to stuff my face into oblivion."

Birdie stood beside her and applied lipstick.

"Yikes don't look at the center of the mirror. Did you forget about the ghost of Jodie Boyle?"

"Oh yeah, I completely forgot about Jodie Boyle." Isabel said, with a chuckle.

"Don't say her name again, three times would summon her."

"Shit, sorry."

Everyone who grew up in town knew the story of Jodie Boyle.

In the 1890's, the One-Eyed Raven Hotel and Saloon stood where the bingo hall currently resides. Jodie Boyle had been a prostitute there and was particularly popular with the cowboys. It was said that the bathhouse was located where the women's restroom now resides. Jodie had been bilked by a client, who refused to pay. When she

108

demanded payment, he chased her into the bathhouse and cut her throat in front of the shaving mirror. Legend has it that Jodie's ghost haunts the mirrors in the building, her favorite place to appear is at the center of the mirror in the lady's room. If her name was called three times while looking in the mirror, a bloody and weeping Jody would appear.

It was common practice for local girls to dare each other to say her name in the mirror. In Isabel's Junior year of high school, she and Birdie pushed Diego into the bathroom during Spring Formal. They shouted Jodie's name and pushed him through the door. Moments later, Diego rushed out of the room, his face as pale as death. He was obviously spooked, but he refused to answer if he had seen Jodie's ghost. Isabel stopped questioning him once she realized he was legitimately disturbed.

He didn't speak to her for a few days after that, and she had to resort to a grand romantic gesture to get him to forgive her. She recreated the famous scene from the movie Say Anything, where John Cusack's character holds a boom box over his head in order to win back the girl he loved. She couldn't find an actual boombox, but her old stereo did the trick. She played the Bouncing Souls song, "The Something Special," as loud as she could. She had chosen that particular song because they loved the band had become the soundtrack for their high school years.

By the time he finally woke up and heard the song, she had been out there for almost fifteen minutes. She had replayed the song almost six times, while she waited. Sleepily, Diego lumbered to his window and stared out at her. She could see his expression of exasperated anger fade to an affectionate smile. He lingered at the window, making her play the song again, before he vanished behind the curtains.

Frustrated she yelled over the music, "I'm not going anywhere Diego, I can do this all day. I'll play this freaking song a thousand times if I have to. I'm sorry!"

She desperately hoped he wasn't going to make her play the song a thousand times, her arms were already shaking. Out of shear discomfort, she had to lower the stereo a few times while she waited for him. There was no reply, and he didn't come back to the window; it was clear he was torturing her. She wanted to cry but instead she told herself, "*Sé fuerte*."

Isabel began to sing along with the chorus. Unfortunately, Isabel was a terrible singer. She was off key, but she sang her heart out. Before the song reached the second chorus, he ran out to the front lawn and scooped her up in his arms.

"You are too much, but I love you Isa."

"That stereo is heavier than you think. I may not be able to move my arms tomorrow. Wait, what did you just say?"

"I said I love you."

Isabel beamed at Diego and said, "I love you too."

That was the first time that they said they loved one another. Although, she had loved Diego since they were kids, it was indescribably liberating to say it out loud. She never mentioned Jodie Boyle to Diego after that. The memory of Diego's fear and the lingering question of what he had seen in that night seemed remote and unimportant compared to newly professed love.

The rosy, sweet memories of her youth were all the more welcome considering the flood of terrible recollections that had resurfaced over the past few days. Isabel inspected her newly applied make-up in the mirror, careful not to look in the center. Birdie handed the lipstick to her and said, "Did you ever manage to stay in here and say her name three times? I never could."

"No, the closest I came was saying her name two and a half times. I couldn't bring myself to finish."

"When I walked in, the way you were staring in the mirror made me wonder if you were working up the courage to say her name. Now that we're all grown up, do want to give it a try?" Birdie said with a wink.

"What? You mean actually say it? Come on. Remember what we did to Diego? He ran out of here like a bat outta hell. He was so pissed at me because of what we did, he stopped talking to me for days. I'm not sure I want to see what he saw?"

"I doubt he saw anything. Diego was in the bathroom for like a second before he ran out. He was probably just embarrassed to be in the girl's bathroom. My guess is he took one look at the tampon machine and freaked out. Besides, Diego was always kind of a jumpy kid."

"Ugh, I don't know, I'm not sure I am up for kid games."

"Are you scared?"

Not wanting to sound superstitious or divulge the truth of her strange encounters, Isabel shook her head.

Are adults supposed to buckle under peer pressure?

"On the count of three. One, two, three." Birdie said.

They exchanged nervous glances before turning their gaze to the center of the mirror.

Best case scenario, Jodie appears and proves that ghosts are real. I'm not going crazy but that means I'm being haunted.

They both stared into the mirror, waiting for the other to begin. An electric tension that flowed between Isabel and Birdie. The anticipation reached a fever pitch as Birdie burst out laughing. Relieved, Isabel joined in the chorus of snorting laughter. The release of rapturous giggles made Isabel even more grateful for Birdie's steadfast presence.

"Thanks, Bird. I needed a good laugh."

"So, if you weren't summoning you know who, what were you thinking about so intensely?"

"I wasn't summoning spirits; I was thinking about Estella. I have so many unanswered questions. I wonder if cancer changed her that much? When people talk about her and knowing how she died, it feels like they are talking about someone else. I wonder if I ever really knew her."

"I'm sorry, *chica*. I think you know who Estella was, but if you are looking for answers then I recommend talking to some of her friends out there."

"Fuck, that's a great idea. Rosa was her best friend; she may have some insight into Estella's state of mind."

"There you go, start with Rosa."

"Thanks Bird, you're a genius."

"You know it. Alright then, let's get out of this creepy bathroom. We can get some pie and you can ask Rosa some questions."

"That sounds like a plan, let's get some pie and leave poor Jodie…"

"Don't say her name." Birdie said, cutting Isabel off before she could finish.

"Sorry! Let's just leave you know who, to her business."

The bingo hall was full of mourners feasting on tamales, chile rellenos, and sopapillas. The dessert table was overflowing with pan dulce, flan, and pies. Norma outdid herself. There were over twenty different pies ranging from fruit-filled to every flavor of cream pie imaginable. Most of the town filled the bingo hall. Apparently, almost everyone skipped the memorial at Debbie's bar. Floral arrangements of pink tulips, Estella's favorite, and dusky pink tablecloths adorned the circular banquet tables. A photo-collage of Estella was situated on the stage in place of the bingo ball cage.

Isabel held a plate filled with flan and four slices of pie. She balanced the overflowing plate on her palm as she stared at the pictures of Estella. At the center of the collage was a photo of Estella holding her blue ribbon from last year's chili cook off. She was rail thin and pale, but her smile was beaming from ear to ear. For as long as Isabel could remember, Estella had won the chili cook-off every year.

When Isabel asked Estella her secret for winning, she winked and said, "The secret is in the green chiles, you've got to fire roast them before putting them in the pot."

"Come on auntie, I know your secret isn't the chiles."

"What are you talking about Isa?"

"Your secret isn't the roasted chiles. Your chili is so delicious because of the love you put into your cooking. I've watched you labor over so many pots of chili and I've seen how you put your heart and soul into your food. You can taste the love in every bite. Love is your secret, isn't it?"

Estella's cheeks turned bright red; she was rarely taken back by flattery.

"You are too smart for your own good," Estella said with a chuckle.

Over the years, when she was particularly homesick, Isabel would try to duplicate Estella's chili recipe. Estella showed her how to cook it, but it never came out quite right. Her chili was adequate, but it wasn't Estella's chili. There was something missing, it was her aunt's love. Isabel couldn't replicate it, so she gave up on cooking entirely. Estella's chili was now only a delicious memory: unattainable yet vivid. If she thought hard enough, she could still taste the char from the roasted chili and the sweetness of the onions grown in Estella's garden.

She smiled at the photo of Estella; it was good to see her smile her real smile. Tears filled her eyes, obscuring her vision and she brushed them away with her fingers.

A hand gently rested on her shoulder. She sniffled, dried her eyes and turned around. Maria Flores, president of the women's auxiliary was there. Maria was in her late sixties, but her back was straight, and shoulders set. She had been a dancer in her youth, and her posture had not diminished with age. Her hair was white, worn in the same pixie haircut she had since Isabel was a little girl. Her brown skin was soft and well moisturized. Isabel wished she could look half as good at Maria's age. For reasons beyond her comprehension, it was hard for her to fathom living that long. Isabel's life had been harsh, and she assumed eventually all the trauma would show on her face. She tried to imagine herself old and weathered, but soon the image of herself faded to a skeleton. Isabel pushed the gruesome imagining away and smiled at Maria.

"*Lo Siento, chiquita.*" Maria said.

"*Maria, gracias por todo esto, es muy hermoso.*" Isabel said.

Isabel's use of Spanish was slow. She was regretfully out of practice, rarely utilizing conversational Spanish other than ordering at her favorite taco shop. She was fluent in Spanglish and that's about the height of her fluency. Isabel reached back in her recollection, trying her best to conjugate verbs because she desperately wanted to issue a thoughtful expression of gratitude for the lovely reception Maria had created for Estella.

"Do you like the pictures? We collected quite a few over the years." Maria said. She must have sensed that Isabel was struggling with her Spanish.

Feeling that she failed to articulate herself well enough. Great I chocked and now we are speaking English.

"Yes, they're wonderful. *Gracias* for putting all this together. Estella would have loved everything. She would have adored the flowers and pie. It's perfect."

Maria tapped the center picture with her index finger and said, "That was a good day. It was really hard for Estella to get around and socialize at the end. Good days were few and far between. I want you to know that I don't—"

Maria couldn't finish her sentence; she closed her eyes and tears rolled down her cheeks. Composing herself, she pulled a handkerchief from her pocket and wiped away her tears.

"I don't judge Estella for what she did. I can't imagine the pain she was in. I just wanted you to know that no one here stands in judgment. She was a friend and a good woman."

"*Muchísimas gracias*. Honestly, I hate to think of people forgetting everything that made Estella wonderful and only remembering her for how she died."

Maria hugged Isabel with surprising force.

These are good people, and this is a good place.

"You are welcome to take the photo collage after the memorial. I made it with the intention of giving it to you. But I would like to keep the photo of her from the chili cook off. I want to hang it in the Women's Auxiliary office. Estella had quite the winning streak and I don't want people to ever forget that."

"Thank you, I would be honored. Please take the picture. I'm sure Estella would have been tickled to have her photo on display in the office."

"Well, I'll let you get back to your pies, but just in case you decide to stick around town, you are always welcome at bunco night. Birdie and a few other ladies your age are regulars."

"Thank you for the invitation, I'll think about it."

"Just remember you are always welcome here." Maria said, as walked toward the dessert table.

Isabel sat down at the table closest to the photo collage and set about devouring every last bite of flan and pie on her plate. She needed to drown her sorrows.

By the time The Temptations' greatest hits played over the speakers, Isabel was on her second plate. Her stomach was full, and her dress felt smaller than it had only a few hours earlier. She wished she wore something that was stretchy instead of form fitting considering how she expanded with each slice of pie.

I can't breathe, I can't think, and I'm just too full. I need to go directly into a food coma.

Full of regret, Isabel stared at the dessert table. "That last slice of pineapple cream pie was one slice too many."

Though she was full, she planned on taking the rest of the pineapple pie back with her to the farmhouse and devouring it after midnight, like a gremlin. Maria Flores tapped the microphone at the bingo stage.

"Excuse me, I'd like to take a moment and share some of my memories of Estella with you all. Afterward, everyone's welcome to share their memories, thoughts, and prayers."

The music was cut in the middle of the chorus of Commodores' "Night Shift." With the exception of forks rhythmically tapping glass dinner plates, the room was silent.

"We all remember that Estella was one hell of a cook. Each year during the chili cook-off, we all knew that second place was the best we could expect when up against Estella's chili. When I asked her what her secret was, she said that she put her heart and soul into her cooking.

Isabel smiled and whispered under her breath, "I knew it."

"Each bite was filled with love. That was Estella, when she did something, she did it with love. She was a kind and gracious friend. When I think of her, I'll remember her love."

The crowd applauded and sniffled. A few others spoke. Kind words and happy memories filled the room. Each speaker had nothing but positive things to say about Estella. She would have blushed and been mortified; Estella was never one to accept compliments with ease.

Estella was humble and she didn't like people to fuss over her.

The microphone made its way to Isabel. She held it far from her face with unsteady hands. She stared down at the microphone, debating on whether or not speak. She cleared her throat and stood up with no concept of what was going to come out of her mouth.

"Being home has stirred up a lot of memories, some wonderful and some painful. After my parents died, I had nightmares and was sleepwalking so much that I was afraid to fall asleep. One night, I was pacing around my room trying to stay awake. Estella heard me from downstairs and came to tuck me in. She told me something that I'll never forget. She said that maybe I was sleepwalking because I wasn't dealing with my emotions. She told me that I needed to feel the loss. It was okay to be sad, and it was definitely okay to cry.

"She was honest with me and never sugarcoated things, especially when it came to loss. She said you never get over it, you just get used to it. Let the pain make you stronger, harder. You can survive anything if you can survive this. Take the tragedies of your life and turn them into something meaningful. She would always tell me *sé fuerte*, be strong. Estella guided me and helped me. Those words shaped who I am today. Listening to your stories about her, I see that she did that for everyone. I think she would have wanted me to tell you that it's okay to be sad. It's okay to cry, but not to linger in her loss. She would tell you *sé fuerte*. She would want you to turn your pain into something meaningful. To take the lessons of her life and death and learn from them."

Isabel swallowed back tears and cleared her throat before continuing. The room was as silent as a graveyard after midnight.

"So, tell the people closest to you that you love them and don't hide the truth from them, no matter how ugly or scary it is. Hold them close and never let them go. Thank you all for your kindness and support."

She placed the microphone on the table. The room was dead silent, and every eye was on her. She was exposed, she blinked hard as numerous eyes without faces stared at her throughout the dimly lit bingo hall. She wanted to crawl out of her skin or run away.

Oh fuck, I think I overshared.

The room filled with a ghostly ensemble of whimpering and sobs. There wasn't a dry eye in the house. Everyone knew Isabel's loss and they grieved along with her. She picked up the microphone and handed it to the DJ who had quietly made his way beside her. She sat down and stared at her empty plate.

Birdie patted her on the shoulder and said, "Wow, that was unexpected. You were really going for naked honesty there."

Isabel rested her head on the table. She fantasized about crawling under the table and hiding under the dusky pink tablecloth for the rest of night, possibly forever. She could be the phantom of the bingo hall, only appearing to forage for food from party buffets. She could make friends with the ghost of Jodie Boyle and spend the rest of her days hiding from the shame of an all too honest eulogy.

"Oh god, I'm not sure of what just came out of my mouth. Was it really bad?"

"No honey, you didn't say anything that wasn't true."

Birdie patted the back of Isabel's head and laughed.

"I'm so glad you're back. You always kept things interesting." Birdie said.

The music turned on and the Commodores' silky voices echoed across the room. The mood was decidedly somber. Rosa was sitting at a table in the corner of the room, closet to the exit.

"Look, Rosa is sitting right by the exit; you can go talk to her then get the hell outta here." Birdie said, brightly.

"Thanks Bird, that's a good idea. I'll see you later."

"You bet your ass you will. Don't forget about dinner tomorrow."

"I wouldn't miss it; I'll see you tomorrow." Isabel said as she slowly stood.

She was too full to move at maximum speed. Rosa watched as Isabel approached. She slid her plate away and then rubbed the tears from her cheeks. The torrent of questions pressed down on Isabel as she approached. She tried to prioritize her questions before speaking. She wasn't optimistic enough to believe Rosa had all the answers but hoped she could at least lend guidance into understanding Estella's motivations. At best, Rosa would have enough insight into Estella's actions or confirm her suspicions about Joe. Diego pulled a handkerchief from his pocket and handed it to Rosa. He looked up at Isabel who was silently fidgeting over the table.

"You look like you could use that drink now." Diego said.

"I want to talk to your Mom first, but I'd love a drink after." Isabel said as she sat in the chair next Rosa then quickly turned back to Diego. "I really want a drink, but I don't want to go to Debbie's bar."

120

"Don't worry I'd never go to Debbie's bar. We can pick up a six pack and meet at my favorite place." Diego said.

Isabel knew that Diego's favorite place in the whole world was the far west bank of the river on his family's farm. The sight was stunning. A lush pasture touched the river's edge, and the tree line led your eye to the perfect view of surrounding countryside. The edge of the field was filled with wild lavender and sage, the aroma wafted in the breeze adding to the multi-sensory splendor. Isabel and Diego spent many happy hours together there.

"I'll give you and Mom some time to talk. Ma, I'll get the truck."

Isabel slowly approached Rosa, trying to summon the courage to ask about Estella's mental state. She started to speak but stammered, her throat was suddenly dry. The words were stuck, refusing to budge. She needed to be brave.

She cleared her throat and said, "You were Estella's best friend, so I would assume she shared her thoughts with you?"

Rosa cast her gaze to the ground.

"Well, we were raised in a different time, when people kept their problems to themselves. It wasn't appropriate to talk about personal issues. When I tried to ask her about sensitive subjects, Estella would just shut down on me."

"Did you know that Joe abused her?"

Rosa nodded and choked back tears. "I would see bruises on Estella, but she always covered for him. Deep down, I think I knew, but she would never admit to it."

"Did she talk to you about wanting to kill herself?"

The words tumbled out of her mouth before she could doubt them. She didn't intent to cut to the chase so abruptly, but it was too late to go back now. The answer was coming, and she needed to be ready for it.

Rosa grabbed Isabel's hands and shook her head, "No, she never said anything to me about wanting to kill herself."

"I found a bunch of prescription medication, the combination of taking all those drugs would have made it hard for her to think straight, was it possible that she may have taken her own life in an intoxicated state?"

"No! She hated taking all those medications. She told me she only kept them because Joe suffered from chronic back pain and his doctors cut him off. Being an ex-hippy, she was into the natural stuff, so she smoked a little, but it was only for medicinal purposes."

"Do you think Joe might have pushed her to commit suicide?"

"That man is a nasty beast. I believe he was capable of doing anything to get her money. When I found out how she died I spoke with the sheriff. He thought there was no reason to believe Joe had any involvement in her death, but my heart tells me otherwise."

"So does mine."

Isabel began to sob. Her dark suspicions about Joe were mounting. An unbearable pressure weighed heavy on her chest. The terrible implications were too much for her to bear.

Did he push her into doing it or did he just kill her?

Rosa wrapped her arms around Isabel. She sank into Rosa and cried. Rosa rocked back and forth, as she held Isabel.

"Let it out, *mija*. You don't have to hold it in." Rosa said.

"Joe said Estella didn't tell me about the cancer because she didn't think I could handle it." Isabel said between sobs.

"No, Estella wanted to protect you. She knew that if you found out she was sick; you would have left school to take care of her. She had big plans for you. She wanted you to have a good life and be happy."

"No, she thought I was weak." Isabel said.

"Listen to me, she wanted to call you so many times, but she didn't want you to see her like that. Estella thought she would contact you once she was in remission, but the cancer kept spreading."

"Why didn't you tell me?"

"I wanted to. I almost called you a few times over the years, but Estella begged me not to. She was my best friend in the whole world, and I had to respect her wishes. I'm sorry."

Isabel felt no anger at Rosa's admission. Estella was her best friend, and friends support each other. She couldn't resent or argue with their code of sisterhood.

"I should have been there for her. I should have fought harder to stay after our fight. I gave up on her. I tried to get her to leave Joe, but I failed. I failed her and I left her alone with him."

Isabel slumped into the chair next to Rosa. She held her face in her hands and Rosa rubbed her back.

"There was nothing you could have done. Estella was stubborn. When she made up her mind about something there was no changing it. She knew Joe wouldn't leave. He depended on her for money. She thought he would take care of her, and she didn't want you to be her nursemaid. She wanted you to become who you are, a successful and strong woman. She was proud of you."

"You really think there's nothing I could have said that would have changed her mind?"

"No. Nothing I ever said did."

Rosa hugged Isabel hard. Her breath was squeezed from her chest, by the strength of Rosa's wide fleshy arms. The knowledge that Estella hoped to reconcile was a hollow kind of comfort. There was too much left unsaid between them for it to be anything more. The familiar ache of loss echoed the pounding of her heartbeat in her ears. She felt small and inescapably alone, without family or love.

"We should get going." Rosa said.

She helped Rosa to her feet, and they made their way out of the bingo hall and down the front steps to the parking lot where Diego's old pickup truck rumbled to a halt beside the two crying women. Rosa gave Isabel another smothering hug, as Diego jumped out of the truck. He walked around and opened the door for Rosa.

Rosa brushed the tears from Isabel's face and said, "*Ten cuidado*, I know we have your suspicions about Joe, but if we are right, then he is dangerous."

"Thank you, I will."

"What are you going to do?"

"I don't know. Try to find some concrete proof, maybe Estella kept a diary or documented her cancer and diagnosis. It might prove her state of mind. It might tell us if she was really suicidal?"

"I don't know if she kept a diary, but if she did, then I hope you find it. Good luck. I'm sorry for your loss. I wish I could take it from you, but I'm not a Burden Eater." Rosa said.

Rosa kissed her cheek, then climbed into the truck with Diego's assistance. He closed the passenger door.

"How did it go? Was Mom able to answer your questions?"

"She gave me a lot to think about but right now, I could really use that drink."

CHAPTER EIGHT
Ghosts Of The Past

Isabel and Diego walked along the pasture on his farm, avoiding cows until they reached the grass field. The river ran along the edge of the entire county, cutting through farms and the undeveloped countryside. Isabel slung her high heels over her shoulder, as she strolled beside Diego.

Her foot was swollen and sore from her injury and she could no longer suffer the confinement of high heels. The cold grass beneath her feet was soft and soothing to her arches. She stepped lightly avoiding putting too much pressure on her injured heel. Even if she wasn't injured, she would have happily abandoned heels at this point in the day. She wasn't accustomed to wearing them. Her go-to shoes were Chuck Taylor Converse. She had a pair in every color. She appreciated the clean lines and practicality of sneakers; heels on the other hand were all form and no function. Two steps in the field with heels, and she would have broken her ankle.

The soft echo of cicadas humming and rushing river were familiar and comforting. The field remained the same, the countryside shaped the skyline in rhythmic patterns she knew all too well. The view had not changed, but the same could not be said for her. The hopeful girl that once walked through the field with the boy she loved was far from who she had become. Now, her youthful optimistic worldview and joy seemed willfully ignorant. She paused to reconsider her morose view of her youth.

Everyone is optimistic until the world gets its hands on you. Give yourself a break at least you were happy at one time.

Taking a cue from the younger Isabel, she took a deep breath and set her mind to enjoying the path she was walking.

They found a small clearing and sat down. Diego used an old bottle opener on his keychain to pop the cap off a bottle of beer, handing it to Isabel. He opened another for himself. The sky was getting darker, thick gray clouds filled the skyline, which reflected off the river's rippling waters. She sat for a moment, lost in its hypnotic rhythm.

A storm was approaching. Their peaceful time by the river was limited. Soon, the weather would turn on them. She took a deep breath and tossed her heels in the grass. Maybe with Diego at her side she would finally be able to relax, free of ghostly voices and nightmares. He stared at horizon and loosened his tie.

Diego was good company. He wouldn't pressure her to talk if she didn't want to. She could just be. She absently peeled the label from her beer and took a sip, trying not to think of Estella drowning herself, or worse, Joe killing her. The beer was still cold and chilled her throat as it went down. It had been a long time since she drank a beer while relaxing with Diego.

The landscape was majestic; walnut trees blew in the breeze and the tall grass rustled. The river stretched out in front of them, leading to the untamed countryside. From where they were sitting, the river seemed calm. A cold tingling crept down Isabel's spine. Estella died nearly four miles downriver from where she was sitting. She shook her head, trying to push the gruesome notion from her mind.

"I was terrified by this river when we were kids." Diego said, as he stared into the distance.

"Well, I'm sure the fact that I almost drowned in it didn't help." Isabel said.

Diego nodded and took a sip from his beer. They sat silently, watching the current drag fallen leaves downstream.

Isabel took a large gulp from her beer. When she closed her eyes, the dead children on the bank were there. She shook her head, hoping to jostle the image out of her mind. Her nightmares persisted into the waking world, clinging to her quite moments. Out of the corner of her eye, she could see La Llorona standing over her. She was being haunted by a nightmare. La Llorona's pale flesh, the veins underneath her dead blue eyes, were engraved in her memory.

An old dirty piece of cloth traveled downstream. It spun and floated like a ghost dancing down the halls of a Victorian castle in a Vincent Price movie.

As the cloth tangled on the reeds in front of her, Isabel choked. She lunged forward coughing as beer dribbled down her chin. Diego grabbed a stick and fished the fabric from the shallows.

"People gotta quit dumping their shit in the river." Diego said.

"What is it?"

She wasn't sure she wanted to know the answer but asked all the same. Diego turned it over, inspecting the cloth.

"I think it's a shawl, or maybe a veil?" Diego said as he placed it on the ground.

You gotta be kidding me, this can't be real. I'm being fucked with.

Isabel couldn't respond, La Llorona wore a similar lace veil with the same floral pattern and delicate bead work. The image of the spirit lifting her veil, revealing her ghastly, face was burned into her consciousness. Isabel winced and bit down on her bottom lip. Her chest was tight, and her hands shook, forcing her to put down the beer. She took a slow deep breath, holding back the rapid breathing that proceed a panic attack.

Don't lose your mind in front of Diego. It's just some garbage that washed down stream.

"Maybe it's La Llorona's veil?" Isabel said.

She looked away from the veil and watched Diego's reaction. He smirked with an expression of amusement. He must have thought she was being dark or joking. She turned the appearance of the veil over in her mind. This wasn't a delusion, Diego fished it out of the water. But, if she suspended her rationality, she could assert the appearance of the veil was the work of La Llorona.

Stop indulging the crazy, you've got to think your way through this.

She can't suspend reality, not now. It was dangerous to give fear and superstition credence. The nightmares, sleepwalking, ghostly voices, and visions of shadowy figures were not signs of a haunting, but more likely possible symptoms. She might be hallucinating, not haunted. The veil wasn't a sign. It was just an unfortunate coincidence, which resulted in her further questioning her reality and sanity. She took another deep breath, hoping to dismiss the appearance of the veil and waited for Diego to change the subject.

"You know my mom used the story of what happened to you to keep me from playing near the river's edge. Mom told me that La Llorona almost got you." Diego said.

She wasn't particularly in the mood to discuss her near-death experience, but Diego seemed interested. Diego enjoyed listening to her stories when they were young, and she always obliged him.

"There are so many popular Latin American folktales circulated in this part of the country; there was the *Cucuy*, the burden eaters, and of course La Llorona." Isabel said.

Diego was staring at the river, saying nothing, but Isabel could tell he was listening intently, patiently waiting for her to continue.

"When I was little, Estella would read a book called *Latin American Folktales* to me. I was absolutely fascinated by the legend of the weeping woman. I'd walk along the river's edge looking for her, listening to hear if she would call my name. The day that I fell in the river, I was searching for her."

"Why on earth would you go looking for La Llorona?" Diego said.

Isabel shrugged and sat in silence for a moment. Unsure of her original motivation, she assumed it had something to do with wanting proof there was existence beyond death.

"I think I wanted to know if ghosts were real because if La Llorona was out there then maybe my Mom wasn't gone forever."

"I knew you were a little morbid as a kid but had no idea you were actually looking for ghosts."

"Maybe I was too embarrassed to tell you. I can only guess at my ghost hunting motivation, but I missed my Mom and was desperately hoping she was still out there. I would have done anything to see her again or just know that she wasn't gone forever. Honestly, I don't care what happened to my Dad. Part of me hopes that there's nothing beyond this life, because I would hate to think of his ghost haunting our old house."

"That would definitely suck for the new family that moved in. Did you ever go back to that house?"

"No. You know me. I tend not to look back."

Diego sat in grim contemplation as Isabel remembered how much she missed her Mom and hoped she could still be out there. She sought out La Llorona as proof of an afterlife. If her nightmare wasn't a stress induced hallucination, then she had in fact found the weeping woman in her youth.

Biting down on the side of her lip she scolded herself. Before Estella's death, she considered herself a rational person, but all of the eerie occurrences and night terrors had her on edge. She stared at the river, fearing La Llorona would rise from the water.

"Enough about my ghost story, don't you have one to tell?" Isabel said.

"What are you talking about?"

"Jodie Boyle. Did you see her that night during winter formal?"

Diego gulped his beer and shook his head. Silent, he looked off.

"I can't talk about it, Isa. Do you even believe in ghosts?" Diego said.

"I wanted to believe in ghosts when I was young, but I never saw one, so I stopped believing. They became a useful plot device in my writing, nothing more. I didn't really question the possibility of their existence until a couple of days ago. Now, I'm not so sure."

"Maybe when you make up your mind about ghosts, I'll tell you my story. Until then, I just can't talk about her." Diego said.

The veil caught the breeze, rolled several inches and finally rested at Isabel's feet. She had heard the phrase "blood running cold," but this was the first time she experienced it. Chills ran through her body. She grabbed her beer, gulping it, trying to regain some warmth. She wanted to be honest. Maybe if she voiced her concerns aloud, she could hear how ridiculous they sounded, and she could demote them from legitimate concerns to the product of an overactive imagination.

"Can I be honest with you? I've been experiencing some really strange things lately and I think that I'm either haunted or grief is driving me crazy. I've been mentally torturing myself over Estella's death. It has me questioning everything. I can't sleep, and when I do, I'm plagued by nightmares."

"Holy shit, how long has this been going on?"

"Right after I found out Estella died. Last night, I was sleepwalking, and I woke up outside at the edge of the riverbank. I think that Estella's death might have caused me to finally lose my mind."

"You're still worried about becoming like your Mom and Dad?" Diego said.

"Yes."

"I think you're grieving, and you feel a lot of guilt."

"The things I have been experiencing seemed so real. I don't trust my own judgment anymore."

"If you think you are being haunted by a ghost you need to figure out why? You didn't say their name while looking in a mirror, did you?

"No, I didn't say a name in the mirror or anything like that, but I've been seeing some weird shit."

"Well, what do you mean, specifically?"

"It started with seeing shadows and hearing voices; then the nightmares started. The night before I came her there was a shadow in the mirror and wet footprint on the floor, everything just got worse after that. Oh, and there's the black sludge that appeared in my sink and at the farmhouse."

Isabel could tell by the look on Diego's face that he was skeptical.

I'm rambling, he doesn't believe me, but can I really blame him? Hearing it out-loud I sound crazy.

"Okay, so if this is a legitimate haunting, you gotta find out why the ghost is appearing to you. But if you are really concerned that you are experiencing symptoms, you should talk to your doctor about it. You are not alone. I'm here for you."

"I've never felt so alone and honestly you just sitting here listening to me is the best I've felt in days."

"Instead of being haunted, maybe what you are experiencing is grief. You don't really deal with heavy emotional shit like pain. You push it down and lock it away. Your trauma could be presenting in weird ways?"

"I don't really know what is happening to me?"

"Well before you go ghost hunting or lock yourself away in a mental hospital, I think you might want to start by coping with your loss and dealing with whatever misplaced guilt you're carrying."

Isabel kicked a rock into the river and said, "Oh the guilt isn't misplaced, the blame stands squarely on my shoulders, just like everything else. It wasn't the weeping woman's fault that I almost drowned in the river all those years ago, the fault lies with me. As does my estrangement from Estella, I am at fault for the state of our relationship. If I could have convinced her to leave Joe, then maybe none of this would have happened."

Overcome with self-loathing, she took a hard sip from her beer.

"None of this is your fault." Diego said earnestly.

"There's something else bothering me. I think Estella's death wasn't a suicide. Joe may have coaxed her into killing herself or worse."

"Why do you think that?"

"Joe had been abusing her for years. She stayed with him so he could care for her, but there were signs of continued abuse all over the house. He punched holes in the walls, and she had been sleeping in my old room. Her old revolver was out of the case and loaded. I think she was afraid of him. Maybe she was worried he might kill her. Oh, and she left him out of her estate. He thought he would get everything when she died. He was bragging to Debbie about what he was going to do with the money and the farm."

"I had no idea he was abusing her, but that's not necessarily evidence she didn't commit suicide."

"Rosa said she didn't believe Estella was suicidal. And given how my parents died, I don't think she would ever do that."

"If you really think this is a possibility, go talk to the sheriff." Diego said.

"I don't know if it's enough to bring to the police. All I have are my suspicions. I need more proof than a gut feeling. Maybe I'm just being paranoid or in denial, but this feels real."

"We can figure this out Isa."

"We can?"

"You don't have to go through this alone." Diego said.

"I hate to admit it, Diego, but I've always been better at dealing with imaginary darkness than the real thing. I manufacture monsters and ghosts because real evil is too hard to bear. After my parents died, I retreated into my own imaginary world. Estella believed I was too weak to deal with the news of her cancer diagnosis. She didn't think I could handle it."

"I'm sure she didn't think that."

"Joe said as much at the funeral."

Isabel pinched the bridge of her nose, trying to force back tears. She didn't want to cry over Joe's words, but they cut too deep.

"It's not surprising she kept so much from me. When Estella was abused, I abandoned her, and now instead of dealing with the pain of her loss, I concocted the notion that I'm being haunted. I am imagining ghosts and hearing a voice call my name."

Diego reached out to Isabel, softly touching her hand.

"We all deal with grief differently. It can come out in strange ways. You didn't abandon Estella; she exiled you. None of this is your fault. We'll get this figured out."

Isabel couldn't bear to look into Diego's eyes. His words were kind and understanding. She hated herself and didn't believe she deserved his compassion. Her stomach twisted in several knots. Although she felt no reprieve from her guilt, her resolve was stronger than ever. Having laid out all of her suspicions, she was left with the arduous task of finding substantial evidence which she would then bring to the authorities. She needed to scour the farmhouse to find something concrete.

"I hope Estella kept a journal, or maybe I can find some other evidence that she didn't kill herself. It's a long shot, but I have to try."

"So, you're looking for written evidence like a diary or letter? Where would Estella keep something like that?"

"I'm not sure, but I am going to search the entire farmhouse before I leave."

Isabel.

The sound of her name floated along the current of the river. Isabel sat up straight and nervously searched the darkness of the river, trying to locate the weeping woman. She looked at Diego to see if he had heard the disembodied voice, but his eyes were firmly set on her. She knew he heard nothing. Isabel assumed that the ghosts of her imagination were once again calling her away from the present emotional distress. Isabel stood; her gaze drifted along the horizon.

She scanned the tree line, fog was rolling in, obscuring the treetops. Although dark clouds loomed overhead, the peaceful scenery stood in direct contrast to her inner turmoil. A growing storm of anxiety collided in her mind, she feared what her search would reveal, but she was committed to facing the dark road ahead.

"There you go again, Isa. You're a million miles away."

Shaking herself from her introspection, she gave Diego a weak smile. "I'm sorry for being inside my own head so much."

"It's just who you are. Your imagination has always taken you away."

Isabel sat beside Diego. She picked up a twig and fidgeted with it. Time had changed Diego. He was open and forthright. His understanding was disarming, and she couldn't resist asking the questions she had pondered for years after their breakup.

If I was bold enough to ask about Jodie Boyle, then I should be brave enough to ask an even scarier question.

"But you never tried to stop me from leaving. Why didn't you ask me to stay?"

Looking into Diego's eyes, his expression was somber.

Isabel turned back towards the river, absently playing with the twig, avoiding Diego's gaze. He rubbed the back of his neck, an indicator that he was uncomfortable. Diego followed Isabel's lead of avoidance. He placed his beer on the ground, carefully choosing his words.

"I never stopped you from leaving because I knew that your imagination would bring you the world. How could I compete with that?"

Isabel stopped fidgeting with the twig and stared at him. She was completely caught off guard by his response.

He didn't end their relationship because of distance or falling out of love, but because he felt a sense of responsibility for her future happiness. It was noble yet maddening.

"Estella pulled me aside before graduation. She had big plans for your future. She said that you needed to go to college, see the world, and that if I truly loved you, I wouldn't ask you to stay here with me." Diego cleared his throat. "I loved you, Isa. Estella told me that love is not selfish, so I couldn't be selfish with you. If I had asked you to come back after college, do you really think you would have been happy here?"

Without any reluctance, Isabel knew the answer to Diego's question. She had asked that same question of herself many times over the years. A string of terrible relationships and failed romantic entanglements were proof, Diego had been the love of her life.

Although they had lost touch over the years, Isabel often wondered what her life would have been like if they had stayed together. She assumed that their youth and distance was the reason behind their breakup, but Diego's revelation gave her clarity. She took a deep breath as the weight of unanswered questions lifted.

Her reply was an easy one. "Yes, I could have stayed. I'm a professional writer, the benefit of being a writer is that I could write from anywhere. Since Estella left everything to me including the ranch, I plan on turning one of the rooms in the farmhouse into my writing room."

"So, you're staying then?"

"Yes, I am. I should have come home years ago. The ranch was Estella's pride and joy. She left it to me and so I plan on taking good care of it."

"No, Isabel, you were Estella's pride and joy." Diego said.

The warmth of rekindled friendship enveloped Isabel and in that moment, she realized how much he had missed Diego's company.

Isabel gave him a beaming smile. She envisioned herself living at the farmhouse once again. There was happiness still to be felt. Filled with optimism, Isabel dreamed of her future living and writing at the farmhouse. Isabel pulled herself from her dreams of the future by snapping the twig she was holding in half and discarding the broken pieces.

They fell silent.

God, I wish we had this conversation much sooner.

She felt the sharp pang of regret and longing, momentarily mourning what could have been. Isabel looked at Diego and wondered, was it too late to start again? He opened another beer from the six-pack and took two large gulps. It seemed to her that their lives curiously mirrored one another. Both Diego and Isabel's life-paths were guided by tragedy, loss, and family. Both of their lives were shaped by elements beyond their control, yet they attempted to make the best out of their circumstances.

The clouds loomed dark and low; a storm was imminent. Isabel's hair caught the breeze, the air was filled with a static electric energy. High topped thunderhead clouds filled the sky.

"I think we should get inside," Diego said, as she examined the ominous skyline.

Isabel stood up.

"I think I'll walk home and enjoy the fresh air. I don't mind the rain."

Diego slowly stood up. Isabel collected her shoes and purse. She looked around to make sure she wasn't forgetting anything, intentionally delaying their goodbye. A moment like this with Diego was something she had not experienced in a long time. It was intimate, comforting, and familiar. She didn't want it to end. Diego collected the empty beer bottles and placed them in the case. They scanned their surroundings, making sure not to leave any trash behind. Diego walked over to the discarded veil and picked it up.

"Can I have that?" Isabel said.

"Why?"

"I don't know."

Diego shrugged and handed the veil to her. She lied; she knew exactly why she wanted the veil. She wanted to throw it in the fireplace and burn it. Maybe if she burned the veil, it would destroy all memory of La Llorona, erasing it from her nightmares? And, perhaps, all the strange occurrences would stop. It wasn't rational, but it felt right. She folded the damp veil and slung it over her shoulder.

"Would you like me to walk you home?" Diego said.

She stood on her tiptoes to kiss Diego on the cheek and said, "It's okay. I think I need to clear my head, but I would like to have dinner with you later."

Encouraged, a smile stretched across Diego's face, "Dinner sounds great. I'll pick you up at six."

"See you at six."

Isabel and Diego held each other in a lingering hug. Both looked back several times before taking their separate paths home.

She walked along the side of the riverbank. The current hummed steadily beside her. Isabel picked up a long stick, using it to balance herself as she walked along the pebbled and muddy bank. It was a welcomed walking companion, take some of the weight off her injured foot. The familiar setting was comforting, but the feeling slowly drifted away the closer she got to the farmhouse. She caught sight of the veil in the corner of her eye. Pausing for a moment she considered throwing it back in the river but returned to her original plan of burning it.

She continued her trek to the farmhouse and thought of Estella as she walked along the bank of the river. Estella was a complicated woman, but Isabel loved her, distance and even death would never change that.

Isabel considered the monumental undertaking of uncovering the truth. She went over her the list of possibilities. Estella taking her life stood in direct opposition of Isabel's notion of who her aunt was. Would she ever be able to reconcile the opposing aspects of Estella's nature? Her questions about Estella's death were only furthered by her conversation with Rosa and the bizarre interaction with Joe regarding Estella's estate. If Estella had left nothing to Joe, then the state of their marriage must have been dire. And there were the holes punched in the walls and Estella's loaded revolver. Was Estella afraid of Joe? Did she load the gun for protection? There were too many unanswered questions. Was Joe capable of killing Estella for the inheritance?

Her mouth was dry, and a lump welled in her throat. All the unanswered questions made her blood run cold. She used to believe blood running cold was just colloquialism, but it really was a sensation. Ice pumped through her veins, causing tremors of cold to reverberate through her body.

She wrapped her arms around herself as she made her way to the back of the farmhouse.

The storm was fast upon her. She could taste the moisture in the air and her hair became frizzy with static electricity. Approaching the farmhouse, she noticed bed sheets on the clothing lines flapping wildly in the wind. She had avoided looking out the windows last night and hadn't noticed that the sheets had been left out. She was in such a state from sleepwalking, that she must have run right past the clothesline. The sheets cracked in the breeze, like the sails of a ship on a stormy sea.

"The linens can't stay out here."

A sharp twinge of anger reverberated through her as she realized that the linens had been outside for some time prior to Estella's death and Joe had not bothered to bring them in. If Estella planned on committing suicide, why would she start a load of laundry and leave it hanging on the line? She added the sheets to the growing list of things that didn't make sense.

Isabel approached the basket that sat abandoned on the ground. Estella wouldn't leave her wash out like this. Tiny droplets kissed her cheeks as she looked up. Black clouds surrounded the house, seeming to almost touch the roof top. She took the veil off her shoulder and placed it on the ground, under the flapping sheets. After she finished folding the linens, she would retrieve the veil and burn it in the fireplace. Isabel didn't think of herself as a superstitious person but the act of burning the veil seemed ritualistic and symbolic.

The impending storm filled Isabel with urgency as she pulled the first sheet from the line. Cursing under her breath as she fought against the wind to keep her grip.

The sheets whipped wildly in the blustering wind. As she reached the last row, a haunting shadow moved across the sheets and stopped in front of Isabel, etched across the panel. The shadow hovered above the crumpled veil. It bent down over the veil. The bottom of the sheet blew up, revealing a pallid hand.

On pure instinct, Isabel hastily yanked the sheet down. No one was there. Her eyes darted left, right, and then back to center, nothing.

Her hands were shaking. She stood for a moment, waiting with bated breath. The sound of her heart pounding overpowered the sound of the rushing wind. Holding the sheet tight, Isabel paced backward toward the farmhouse. Slow and steady, she retreated, her eyes shifting from side to side. She half expected the shadow figure to be hiding in the periphery. With startling force, the wind ripped the sheet from her grasp. She watched it fly through the damp air.

"What the fuck?"

She inhaled with a shrill wheeze. Her mouth fell open, as she stood in frozen terror, watching the sheet violently hit the farmhouse wall. Looking around and blinking several times, she tried to make sense of what was happening. Like a scared child, she closed her eyes for fear of what she would see next. She could sense, with every part of her being, that the shadow figure was standing by the river. Slowly, she opened her eyes and reluctantly turned her head to look beyond the clotheslines. Where seconds before nothing could be found to explain the eerie shadow, a figure appeared in front of her.

"Isabel."

The specter beckoned; her voice carried on the wind.

The hair on her arms stood up and chills ran through her body. She trembled as tears welled in her eyes. She wanted to scream, she wanted to run, but her legs and voice failed her.

Was this really happening?

The weeping woman placed the veil on her head. She stood for a moment staring at Isabel, then stepped forward and pulled the veil back, revealing her face. Her eyes blazed an unnatural blue, and melancholic tears streamed down her sunken cheeks. The weeping woman's white dress clung to her gaunt figure. The vague scent of decay wafted on the air. Isabel stood motionless, utterly paralyzed by fear. She was the entity that haunted Isabel's nightmares. There was no rationalizing or dismissing this moment.

La Llorona stretched out and grabbed Isabel's face. Unable to fight or retreat, Isabel shuddered as La Llorona's cold hands made contact with her cheeks, forced Isabel to meet her gaze.

Isabel became lost in the swirling blue abyss of La Llorona's eyes. The disorientation enveloped her. Their surroundings blurred until everything around them melted away. The motion was intense as they were pulled through time and space. Dazed, Isabel forced her eyes shut, fearing she would lose consciousness if she continued to watch the world spin around her.

The weeping woman's voice echoed from inside Isabel's mind. "You have my story all wrong. You call me La Llorona, now let me show you why I weep."

The vortex came to a sudden stop. Ripped from the chaotic motion, Isabel hit the ground with violent force.

She opened her eyes, expecting to see the world dissolving around her, much like her insides.

I want to get off the ride.

She struggled to her knees, awestruck by the sight before her. The weeping woman had been transformed, she was alive and beautiful. Her skin was soft and brown, her eyes were no longer an unearthly blue, but a warn chestnut. Her skeletal figure was now full and shapely. La Llorona's cheeks rested high on her cheek bones, filling out her face with a youthful beauty.

Where are we, am I reliving one of La Llorona's memories or did we travel back in time?

There was an odd sensation of distance and detachment here. La Llorona walked through Isabel as if she was a ghost. Shivering, Isabel wrapped her arms around herself.

"Hey, what's happening here?"

The weeping woman walked past her without any sign of recognition or acknowledgment. Isabel was merely a spectator.

"Where am I?"

Isabel surveyed her surroundings. A lush green pasture led to a red terracotta farmhouse. The farmhouse was expansive with courtyards extending around the exterior of the house, mirroring the long stretch of the surrounding mountain range. Beyond the pasture, fields of marigolds stretched as far as the eye could see. Blossoms bloomed on the surrounding trees and sweet scent of spring caught the breeze.

The weeping woman continued to walk past Isabel and stopped near the side of the farmhouse, calling for her husband and children in a soft, motherly tone. Unconditional love filled every word.

"Roberto, could you please get the kids, it's time for lunch."

Her calm expression turned to worry, hearing no reply from Roberto or their children. La Llorona called again, this time with urgency in her voice.

"Roberto, are you with the kids? Jose! Amelia!"

She turned her head toward the river to listen. Isabel paused, mimicking the actions of La Llorona. She heard what sounded like frantic yells and splashing in the distance. Stricken with dread, La Llorona sprinted toward the source of the sound. The wind blew hard, whipping her black hair around her face as she ran. She made her way up a small hill that broke sharply, leading to the river. La Llorona reached the edge of the embankment and let out a whimper of shock as she saw Roberto viciously holding Amelia's head underwater. Her daughter's legs kicked frantically, breaking the surface of the water. Her small hands flailed. Unable to comprehend the gruesome scene, the weeping woman was momentarily motionless.

"Roberto…what?"

Regaining her senses, she let out an ear throttling scream. Within seconds La Llorona, sprinted down the hill toward the bank of the river. Amelia's small hands went limp and receded into the water. Running with reckless abandon, Llorona tripped as she made her way down the riverbank. With a crunching thud, her face hit the pebbled dirt and sparse grass. The impact was jarring, and she had trouble pushing herself to her knees. La Llorona wiped her hand across her forehead, to remove the dirt and gravel.

Blood dripped from her the back of her hand and into her eyes. The weeping woman glanced at her bloody palm.

The object Llorona tripped over was large but had some give as she fell over it. She turned to see that she had toppled over Jose's lifeless body. The weeping woman shrieked. Choking on her tears, she reached out to her lifeless son. Brushing her hand across his pale cheek, her blood smeared across Jose's corpse.

"Roberto, what have you done?"

Hoping to save her daughter, La Llorona dove into the water. She wildly attacked Roberto and knocked him off his feet. Frantically she grabbed Amelia limp body as it began to float down-stream. La Llorona made it to the shore, clutching her daughter's corpse. She dragged Amelia and herself through the reddish mud next to Jose.

"Please, God help me. Don't take my babies!" La Llorona pounded on Amelia's chest, trying to push the water from her lungs. Utterly broken, she raised her head to the sky pleading, "No, please God! Have mercy!"

Her efforts were futile. Amelia was dead. The weeping woman crawled between Jose and Amelia, she grasped both of her lifeless children, embracing them as she screamed and rambled incoherent pleas.

"No, please no!"

Isabel knelt down beside the weeping woman.

I know these children; I've seen them before.

"I know where we are, this is how you died. I felt your death in my nightmare."

Isabel's chest tightened as she noticed that La Llorona's white dress was covered in blood and orange river clay. The clay mingled with the blood on her dress, giving it a horrific crimson hue. Isabel couldn't look away. The legend of the weeping woman from her childhood was wrong. La Llorona wailed as she rocked back and forth, cradling her children, unaware that Roberto had emerged from the river.

"Look out, he's coming!" Isabel said.

La Llorona couldn't hear Isabel's warning. Roberto grabbed his wife by her hair and dragged her waist deep into the river. He shoved her head under the water. Isabel watched in terror, with the realization that the nightmare in the tub was no nightmare, but a vision of La Llorona's murder. She had seen La Llorona's death, she experienced it firsthand. She knew the weeping woman's fate, yet she couldn't sit back and watch.

"Stop!" Isabel said, desperately.

Isabel ran into the water. She furiously punched and clawed at Roberto, but her actions made no impact. Powerless to help, she fell back into the reeds. She was an observer in this vision, nothing more. Helpless, Isabel was forced to watch the horrifying scene conclude.

The weeping woman stopped struggling, her arms and legs went limp in the water. Her hand floated lifelessly. La Llorona sank beneath the surface of the water. Roberto vanished and the sky turned dark. Isabel looked into the black waters trying to locate the weeping woman. With a gasp, the familiar ghostly figure emerged. La Llorona's eyes burned bright blue; all signs of life left her body.

The weeping woman stared at Isabel as she made her way to the shore, her expression was unreadable.

"Do you now see why I weep?"

The world began to swirl as La Llorona lead Isabel through the tornado of time. Her body vibrated and her stomach lurched in her throat like hitting the drop of a roller coaster that flew off the rails. Within a blink of an eye, they were standing in front of the red terracotta farmhouse.

The weeping woman pointed and said, "Now come see the reason why he murdered my family."

As the two approached the farmhouse, Isabel noticed that the lush green of spring had vanished. Red and brown leaves were scattered across the yard and blowing in the crisp, fall breeze. Bare spindly trees scraped the skyline. It was apparent that time had passed. They reached their destination and approached a curvaceous brunette woman. The woman methodically placed laundry on the clothesline as she hummed an old nursery rhyme. Isabel stood beside La Llorona, puzzled by the scene.

"Who is she?" Isabel said.

Llorona scowled at the woman, speaking in a hiss she said, "This is Vanessa. She was my husband's mistress. Roberto was an abusive, cheating drunkard. He disgraced our marriage time and again, but I thought as long as he only beat me and not the children, I could endure. As Amelia got older, he took an obscene interest in her. I stopped him; I would not abide harm to my little girl. When I confronted him, he beat me and raped me. He almost killed me that night. After attacking me, he disappeared for four months. He returned home with Vanessa, putting her up in the finest hotel in town. Vanessa was something of a provocateur and disinherited heiress. She loved scandal almost as much as money. Roberto was desperate to please her but couldn't sustain her expensive tastes."

"Why didn't you leave him."

"Divorce simply wasn't done then. I demanded that he leave. Desertion was almost always preferable to the alternative of staying in a broken union, but he refused to leave. My family was wealthy; the money and the farm were mine."

The weeping woman walked around Vanessa; her voice filled with rage. Roberto wanted to be with her, but if he left me, he would have been penniless. Roberto and Vanessa devised a murderous plan, and he executed it. He told everyone that I killed the children out of revenge over his affair. He murdered my children, killed me, and ruined my good name all so he could keep the ranch."

La Llorona's body shook with feral rage. "I took my revenge, but instead of freeing my restless spirit, I became bound to rivers that carried despair."

Isabel turned to La Llorona. "How did you get your revenge?"

"Keep watching," the weeping woman said, as a grim expression spread across her face.

The wind blew furiously, knocking a white shirt from the clothing line. Vanessa followed after it as the wind carried it past the hill, near the edge of the river.

Vanessa muttered under hear breath, "Shit, it's ruined!"

She bent over to pick up the mud-soaked shirt. As she leaned down, La Llorona sprang from the river, grabbing Vanessa by the hair and pulling her into the water. Vanessa's screams were carried by the wind, echoing across the field. Roberto emerged from the farmhouse. He drunkenly stumbled, as he followed after Vanessa's screams.

"Vanessa, are you alright?"

He looked around the yard. Vanessa's face broke the surface of the water and she wailed for help. The splashing and screaming drew him to the edge of the hill.

"Vanessa!"

Roberto ran into the river, unaware that Llorona waited beneath the surface. As he entered, the rushing waters turned red as pieces of Vanessa's body floated to the surface. Her broken torso and severed head bobbed in the current. Roberto grabbed what was left of Vanessa, yowling and crying as he held her head in his hands. He dropped it upon realizing that her eyes had been gouged out.

His screams became a wheeze in his throat, as the weeping woman emerged from the depths of the river. Her blue eyes blazed as she reached out for her murderer.

"Oh God, no, please." Roberto said.

Roberto tried to swim away, but his efforts were in vain. La Llorona sank back into the water in pursuit of him. Roberto struggled through the bloody current. One of Vanessa's eyes floated to the surface and drifted in front of him. He screamed, splashed, and choked as he inhaled a grotesque combination of blood, silt, and water.

There was a strange voyeuristic satisfaction in watching his last moments. Isabel felt no pity or sympathy, as she watched Roberto struggle. Isabel thought of Joe as she watched Roberto struggle. Would she hope for that kind of reckoning if Joe killed Estella? Goosebumps erupted across her entire body as the darkest part of herself acknowledged the desire for vengeance.

He pleaded as he was pulled beneath the surface of the water. Large air bubbles rose to the surface. His blood filled the water and bits of Roberto's body surfaced. Isabel covered her mouth in disgust as she watched as his head and one of his arms surface and float downstream.

I don't want to see any more of this.

Guilt rose as she doubted her moral judgment. Was death like this too gruesome to be just? Isabel's stomach dropped at the thought of the poor soul that found Vanessa and Roberto's body parts once they washed up on shore.

La Llorona rose from the shallows of the river and stood beside Isabel. There was no sign of satisfaction or peace in her face. Her eyes were distant, her expression full of regret. She placed her hand on Isabel's cheek and the water swirled around them, rising up to the sky. Isabel was once again pulled from the vision and brought back to her own time. She closed her eyes and braced herself for the fall.

La Llorona released Isabel's face, the jarring rush caused her to collapse. She was reduced to a quivering mass on the ground. The weeping woman bent down to her. Isabel reached out, clasping the offered hands, "I am so sorry; what happened to you was horrible. You deserved your revenge. Why are you trapped here?"

The weeping woman shook her head, "I am bound to this river because revenge is a terrible trap. The wedding veil and the white dress are part of my torment and punishment. I have become the bride of darkness. There was a light that beckoned me home, but I turned away because I wanted revenge. Revenge is a curse which will snare your soul and never let you go. My rage is the reason I will never see my children again."

"What do you mean when you say you are a bride of darkness?"

"The world before the light was filled with a malevolent darkness. It covered the earth, but when the light came, it was banished to anther realm. However, the barrier between our world and the other realm is thin. What remains of the darkness is a shadow that whispers to us and encourages our most heinous impulses."

"How did the darkness speak to you?"

"As I died, I heard a voice. It was like my own but different, whispering to me from the void. It was the darkness speaking. I saw the light that would lead me to peace, but the darkness told me to turn away. It said that if I turned from the light, it would give me the power to take my revenge."

Images of Isabel's mother arguing with the darkness days before she died raced through her mind.

Was Mom speaking to the same darkness? Had it twisted her into something else, something like La Llorona?

"Does the darkness only speak to the dead or can it whisper to the living?"

"Everything the darkness touches, it stains. I see the stain of the darkness on you. You've heard it; you know its touch. The darkness stained and damaged my soul. I turned myself into a monster when I gave into it. I cursed myself, and now I am nothing more than a harbinger of death. I may not take innocent lives, but I am drawn to waters that carry death."

"But you're not a monster. You saved me when I was a little girl."

"Yes, I saved you. I don't want children to drown. It's easy to scare children away because of how I look, but you were different. You, Isabel Martin Del Campos were seeking me out. You were drawn to my tragedy just as I was drawn to this river by yours. Your sadness was so profound it was like a storm raging across distant waters, calling out to me like thunder."

The weeping woman looked up as rain fell. Lightning split the sky and thunder cracked vibrating the ground.

"Roberto told everyone I was a murderer and they believed him, especially after their dismembered corpses washed up on shore. My story eventually became legend, and I am now a boogeyman of sorts. And why shouldn't I be considered such? What I did to Roberto and Vanessa was truly monstrous."

The two held hands. As hard rain pelted Isabel, she considered the moral dilemma.

The weeping woman deserved her revenge.

Isabel sympathized with the La Llorona, and if placed in the same situation, would she have done anything differently? The price was high, but Isabel understood the weeping woman's desire for reckoning. Anger and hate were more appealing than the gaping pit of sadness that consumed Isabel by since Estella died.

Was being ruled by vengeance and anger any better than grief?

"I know the truth now; you are no monster. Yes, you took a terrible vengeance, but there is still good in you."

"No, there's nothing but remorse and sadness. If I ever had goodness in me, it was extinguished by my actions."

"But you saved me."

"Saving you does not absolve my darkness."

The spirit's expression softened. La Llorona released her hand and gently grasped Isabel by the shoulders.

"I am not here just to share my story with you. I am here to deliver a warning. You are in danger." La Llorona said, firmly.

"What do you mean I'm in danger, how?"

"Estella did not kill herself; she was drowned in the river by Joe."

"I knew it!"

Isabel's heart sank with the realization that her worst suspicions were true. Joe murdered Estella.

"He was having an affair with a woman named Debbie. Joe wanted to be with Debbie, but he also wanted Estella's money and the ranch. He dragged her into the river and drowned her while Debbie watched from the bank."

The truth was worse than she could have imagined.

La Llorona's head jerked to the side in frustration and said, "The past repeats itself. The same tragedies occur over and over again. Greed is timeless."

Isabel shook her head as she tried to prioritize the earth-shattering information.

"How do you know all of this?

The weeping woman replied, "I wasn't able to save Estella. She was dead by the time I came across her body in the river, but her spirit spoke to me. She told me that Joe and Debbie murdered her. Estella feared he was going to come after you next."

"Holy shit. Is she a ghost now or something? Is her spirit lost or forced to wander?"

"No, she is at peace, but before Estella's spirit would cross over to the realm of the dead, she begged me to warn you."

Isabel fell to her knees with the weight of La Llorona's words. The rumble of thunder was deafening, and she flinched with each detonation of sound. Lightning flashed across the sky, illuminating La Llorona's face. Beyond the cracking thunder, a voice called out to Isabel. It whispered to her. The voice was her own, yet different. The same refrain repeated softly, then each word roared above the thunder.

Kill them both, Take your revenge on Joe and Debbie. Make them suffer as they made Estella suffer.

Isabel clinched her fist and screamed, "That motherfucker, I'm going to kill him!"

La Llorona bent down to Isabel and said, "The darkness is speaking to you now. It wants you to take revenge on Joe. Don't listen to it and don't give in. You must leave here now."

"Leave? But Joe and Debbie need to pay for what they've done."

"Don't you see? Revenge won't free you. It is a trap; it has trapped me. I don't want you to share my fate."

Isabel shook her head in protest and anger. The voice of the darkness screamed for vengeance.

"They deserve to die! Joe took everything from me! Estella was the only family I had."

La Llorona turned her head to side, examining Isabel.

"You still have your life. If you stay, he will take that from you as well."

La Llorona's electric blue eyes reflected the bright, crawling lightning above. The weeping woman pulled Isabel to her feet with surprising force. Isabel winced.

"Leave now; I promise that when Joe and Debbie come close to the river, I will take them. Please try to take comfort in the knowledge that they will suffer."

Not wanting to argue with a vengeful spirit, Isabel relented.

La Llorona released Isabel and said, "Now go."

Isabel nodded and ran back to the farmhouse. She threw open the door but before entering she turned back. La Llorona retreated into the river the storm crashing wildly around her.

CHAPTER NINE
The Darkness Calls

Isabel ran through the farmhouse and bolted up the stairs, ignoring the flickering hall lights as she hurried to her bedroom. In a scramble of clothes and accessories, she collected her belongings and threw them into her suitcase. The flurry of panicked action came to a crashing halt when, as if compelled by some unknown force, she stepped out and went to the hall closet to retrieve Estella's revolver. Isabel stared blankly at the weapon; she was unsure why she grabbed the gun. She placed the revolver in her coat pocket and headed to the front door.

Within arm's reach of the doorknob, she had no clear plan of where to go or what to do, but she took comfort in knowing that Joe and Debbie's days were numbered. A course voice echoed through the room, startling her. Isabel flinched and slid her hand into her coat pocket.

Sé fuerte.

"Where do you think you're going?" Joe said.

I'll stand my ground and face down the darkness. I'm not running anymore.

She turned around to face Joe. He stood lurking in a darkened corner of the room, emerging from the darkness as if he was part of it. She dropped the suitcase, pulling the revolver from her pocket. It felt surprisingly light as she raised it. This was the second time she had pointed a gun at Joe. The first time she acted on instinct to protect Estella, but now she was holding the gun to protect herself.

The malice in Joe's eyes and his cruel sneer revealed his deadly intentions.

He's here to kill me.

A mad excitement glinted in his eyes. He looked positively tickled by the idea of murdering her. Was Joe's wicked nature the influence of the darkness or had the darkness always been a part of him? She stared into his cold eyes. Her hand trembled as she raised the gun to his face. His cold eyes gleamed in the dimly lit room. There was no doubt in Isabel's mind that he chose the darkness long ago and he enjoyed it. He wore it darkness like a second skin. The origins of Joe's malevolence would be a question for later consideration. Isabel was in danger and she needed to focus on the moment at hand, existential questions about the nature of evil would have to wait.

Joe smugly snorted, stepping forward as he glanced down the barrel of the gun.

"Your bitch of an aunt couldn't pull the trigger, and neither could you."

"You killed Estella, you piece of shit!"

"You can only wipe someone's ass so many times before you can't take it anymore. Estella was dying anyway. The cancer was killing her; I just put her out of her misery."

"You sick motherfucker, you are going to jail. You just admitted to killing Estella. I'll make sure you die in prison."

"Shit, you aren't going to live long enough to tell nobody."

"Oh yeah? I'm the one with the gun."

"Is that so, well then I guess you got me." Joe said as he tilted his head in the direction of the door.

It creaked as it opened behind Isabel. She swung around just in time to see Debbie smashing the butt of a shotgun into her face. The crunch of her left cheek reverberated through her entire head as white-hot pain shot through her temple. Isabel toppled to the floor, her cheek split open and her face throbbed. Warm slithered in a stream down her neck.

"Oh, I got ya good." Debbie said.

She could barely hear Debbie's goose-honk of a laugh over the ringing in her ears. Isabel was disoriented, but she had managed to keep hold of the revolver. With shaking hands, she raised the gun, firing it randomly in Joe's direction. The kickback of the revolver rattled Isabel's entire arm. The bullet grazed his leg, taking a large chunk of flesh from his shin.

"You fucking shot me." Joe said, as he fell to the floor with a resounding thud.

Blood seeped from his wound. Debbie kicked the gun out of Isabel's hand, before she could manage a second shot. The revolver slid across the floor, smacking against the rocking chair. There was no way Isabel would be able to reach it before Debbie shot her.

I'm fucked.

"You little bitch!" Debbie said, as she pointed the shotgun to Isabel's head.

Isabel looked up at Debbie. She couldn't help but focus on the bright pink bandanna tied around Debbie's neck.

Oh God, I'm going to be killed by a racist wearing a pink bandanna.

It was admittedly a strange observation, considering her imminent death.

"Debbie, stop! Don't shoot her, not yet!" Joe said.

"What are you talking about? This bitch just shot you!"

"No! We need to make it look like suicide." Joe said.

"Whatever." Debbie said as she lowered the shotgun.

Dazed and unwilling to accept death at the hands of these two morons, Isabel struggled to get to her feet. Debbie snorted and chuckled as she watched Isabel try to stand.

"Oh, no you don't." Debbie said in a cruel chuckle.

She kicked Isabel in the ribs, knocking her back to the floor. Isabel wheezed and coughed. She glared up at Debbie, wishing she could choke her to death with her pink bandanna.

"I think I'm gonna enjoy watching you die even more than I did watching Estella. To be honest, Estella wasn't able to put much of a fight, not like you did."

"Fuck you!" Isabel said.

"Night, night sweetie." Debbie said, in a mocking tone as she delivered another blow with the butt of the shotgun to Isabel's head. Her ears buzzed, filled with a sound that was akin to bells ringing. Her vision blurred and everything went black.

CHAPTER TEN
Blood in the Water

Isabel slowly regained consciousness. She tried to take in her surroundings, unintelligible voices echoed above. Everything else was a blur. Her anxiety spiked at the thought of what laid ahead.

What's next, murder, death, or worse, the darkness.

Pebbles and mud scraped against Isabel's back as Joe and Debbie struggled to drag her by the legs. The rain pelted her sore face, and the coppery taste of blood filled her mouth. Slowly Isabel opened her eyes, lifting her head to see the blurred figures of Joe and Debbie. Debbie's pink bandanna was wrapped around Joe's wounded leg. They were arguing, and Joe was limping while cursing at Debbie.

"You almost blew everything, ya dumb shit. It wouldn't look like suicide if you blew off her head with the shotgun." Joe said and he lumbered through the mud.

"Just shut the fuck up. I didn't shoot her, did I. Besides, people have blowed off their own heads with shotguns before."

"She wouldn't have the gunshot residue on her on her hands. Don't you remember watchin' those forensic

162

shows? Anyway, who shoots themselves standing by the front door. You just don't got no sense do ya?"

"Don't you treat me like I'm stupid Joe. I'm the one who thought of killing Estella in the first place. You'd still be putting up with her shit if it weren't for me."

"Shut up and help me pull this bitch to the river. We ain't getting no money if we don't make this look right." Joe said in a wheeze.

"That dirty brown bitch is dead and still causing you all kinds of trouble. After everything you did for her, I can't believe she left you with nothin."

"We'll make it right, we just gotta kill this bitch first and all our troubles will be behind us." Joe said.

"When you sell the ranch, you better make sure you sell it to a good white family. This land belongs to true Americans, and we don't need any more disease-ridden immigrants taking what is ours."

"Once I sell this place, I'm finally going to be able to write my own ticket. I'm tired of nothin but scraps. I'm sick of pretending to love these nasty old bitches. I wasted so much time with Estella, but she was by far the richest. I was sure I was getting all the money, but she was a sneaky little whore."

"You can't trust Mexicans; I told you a thousand times." Debbie said.

"No, you can't." Joe said.

"You're gonna buy me a new pink bandanna after all this."

"Baby, I'm gonna buy you whatever you want. You can have a million bandannas my beauty queen."

163

Thunder boomed overhead, Debbie jumped and dropped Isabel's leg. She let out a torrent of slurs and scrambled to grab Isabel's limp leg. Regaining her grip, Debbie's nails dug in the flesh of Isabel's ankle.

"I hate the sound of thunder." Debbie said.

"Just keep pulling; we're almost there."

The rushing burble of the river echoed on all sides of Isabel, and within an instant their plan became clear. Joe and Debbie would drown her in the river. Joe would claim she committed suicide, following the death of Estella. In her mind, she could hear Joe explaining her death to the sheriff.

She just couldn't take the guilt of abandoning Estella. She was always weak and running away. She couldn't handle it. Besides crazy runs in the family. It's a wonder she didn't kill herself years ago.

Acid rose in her throat, she wanted to spit venom. In the event of her death, Joe would inherit the ranch. She had to admit the simplicity of the plan and symmetry of her death would make Joe's case believable. The Martin Del Campos family had a long history of suicide and Isabel would be just another crazy woman added to their ranks. The weeping woman's words echoed through Isabel's mind.

It's amazing how the past repeats itself. The weeping woman was killed for her wealth and so was Estella.

Would Isabel join La Llorona in the darkness? She doubted if she could resist the temptation to take vengeance. She thought of the floating pieces of Vanessa and Roberto in the river after La Llorona took her revenge. The weeping woman found no peace or solace in their deaths. She told Isabel that revenge was a trap.

Would I be willing to lose my soul and become a bride of darkness to do the same to Joe and Debbie? No, I've got to fight, I have to survive.

She couldn't think about the darkness or revenge, the only thing that mattered was survival.

Isabel grasped and clawed at the mud, trying to stop their advance to the river. Joe and Debbie cursed as they fought against Isabel's resistance. Joe exhaled laboriously, as they stumbled and slipped in the mud.

Lightning split the sky, illuminating the black night. With a second bright bolt of lightning and the boom or thunder, Debbie lurched forward and dropped Isabel's leg.

"Keep hold of her, God damn it!" Joe said.

He slipped in the mud and fell to the ground.

"Get up Joe." Debbie said.

"I'm tryin' to, but my leg hurts. Help me up." Joe said, as he rolled over and slipped.

Joe was down on the ground, right beside Isabel. If there was a right time to make a move, this was it. Isabel sprang into action. She jumped on top of Joe and wildly threw punches at him. He tried to block her barrage of punches, screaming at for Debbie for help.

"Get this bitch off me!" Joe yelled at Debbie.

Isabel hit whatever she could manage. His face, chest, and arms were all fair game.

"Get off him!" Debbie said.

Debbie scratched and yanked at Isabel as she tried to pull her off of Joe. She grabbed a handful of Isabel's hair and yanked down with all her might. As hair ripped from her scalp, the force caused Debbie to slip and fall back in the mud. Water splashed Isabel's face as Debbie landed in a large puddle. Free from Debbie's grip, Isabel jammed her thumb into Joe's eye. He wailed as she dug her thumb into his eye socket. His eyeball popped under her finger. His screams reached a piercing octave. Debbie writhing in the mud and the pitch of Joe's squeal reminded Isabel of frenzied pigs at the trough.

"Stop!" Debbie said.

Debbie clamored back on her feet and tried to grab hold of Isabel. Isabel turned, punching Debbie in the ribs. She was knocked on her back falling with a splat in the same puddle. Isabel couldn't stop, she just kept punching. She knew it meant death if she did. She knew by the ringing in her ears and searing pain in her cheek, she had a concussion and a broken cheekbone.

I'm outnumbered, I'm injured, it doesn't matter. Don't let up, keep fighting. Don't stop!

Isabel saw red, she lost control and screamed incoherently.

"You killed her. You took Estella from me. You stole everything!" Isabel said as she continued to lay a torrent of punches into Joe.

Years of anger and resentment poured out of her as she smashed her fists against his chest. Conscious thought dissolved. She couldn't hear the voice of the darkness. She was only able to perceive the wet slosh of her fists, crunching against Joe's face.

The lightning cracked across the sky revealing Joe's face. His blood looked almost black in the darkness of the night. Mud and blood-stained Isabel's hands during her savage attack. She could feel the pop of Joe's nose and cheek bones shattered under the impact of her fists. She lifted her knee, placing all her weight on Joe's wounded leg. Joe lurched forward, screaming in agony.

"You bitch! I'll kill you!" Joe hissed.

Joe reared up, punching Isabel in the same spot where Debbie hit her with the butt of the gun. Her head snapped back; blood spurted from Isabel's ruptured cheek.

"Debbie, get off your ass and git over here."

Debbie managed to get back on her feet and she pulled the dazed Isabel off of Joe. Debbie struck her several times in the back of the head. Isabel rolled off Joe and collapsed in the mud. Her vision turned to a misty blur. She wasn't sure how much more her body could take. Joe was sprawled out on the ground, muttering and cupping his damaged eye.

"That bitch, fucked up my eye." Joe said, and he rolled over and pushed himself up.

Joe staggered to his feet, grunting as he limped over to Isabel, using Debbie's shoulder to steady himself. He hovered over Isabel. Her vision was blurred, but she could see his eye socket was sunken in and his nose bent sharply in the right. He was in sad shape. Joe leaned hard on Debbie, causing her to wobble as he kicked Isabel in the ribs. The pop of her ribs breaking, joined the chorus of ringing in her ears. She grabbed her side and gasped, unable to breath.

Joe bent down and grabbed Isabel by the leg. Isabel pulled her knees to her chest in a defensive posture. Joe yanked on her leg and motioned to Debbie to do the same. Joe and Debbie proceeded to drag her to the edge of the riverbank. Isabel struggled as rocks scraped the back of her neck and arms as they pulled her into the shallows of the river.

The water level had risen during the storm and the current was fast and choppy. Isabel resisted, pushing and kicking in an attempt to keep her head above water. The stabbing pain in her ribs from Joe's kick and her inability to breath made it hard for her to remain conscious. Their faces were a blur as they held her tight and thrust her head underwater. The voice of the darkness called out to her.

"You are going to die. You can't stop them, but I can help you get revenge."

Don't listen to it, just keep fighting.

Isabel reared up, gasping for air. She tried to fill her lungs before they shoved her back down, but her ribs were like a vice around her abdomen.

Joe grabbed Isabel by the collar of her dress and again shoved her head underwater. From the darkness, a skeletal hand reached out for her. The blackness of the water was disrupted by the billowing glow of La Llorona's white dress. Isabel's lungs burned; she was drowning. She reached out for La Llorona. The weeping woman looked to the surface of the water and disappeared.

Isabel's arms thrashed wildly, trying to fight against Debbie and Joe. The metallic taste of blood and muddy water filled her nose and mouth. Feeling began to leave her extremities and her body was unable to continue fighting. She had nothing left; she was too weak to fight. Her death was close at hand. The void tugged at her. She was fading, no longer conscious but aware that she was slipping away. The only thought that traveled through her vague awareness was that she wasn't ready to let go.

The lightning illuminated the surface of river. Light seeped through the water and surrounded Isabel. The tendrils of light slowly broke the surface of the water.

Carried through the lightning, a bright tunnel opened. It called to her, beckoning her forward. The pain had stopped, she was no longer drowning. Isabel reached out toward the tunnel, but the darkness called to her once again.

"Turn away from the light and you will have the power to take your revenge."

The light was beautiful and warm, she ignored the darkness and swam forward. The light enveloped her.

I'm going home.

The sound of cicadas buzzing and wind chimes clattering echoed from the tunnel. She moved toward its entrance. It was a brilliant, serene illumination, but she couldn't pass through it. She smacked her fist against an invisible barrier. Estella's voice called out to her.

"Don't listen to the darkness. Don't run from your pain. Face it. It's not your time yet, *mija*. Keep fighting. You still have an important job to do. You're not done yet, *Sé fuerte*."

The tunnel of light shrank as it pulled away from the water and disappeared into the storm clouds above. Once again surrounded by black waters, consciousness returned.

Joe and Debbie's grip on Isabel loosened, allowing her head to break the surface of the water. The cold air stung her lungs as she spat out water.

"What was that?" Debbie said.

"There's someone here with us." Joe said.

The tunnel of light was gone, darkness filled the sky. Though the light was now absent, Isabel was still blind from its intense glow. Her eyes tried to adjust, but all that she could see was Joe and Debbie's blurred silhouettes.

"Joe, did you see that?"

"It wasn't human. We need to get the hell outta here." Debbie said, frantically.

Debbie's scream was garbled as she was dragged beneath the surface of the water. Seizing on the distraction, Isabel swam for the riverbank with all her might. Just as she reached the shallows, her muscles gave out. Unable to swim any further, she collapsed into the muddy reeds at the river's edge. She was on the verge of passing out. She panted and wheezed as she struggled to grip to the slick reeds.

The lightning reflected in the water, lighting up the night. Joe was panicked and looking for Debbie, who was nowhere in sight. Joe swam past Isabel as he desperately screamed for Debbie.

"Debbie, Deb! Where are you?"

Isabel watched as Joe dove beneath the surface, searching for her. She remembered the sight of La Llorona beneath the surface of the water.

The weeping woman must be making good on her promise.

Joe swam in aimless circles as he called out for Debbie.

"Debbie, where are you?"

He screamed as her mutilated body floated to the surface. Caught in the thrashing current, her corpse floated downstream towards Joe. Struggling against the undertow, Joe whimpered as he tried to swim away. Isabel stared in grim fascination. With each flash of lightning, La Llorona was coming closer to Joe. He was unaware of the specter lurking behind him, edging closer and closer through the blackness of the water. He babbled and choked as he swam.

Isabel couldn't look away, she needed to see Joe's reckoning.

"She's coming for you." Isabel said as she pointed behind Joe.

Directing his gaze to the advancing ghost, Joe screamed as he smacked into Debbie's body tangled in reeds. He pushed her aside and thrashed around in the water trying to escape his fate, but the specter was soon upon him. He looked over his shoulder to see the ghostly figure of La Llorona reach out, grabbing his injured leg. Joe shrieked, begging for help.

"Please no, God help me!"

La Llorona violently pulled Joe beneath the surface of the rushing river. Submerged, bubbles broke the surface as Joe screamed and pleaded for help. Water was filling his lungs and throat. He was nearing death; there was no escape, no reprieve, only the cold grip of La Llorona as she pulled him further into the darkness.

Thunder rolled across the sky and lightning touched the river. Isabel winced at the blinding light. She wanted to raise her hand to shield her eyes from the bright flash but feared losing her tenuous grip on the reeds. She watched the sky turn dark again and turned her gaze back to the river. Isabel was concerned that pieces of Joe's mangled corpse would surface and float around her. Although she was sure he was dead she feared seeing the ravages of La Llorona's reckoning.

Joe's head popped out of the water, followed by his large belly. His lifeless body floated down stream and out of view. Isabel was relieved to see Joe's body intact, but bitterness rose in her chest as she felt no peace in witnessing his demise.

The adrenaline from her fight faded and Isabel felt the full brunt of her numerous injuries. With her fingertips, she gently examined the open gash on her cheek. Her eye was swelling shut. She looked down at the blood on her hands. So much blood had been shed in the river. So much life and hope had been lost in these seemingly endless dark waters.

Thinking back to the weeping woman's promise to Isabel, she stared into the water, waiting for her ghostly savior to emerge. The waters remained still. The weeping woman wasn't coming back. With great effort, Isabel pulled herself up the steep bank. A hand grasped her arm. She screamed and pulled away. Frantically she dug her nails into the muddy embankment as she slid down.

"It's okay, let me help you."

The voice was familiar. It was Diego. He regained his grip on Isabel's arm and pulled her up. She swayed, barely able to stand. Without hesitation he picked her up.

"I saw a ghost or demon or something not human, drag Joe under the water. She killed him. What the fuck did I just witness?" Diego said, his voice quivered.

The color drained from his face. He was paler than one of Estella's sheets. His expression of fear reminded her of the bathroom incident during Winter formal. It was startling how much he resembled the scared kid, who was the victim of her and Birdie's misguided prank.

"That was La Llorona, she saved me. Joe and Debbie tried to kill me." Isabel said.

She grasped her side and went limp in Diego's arms. A sharp pain throbbed in her side; it was likely several broken ribs. Diego looked at the river's edge, Debbie's floating corpse was caught, tangled in the reeds further downriver.

"She killed both of them?"

Isabel nodded, "There is too much to tell you right now, I need to go to the hospital."

"I'll take you," Diego said, breathlessly.

CHAPTER ELEVEN
Scars

Isabel winced as Diego slid her into the passenger seat. He fiddled with the seat belt as she crumpled into the seat, shaking from the cold. Her teeth chattered causing her broken cheek to pulsate and bleed profusely. Not wanting to make his car a bloody mess, she tilted her head back, but the pain limited her range of motion. Diego ran around the truck and jumped into the driver's seat, slamming the door as entered. The vibration shot pain through Isabel's upper body.

"Ouch!"

"I'm sorry."

"It's okay, I'll live. I think."

Isabel gazed out the side window of Diego's truck as they drove. Each bump was agony. Diego apologized and assured her that the ride would be much smoother once they reached the paved road. She stared in the direction of the river, thinking of the ghost who saved her life for the second time.

Why didn't La Llorona surface after killing Joe?

Isabel wanted to thank the weeping woman for saving her life, but there was so much more she wanted to say as well.

As Diego promised, the ride was much smoother as they reached the asphalt road. She was finally able to rest her head against the seat. Diego was still breathing heavy as they raced through town to the hospital. He looked at the bruised and beaten Isabel. He shook his head and clenched the steering wheel.

"They beat the shit out of you."

"Yes, they did, and they killed Estella."

"She didn't commit suicide? You were right."

"La Llorona warned me, but they were waiting for me at the farmhouse. They ambushed me."

Isabel could sense Diego's fear and confusion. With great effort she slid into the center seat and placed her hand on his arm. She leaned her head back and stared out the window.

"So, La Llorona is real?"

Without shifting her gaze from the window, she nodded. Diego glanced at Isabel and shuddered. He took a deep breath and stared straight ahead at dark road.

"If the weeping woman is real, what else is out there?"

The question shook Isabel to her core. She trembled at the horrifying possibilities. Unable to answer, she shrugged.

"Ghosts are real; that's all I'm sure of." Isabel said, her words trailed off to a whisper.

"Yes, ghosts are real and apparently so are some local legends."

"No, the legend of La Llorona wasn't correct. We had her story all wrong." Isabel said, remorsefully.

Isabel paused for a moment and took a small slow breath. The warm blast of hot air from the heater eased the sting of the cold. Her dress and hair dripped all over the seat. The fabric was getting ruined with the water pudding around Isabel.

"I'm sorry for getting your car all wet.

"Don't worry about that; it's no big deal. I'm so sorry I didn't get there sooner. When I drove up to the house to pick you up, I found blood on the floor and the back door open. It was obvious there was a struggle. I was so scared for you."

"You don't have to apologize. You're helping me right now."

Diego pulled an old towel from under the seat and handed it to Isabel. Isabel pulled the towel over herself, but her grip was weak, and she was unable to manage the seemingly monumental task of drying herself. She was exhausted, soaked, and aching.

"I'm so tired." Isabel said.

"Don't fall asleep, you probably have a concussion. Keep talking to me, Isa."

"La Llorona, she's not what we were told." Isabel said.

"What do you mean?" Diego asked.

"The legend was just plain wrong. She wasn't a killer; her husband drowned their children and then he murdered her. She was a victim, but the darkness temped her and she took revenge on her husband and her mistress. She chose vengeance and became a bride of darkness, forever cursed and bound to rivers that are marked by tragedy."

"Holy shit, so she didn't drown her children, but she killed her husband and his mistress. Doesn't that still make her a murderer?"

"Yes, I guess, but not exactly. She was a ghost when she killed them. In life, she wasn't a murderer. She died and then became a killer. She's not the monster we thought. She was the one who saved me from drowning when I was a kid and she saved me again, tonight."

"What did you mean by bride of darkness?"

"The darkness is some kind of force that speaks to us. It encourages our most wicked impulses. It's a part of us, speaking to us in our own voices. It tempts us to do horrible things."

"I may never have a good night's sleep again." Diego said.

"I hope my nightmares will finally stop now that I know the truth. Although, after what Joe and Debbie did to me, I may have a whole new set of nightmares to deal with."

"Hey, at least you now know you're not crazy. All those visions, voices, and nightmares were real."

"You're right. I didn't even think of that. I guess that's comforting. I'm sorry if I shattered your worldview by proving ghosts were real?"

"You didn't shatter it tonight, that happened years ago. I've known ghosts were real for a while now." Diego said, in a somber tone.

"What do you mean?"

Diego glanced at Isabel and quickly returned his gaze to the road. Isabel lifted her head and shifted to face him. Her body pulsed with pain, she welcomed the distraction from her physical and mental trauma.

"La Llorona wasn't the first ghost I've seen. I saw Jodie in the ladies' room during spring formal."

"Jodie Boyle. You never told me that you saw her that night. You were so freaked out, but then were super pissed. You were so mad that you didn't talk to me for days. Once we made up after the Say Anything moment, I was too afraid to ask."

"Your John Cusack moment was adorable, and I honestly didn't want to talk about it. I probably never would have told you if it weren't for tonight."

"I'm so sorry for pushing you into that bathroom. I had no idea."

"After you and Birdie called her name, the lights went out in the bathroom. They turned on a second later and there she was staring at me from the center of the mirror. Just like the fucking story. A second later she was standing right beside me. She didn't touch me or move. She just stared at me."

"What did she look like?"

"She didn't look like La Llorona. She wasn't a glowing eyed bride of darkness or anything like that. She looked like a dead body. She was pale, copper brown blood dripped from her slit throat. Her eyes were dark brown, and her hair was matted with blood. She looked like one of those photos from the old west days."

"What did you do?"

"I froze, I couldn't move or scream. I was stuck in the girl's bathroom with a goddamn ghost. I didn't know what to do."

"Holy shit." Isabel said.

"The scariest part was her expression."

"Was she angry?"

"No. She was sad, so sad. Jodie reached out, like she wanted to talk but she couldn't speak. She cried and held her throat like it still hurt. I felt so bad for her, but I couldn't stand the sight of her. As soon as the feeling came back to my legs, I ran. I got the fuck out of there and didn't look back."

"I'm so sorry." Isabel said.

"The worst part was a week or so after the dance, I kept seeing her. Jodie was everywhere looming just out of clear view, hiding in the periphery. She would just stand there crying. I saw her at home and school. There was no escaping her. The legend said that she had been bilked and murdered, which got me thinking that maybe she wanted something from me."

"What did you think she wanted from you?"

"I didn't know but there's a ton of lore about unsettled spirits in the cowboy days that end with a spirit's need to be properly laid to rest. So, I started researching burial traditions in the old west and I came across several images of Corpse photography. The pictures revealed the key to freeing myself of Jodie Boyle's ghost."

"What was in the pictures that helped you figure out what she wanted?"

"In almost all of the pictures, the corpses had coins over their eyes?"

"What did the coins have to do with Jodie?"

"They placed pennies over their eyes of the dead as payment for the ferrymen to carry their souls across the river to the land of the dead. If Jodie had been robbed, then maybe she didn't have the coins to pay the ferrymen and that's why her spirit couldn't rest?"

"So, what did you do?"

"I went to visit her grave. It was really hard to find. Her grave marker was located in the really old part of the graveyard at base of the hill. Her headstone was damaged and worn. Her name was barely legible. I placed flowers and two old pennies at her grave. All the while I could see her in my periphery. Then, moments after I placed the coins on the ground, she was standing beside me, watching. After I stepped away from her gravestone, she hovered over the flowers. She picked them up and smelled the daisies and then she took the two coins and smiled at me. Jodie placed them in her pocket and walked away in the direction of the river. I guess she was able to pay the ferrymen, because I never saw her again after that. That's why I said that if you really thought you were being haunted, then you needed to find out why the ghost was appearing to you and what it wanted."

"What would you have done If you were wrong about the coins?"

"I don't know. The coins were my best guess, and I remembered my Mom had once told me about an old wives' tale about hauntings. She said that is you are haunted by a ghost they usually wanted something from you, and you would have to appease them in order for the haunting to stop. Luckily, I was able to appease Jodie."

"God, to think of poor Jodie haunting the bathroom looking for someone to give her coins for the ferryman is just tragic. Have you seen her since you put the coins on her grave?"

"No but for a while I thought I did. I saw her in every shadow and in nightmares, but it wasn't really her. It was just my fear, masquerading as a ghost. Eventually, she just faded into an awful memory."

"I wish you would have told me."

"I don't think you would have believed me. If anything, you might have thought I was going crazy."

"I would have been there for you. I wish you had trusted me, I loved you and would have believed you."

"I know you would have been supportive. I think I was afraid that if I said it out-loud, then it would make it real."

"Well now we both know that ghosts are real." Isabel said.

"We're never going to be able to forget them, are we? God, I hope our ghosts won't lurk in our periphery forever," Diego said.

"I doubt we'll ever be able to forget. I think they left their mark on us, and we'll carry the memory of them as long as we live."

"Do you think you'll see La Llorona again?"

"I'm not sure. She said she was there to tell me her story and to warn me about Joe. Now that she's issued her warning, she may be gone. I wish there was a way I could help the weeping woman like you did for Jodie."

"Maybe there is?"

"I don't know. Her spirit is so mired by guilt and sadness. I'm not sure there is a way to free her?"

Stabbing pain reverberated through Isabel's face. Gently, she touched the still seeping wound on her cheek. Exhausted, she rested her head against the window. They drove to the hospital in an uneasy silence, filled with other worldly revelations beyond their comprehension.

Diego's truck came to a skidding halt at the entrance of the emergency room. He ran around the car and waved down a nurse who was smoking a cigarette outside. She ran through the main sliding doors and came back out with two nurses and a gurney. She shivered as the cold air hit her wet skin and dress. Voices yelled over her, speaking in incomprehensible medical jargon as they rolled her into the hospital.

CHAPTER TWELVE
Broken

~~~~~~~

Isabel laid on her back. A tube stretched from the top of her hand and snaked its way around her legs to a pole which held an IV bag filled with fluid. She wasn't sure if the room was hazy because of her concussion or the steady flow of pain medication dripping from the IV. Her dress had been cut off during the triage in the emergency room and she was fitted with a chartreuse hospital gown. The glare from the overhead examination light blared down on her.

Diego was sitting next to her filling out insurance forms and talking to Birdie. Birdie was wiping blood and mud from Isabel's face.

"Oh honey, you're a mess. Look what they did to you." Birdie said, as she pulled pebbles from Isabel's scalp.

"I know Bird, but at least I'm alive. Poor Estella wasn't so lucky."

"By your defensive wounds I would say you're alive because of more than luck. Looks like you gave as good as you got."

"Well, they are dead, so I guess I won?"

"You are a fighter and survivor; Debbie and Joe should have known better."

J.C. COOKSEY

Isabel's swollen face caused her to wince after every word. Though it was painful to speak, she needed to process what happened.

"You are probably going to need surgery to fix your cheek, but I'll be with you the whole time. I'm not leaving your side." Birdie said.

Birdie's gesture made comforted Isabel. She squeezed Birdie's hand as a thank you.

Birdie wore bright pink scrubs, with a Hello Kitty pattern. The pattern made Isabel want to poke the kitties in the face and laugh. Her fascination with Birdie's scrubs was definitely the result of the medication. She had fought for her life and had the injuries to prove it. She welcomed the momentary absence of clear thought as she stared at Birdie's happy little scrubs.

Doctor Leila Trujillo entered, and the room fell silent. Dr. Trujillo was stern but had a reasonably civil bedside manner. She was in her late sixties and received notoriety for being the first female Native American head of surgery in the state. She blew past Birdie and began to examine Isabel's x-rays. Her long white hair was braided down her back and faded into the collar of her lab coat. She hummed and clicked her tongue as she read through Isabel's chart.

"Looks like you'll be needing surgery. It's broken. We'll have to put in a plate to secure it."

"You have to put a plate in my face. What does that mean?" Isabel stammered.

Oh fuck, I'm going to end up looking like the Bride of Frankenstein.

She envisioned herself with scars running the length of her face. She considered whether or not to invest in a Phantom of the Opera style mask, to cover her scars.

"It's a simple enough procedure and you'll be back to your pretty-self in no time. Minimal scarring and six weeks for full recovery. Considering what you went through, I think you'll have more emotional scarring than physical ones. We can offer help with that as well. I'll have the hospital trauma counselor pay you a visit while you're here."

Isabel nodded, still in a haze.

Sure, sounds good.

"Aside from the broken cheek, you have three broken ribs, lacerations to the back of your scalp and a concussion."

That doesn't sound good.

"Holy shit." Diego said.

"Yes, holy shit indeed. You took one hell of a beating, miss. The sheriff and his deputy are here, and they want to speak with you, but I think getting you to the operating room will have to come first. Mr. Gomez they would like to speak to you as well. I told the deputy to wait for you in the hall."

Diego shuffled the papers off of his lap and headed for the hallway. He stopped at the door and said, "I'll be right back, Isa."

"You've had quite a night. Let's get you fixed up," said Dr. Trujillo.

***

Isabel woke up from surgery surrounded by Birdie, Diego, Rosa, Maria Flores, and her agent Ava Pierce. Her eye was swollen shut and she had to turn her head slowly to see her visitors. Their strained smiles failed to conceal their obvious concern.

I must look awful, like the final girl from the Texas Chainsaw Massacre.

Maria was holding a pineapple cream pie.

"Pie." Isabel said. Her voice had a course ring to it. Her throat was dry, and her tongue was like sandpaper. Maria looked down at the pie. Apparently, she forgot she was holding it and looked down at it in surprise.

"I brought you one of Norma's pies, since you liked them so much."

Maria put the pie on the rolling table and poured a cup of water. She hovered the straw over Isabel's lips, and she happily sipped the ice-cold water. The water numbed her throat as it went down.

"Thank you. It's so sweet that you came here and brought me pie."

"Oh honey, we were all so worried about you. The whole town has been baking for you. I imagine you'll be dining on baked goods for months." Rosa said.

"How are you feeling?" Diego said.

Isabel paused for a moment. She tried to sit in bed, her body was heavy, and she struggled to adjust on the stiff mattress. A stabbing pulse shot through her ribs, but it lacked the intensity she felt when Diego was driving her to the hospital. She looked down at the IV tube attached to the top of her hand.

That's why I'm not hurting as much.

She hit the button on the bed to raise her to a seated position. The motion wasn't pleasant, but it was better than trying to sit up on her own.

"I'm a little achy."

Birdie was softly snoozing, collapsed in a nearby chair. A large cup of coffee rested in her lap. Her hair had been in a tidy bun at the start of her shift, but now it was hanging loosely to the side.

"Birdie what are you doing here? You look exhausted. Your shift must have ended hours ago. You should go home to be with the kids."

Groggily, Birdie sat-up and smiled at Isabel. She grabbed her cup of coffee and took a large swig.

"Go home Bird; you should get some rest."

"I planned on waiting till you got up. I wanted you to know that I never left your side. Also, I wanted to ask you about that cute ghost tattoo on your shoulder." Birdie said, with a tired giggle.

"I believe that was a celebratory tattoo to commemorate the sale of your first novel." Ava said.

Isabel turned her head, to get a better view of Ava. She was slender and statuesque. She refrained from sitting and stood beside Rosa, most likely because she didn't want to wrinkle her well-tailored suit. Isabel's first novel had been sold by Ava to a major publisher. She had always been Isabel's most ardent supporter, although she had no issue with delivering harsh criticism when it was warranted. Ava had been calling Isabel since learning about Estella's funeral. Isabel gave her only the basic details and informed Ave that she wouldn't be working on edits for a few days.

"You're right Ava; that's why I got the tattoo."

Isabel tried to glance at her shoulder to look at her ghost tattoo, but her range of motion was severely limited. She remembered how much she loved it. The tattoo was an image of a little white ghost emerging from an old-fashioned typewriter. She got in in celebration of her first novel getting published. The novel was a Victorian era, Gothic tale, complete with a haunted mansion and a murder mystery. Isabel had been so proud of her first novel and although the story was fantastical, she thought her ghosts were realistic apparitions. Considering her newly formed expertise on ghosts, her first novel was tragically misinformed.

Isabel pulled up the sleeve of her hospital gown to show off her tattoo to her visitors. The tattoo was surrounded by bruises and scrapes.

"He reminds me of Casper," Isabel said as she tried to draw attention away from her injuries and onto a more pleasant subject.

The tattoo was cartoonish and sweet. The design of the ghost was similar to the retro Casper The Friendly Ghost comics which Isabel collected during her childhood. Her visitors looked at her tattoo and smiled approvingly.

"It's cute." Rosa said.

"I love it and even Doctor Trujillo thought it was adorable." Birdie said.

"You've been avoiding my calls, but I can see why. You've been busy," Ava said.

Ava was a direct woman, always cutting the chase.

"I'm sorry I didn't answer the phone. Things have been a little crazy."

"It's all right. I'm just glad you are okay."

"I'm a little worse for wear, but at least my fingers didn't get broken so I can still type."

Ava smirked. The tips of her bob haircut swayed as she shook her head and said, "I've put out a statement to the press about requesting privacy and such during this time, but the local news has already reported the story. It's just a matter of time before it goes viral. Once the swelling goes down, you might have to make a public statement."

There was no doubt in Isabel's mind that she would have to discuss her harrowing survival story.

The events of last night would haunt her for years. She would have to discuss it at length during interviews, news reports, and speaking engagements. The public had an insatiable desire to consume tales of real-life horrors like hers. Isabel knew herself well enough to know she would have to oblige.

Her stock and trade were horror and death. Who was she to deny her readers another tales of darkness, even if it was her own. Maybe she could use her platform to discuss domestic violence and the often-brutal conclusion of spousal abuse. She thought back to her speech at the bingo hall. Those words rang truer than ever, "You can survive anything if you can survive this."

"Take the tragedies of your life and turn them into something meaningful, *Sé fuerte*." Isabel said.

"What exactly happened?" Ava asked.

Isabel was adept at thinking on her feet. She would give an acceptable version of the events and omit La Llorona from the narrative. Diego had spoken to the sheriff earlier and surely he had done the same.

"Joe and Debbie ambushed me at the farmhouse. While they were attacking me, they admitted to killing Estella for her estate. They wanted to kill me because Estella left everything to me. If he wanted to keep the ranch and the money, I had to go. Joe said he wanted my death to look like a suicide and so they knocked me out and dragged me to the river. When I came to, I tried fighting them off, but it wasn't enough, and they pulled me in. Luckily, they were intoxicated, and the current was stronger than they expected. They were swept downriver and drowned. In a way, Estella was responsible for saving my life, she insisted I take swimming lessons and I was able to swim back to shore where Diego found me."

She looked around to gauge the reception of her abbreviated, sanitized narrative. Maria was softly weeping into her handkerchief. Birdie was leaning forward, her eyes wide and Ava had a hand over her mouth. It was the first time she had seen Ava, who was normally reserved, visibly rattled. Diego was standing at the foot of the hospital bed; his eyes were cast to the ground. He nodded and gripped the footboard.

There was a twinge of guilt for lying, but the truth was horrifying, and she didn't want to burden them with that knowledge. Isabel's concept of reality had been upended and the fallout almost deprived her of sanity and her life. The sinking realization that there was existence beyond death was something too terrifying to discuss without the guise of fiction. There was a certain amount of relief in the knowledge that Diego had seen La Llorona for himself. She would never have to explain what she saw and experienced to him. The world was forever changed, and he understood that kind of revelation since he had experienced the uncanny years before. Diego would always know her better than anyone. They shared a unique insight into the world.

Diego cleared his throat and said, "When I found Isa, she was crawling up the bank. Joe and Debbie were already gone by the time I came along, and their bodies were floating downstream."

"¡Oh, por Dios, qué horror!" Maria said.

"At least we know the truth about poor Estella. She didn't kill herself," Rosa said.

The room was silent. There was a bleak kind of solace in knowing the truth, but Estella's death was no less tragic. Isabel had watched as Joe and Debbie died at the hands of La Llorona, but there was no sense of satisfaction or peace. Estella's killers had faced a proportional kind of wrath, but revenge was hollow, just as the weeping woman had said.

The curtain pulled back and a sheriff's deputy entered. Everyone stood up straight and stared at the young deputy. Isabel turned her head to get a better view of him. He was tall, with an athletic build. His pale blue eyes scanned over her injuries.

"Excuse me, Miss Martin Del Campos, my name is Severin Wake. I would like to take your statement now if you are ready."

He removed his hat to reveal a head of sandy blonde hair. He surveyed the room and gave a kind smile and a nod to each visitor.

"Looks like you've got a lot of company, I can come back later if you'd like?"

"No, it's fine Deputy Wake, I should probably get on with it."

Deputy Wake cleared his throat and said, "Would you folks please give us a few minutes?"

"We'll be back sweetie; I'm going to make you some *sopa*. If the coffee is anything like the hospital food, you'll need a good meal." Rosa said as she squeezed Isabel's hand.

"Thank you, Rosa."

"See you soon, Isa," Diego said. He didn't look up at her. It must be hard for him to see her bruised and bandaged. She was tempted to ask for a mirror.

Birdie slowly rose from the chair and said, "I'll see you later, sweetie. I'll check in on you during my next shift."

"I'll be by tomorrow to bring you more baked goods." Maria said, with a wink.

"You guys are wonderful. Thank you so much." Isabel said as she waved goodbye to her visitors. Diego was the second to last to leave the room. He turned back and peeked behind the curtain.

"You look better, Isa. They patched you up good." Diego said.

"You take it easy, hon." Ava said.

"Ava, wait. I've got an idea for my next book. It's a supernatural fictionalized account of my story."

"You know you can go non-fiction for this?"

"I know, but I want to include some folklore in the narrative and tie it in with a story about domestic violence and the damage abuse can cause. I want. No, I need to use ghosts as an allegory of the past. I want to tell the story the best way I can. I need to write it the way I know it, but for audiences to accept it, the story needed to be fiction."

"Alright, I'm excited to see what you make out of this."

"I want to give those who helped me justice and a better ending than what they received."

Ava nodded before she disappeared behind the curtain.

Deputy Wake pulled out a notepad and took Isabel's statement. She recited the same story she told only minutes before. The second telling went smoother, and she included small details about the fight and the injuries Joe sustained by her hand. She added a little dramatization to the narrative about fighting off Debbie then Joe and swimming to the shallows. Deputy Wake diligently took notes and nodded at certain descriptive points. After delivering her ghost-free statement, Isabel paused.

"Am I in trouble?"

"No, it looks like this was a clear case of self-defense. We retrieved Debbie and Joe's bodies from the river and the injuries they incurred matched with your description. I am sorry about what happened to you. You are very lucky to be alive."

"I was lucky, but Estella wasn't."

"I'm sorry for your loss. Once you are back on your feet, I would like you to submit a written statement. You can call me anytime if you have any questions or remember any additional details. Sometimes memories resurface after trauma and so please don't hesitate to call."

Deputy Wake walked to the edge of her bed and sat down.

He looked at Isabel and said, "You're lucky to have so many people who care about you. It's okay to lean on them for support. Emotions run high after experiences like yours; be sure to talk about what you are feeling. It's totally normal to want to retreat into yourself, but I'd advise against it."

"It sounds like you've had firsthand experience with this sort of thing."

"It comes with the territory, I see a lot of terrible things on the job, but I also see the good in people, like survivors living beyond the worst day of their lives and thriving. I've had my fair share of traumatic shit. Friends and family got me through the hard times and that's what I'd recommend. Take care, miss."

Deputy Wake adjusted his uniform and walked out, leaving Isabel alone with her thoughts. It was easier to give the false accounting of her story. The sanitized version was simple to digest rather than the otherworldly horror of the truth. She considered the prospect of her next book. It would be her first non-fiction, true-crime story that lurked under the guise of a fictionalized ghost story.

She lowered the head of the bed to recline. She wanted to sleep but feared dreaming.

Would I dream about the river or Estella? Had Joe become my new boogieman; would he make regular appearances in my nightmares?

The image of his corpse floating down-river or his cruel smile as he divulged his murderous plan would no doubt haunt her dreams. She hoped for a dreamless sleep.

Her sleep was anything but restful. The night was punctuated by interruptions from nurses and beeping machines, rousing her to groggy awareness. When she did sleep, it was empty. No dreams, visions, or nightmares; only a black void of unconsciousness.

Sunlight spilled into the room from an open panel in the curtain. Pink light filtered through the window. Isabel wanted to get out of bed and take a look at herself. She didn't want to look in the mirror at night, for fear of seeing a looming shadow standing behind her in the darkness of the room.

There's safety in the light of day.

On unsteady legs, she slowly hobbled to the mirror over the sink. Her pace was slow, and her broken ribs pulsed with each step. She pulled the IV machine alongside her, using it to steady herself. Isabel reached the mirror and took a deep breath before standing up as straight as she could to face herself.

"Oh God, look what they did to me. No wonder everyone was looking at me like that."

She let out a whimper as she observed the full view of the damage done by Debbie and Joe. Her face was a collage of purple and blue bruises. A large black bruise surrounded her swollen eye. She lifted her swollen eyelid, the white of her left eye had tuned a speckled red.

A blood-stained gauze bandage obscured the laceration on her cheek. A smaller piece of gauze was tapped to her temple. She slowly peeled back the pieces of gauze.

"Ouch, ouch."

Dried blood and small pieces of skin tore away with the last of the tape. Her open eye overflowed with tears, she gripped the sink and looked away.

Oh God, they broke me.

Summoning the last of her courage, Isabel looked in the mirror again. Her wrist trembled, straining to hold herself up on the ledge of the sink. She exhaled slowly and raised her face to the mirror. A row of stitches lined her puffy red cheek. Her temple had a smaller row of stitches and some of her hair had been shaved during the operation.

"Well, that's a shitty new haircut. I can't pull off the Cyberpunk look, I'm not that cool."

She lifted her gown to assess the rest of her injuries. Bright red bruises wrapped around her ribs and fresh scabs lined her waist and back. No longer able to stand the sight, she slid her gown down and turned away from her damaged reflection. Scarring would be the obvious outcome of these injuries. Joe and Debbie had permanently left their mark on her. She curled up into the bed and wept.

She would never be the same. Her body and mind were forever altered. The physical scars would be the least of her worries. There were creams to treat superficial injuries, but the emotional scars would be harder to heal. She spent the rest of the morning avoiding her reflection as she prepared to be released later that day.

Isabel was discharged from the hospital late in the afternoon. Birdie was there to assist with all the formalities. When Birdie delivered the discharge papers, she brought a cute little teddy bear holding a balloon. The text on the balloon read "Grin and bear it." Birdie handed her the bear with a smile.

Birdie slid the bag from her shoulder and unzipped it to reveal a fresh change of clothes for Isabel.

"Here, I've also brought you some sweats to wear home. Your dress was ruined, and I thought you could use something clean and soft."

"Thanks Bird, you're the best." Isabel said as she pulled the clothes from the bag.

"Do you need help getting dressed?"

Isabel clumsily slid on the oversize gray sweatpants, then she gingerly pulled the hoodie over her shoulders.

"I think I've got it, thanks."

"Alright, I left a wheelchair in the hall, give me a sec and we'll get you outta here."

"Thanks, Bird. Really, thank you for everything."

Birdie beamed at Isabel as she disappeared. She smacked the wheelchair into the side of the bed as she entered. Isabel slid into the chair and gripped the arm rest, expecting a bumpy ride. Birdie tied the balloon to the wheelchair and briskly rolled Isabel through the halls. The wheelchair almost collided with a patient as they made their way to the exit. Isabel clutched the teddy bear as Birdie rolled her to a thundering halt in front of Diego's truck. The crisp air and fresh breeze were a welcome departure from the stagnant hospital air.

"Thanks for the ride, Mad Max." Isabel said.

"What, you didn't like my wheelchair driving? Excuse me, but I'm a professional. I haven't lost a single patient on a wheelchair run, except for that one time. But that was really his fault, he kept putting his feet down and yelling stop."

Hot bolts of pain radiated from Isabel's temple to her cheek, as she laughed. She winced and clutched the side of her face.

"Geeze, that stings."

"Oh, sorry Isa, I shouldn't have tried to make you laugh."

"No worries, Bird. I needed a good chuckle."

Diego opened the door for Isabel. He cautiously hovered as Birdie helped her out of the wheelchair and into the passenger seat. He gently closed the door and walked around bed of his truck. He gently closed the driver-side door and watched for Isabel's reaction.

"Really, I'm okay. Let's go."

"I'll be sure to take it easy on the bumps and I'll warn you before we hit the dirt road, so you can brace yourself."

"I appreciate that, thanks."

Isabel shifted in her seat, trying to find a comfortable position. Her ribs and face throbbed as she leaned back. Without hope of finding a painless position, she rested her head on Diego's shoulder. The seats had been covered with new blue serapes.

"I'm sorry that I ruined your seats."

"They got soaked pretty good, but I needed to get new seat-covers anyway."

"I've made such a mess of things."

"They were just seat covers, no biggie. Now I'll get you home safe and sound, you just rest."

"Thank you for the lift. I'm happy to be out of the hospital, that place is creepy at night. Every sound and creak made me jump out of my skin."

"After what you've been through, I'm not surprised you're on edge."

"Yeah, I can't seem to relax."

"I imagine you'll feel like that for a while. At least the farmhouse is familiar. Being there might make more comfortable."

"Sleeping in my old bed sounds wonderful."

"Are you planning on staying there while you recover?"

"Yes. The idea of sitting on a plane right now sounds absolutely terrible. I have a lot of work ahead of me if I want to move to the farmhouse permanently, but that can wait till I'm back on my feet."

"How long will your recovery take?"

"Dr. Trujillo told me that it would take six to eight weeks for my ribs to fully heal."

"Shit, that's a while."

"That's not counting the healing time for my face and everything else. I've got a long while 'til I'm back to normal, whatever that means."

Her broken cheek would take eight weeks to heal, and the stitches would be removed in ten days. Her body would be bruised and healing for at least two months. Dr. Trujillo prescribed rest and recuperation. Isabel didn't mind the idea of rest, but she was worried about being alone with her thoughts. She had no desire to sit by herself in the farmhouse and contemplate her near-death experience. There was at least hope that a steady stream of visitors and well-wishers would keep her occupied. During quiet moments, when there were no visitors, Isabel planned on venturing out into the backyard in search of La Llorona. She wanted to thank her spectral savior for rescuing her and delivering reckoning to Debbie and Joe.

"I want to stay here, to be close to the river, in case she comes back."

"She? Do you mean La Llorona? Are you really sure that you want to see the weeping woman again?"

"I need to thank her. She saved me. I want to tell her that I'm going to write her story, her true story. I owe her that."

"It's weird to think that you're friends with a ghost."

"I'm not sure I would call her a friend, but she saved me, and she avenged Estella's murder. I'm grateful to her. If gratitude and mutual understanding is friendship, then I guess I've got a ghost friend. Wow, that's surreal."

"It makes sense in an odd sort of way. If anyone I know would have a ghost buddy, it would most definitely be you."

Isabel resisted the urge to laugh and took Diego's hand into hers.

"I'm just grateful to have living friends, like you."

Diego nodded and kept his eyes on the road. Her stomach growled angrily. She had finished Rosa's *sopa* last night and ate only a few bites of breakfast. Runny eggs and cement thick oatmeal failed to rouse her appetite.

"Are you hungry?"

"I didn't really think about it in the hospital. The food is kinda gross, but I guess so."

"Mom, Maria, and a few other ladies stocked your place with enough food to last a decade. They also took down all the pictures of Joe and packed some of his stuff in boxes. Mom says you're welcome to burn it if you want; the Women's Auxiliary loves to host bonfires."

"Wow, that's so nice. I didn't even think about Joe's belongings, but I'm relieved that I won't have to see pictures of him around the farmhouse. His hateful eyes looming over me are burned into my retinas. I'm worried that I'll never forget his face."

"In time, this will all be just a bad memory and slowly Joe and Debbie will fade into the background. You'll forget the color of his eyes and the sound of his voice. One day, what happened to you might even seem like a distant nightmare. He'll be truly gone from your memory, and you'll be free."

"I hope so. I would rather be haunted by any other ghost than the memory of Joe."

The sky turned a rosy pink, and the setting sun broke through the storm clouds, casting golden rays across the dark landscape. The light was warm and resembled the light from the tunnel to the other world. The glow of the landscape was ethereal.

"It's like staring into heaven." Isabel said.

"I love looking at the sky after a storm; it's beautiful." Diego said.

"I meant it literally, not metaphorically. When I was drowning in the river, I saw the other side. A bolt of lightning broke through the water right in front of me, but it wasn't lightning, it was a tunnel to another place. I was surrounded by the most beautiful light, and I heard Estella's voice calling to me. I feel like we are looking at eternity."

"Maybe we are." Diego said.

In silence, they drove the rest of the way home. Diego and Isabel had experienced the supernatural. They learned of the existence of the darkness and knew that it sought to influence the worst in human nature. They had stared into the void, but would the void stare back? Darkness had left its mark on her. What would be the implications of such an interaction with that otherworldly power, and what where the ramifications of that knowledge? Diego and Isabel were left with more questions about their world than answers, but there was consolation in knowing that they experienced some of the unexplained together.

CHAPTER THIRTEEN
New Nightmares

~~~~~~~~

Staring down the barrel of Debbie's shotgun and Joe shoving Isabel's head underwater melted together in a whirlpool of terror. The smack of the gun hitting her head and the pounding of her fist against Joe's face hit a buzzing pitch as Isabel lurched awake. Soaked in sweat and still kicking, she sat up panting. Isabel waited for the hurricane of fear and memory to pass. Panic squeezed her broken and battered ribs, and she breathed the burning fire of panic from her lungs. Desperate to put distance between herself and her nightmares, Isabel gripped her spasming side and slowly rolled out of bed.

I'm such a horror movie cliché, consumed by inescapable nightmares.

Aimlessly, Isabel waded through the darkened hallway and clutched the rail as she cautiously descended the stairs. With one eye swollen shut, her depth perception was limited. The living room was dark, but she could see the shape of Diego sleeping under a Navajo blanket on the sofa. The steady hum of his respiration filled the room. She tiptoed around the familiar creaking spots on the floor, careful not to wake him as she made her way to the kitchen. Isabel nearly jumped to the ceiling as the grandfather clock chimed five times. By the last clang, she regained her composure and waited to see if the noise had disturbed Diego. He snored and rolled over.

He snores, that's new. I wonder how long he's been doing that?

Isabel entered the kitchen and walked to the window over the sink. Low fog nestled against the ground. It was still dark outside. At this time of year, the sun didn't rise for at least another hour. She proceeded to make a pot of coffee and pour herself a cup. Too excited for a dose of caffeine, she took a sip of the steaming coffee and burned the tip of her tongue. Coughing and blowing into her cup, she opened the door and sat on the top step of the porch.

The cool damp air felt soothing across her face, but she knew the cold would eventually become uncomfortable. She sat for some time and listened to the fading buzz of night creatures give-way to the pre-dawn chirping of birds. The sky was a soft purple by the time her coffee reached a suitable temperature. She watched the river's edge, hoping La Llorona would emerge from the dark waters. Isabel waited until she could no longer stand the sting of the morning air against her skin. Deflated, she returned to the kitchen to find Diego, rubbing his eyes as he sleepily poured himself a cup of coffee.

"What were you doing outside?"

"Nothing, I just needed some fresh air."

The rest of the morning was uneventful, and Isabel was enjoying Diego's company. He left for work around noon, and she busied herself by removing some of Joe's hunting trophies from the hallway. She moved about the house slowly removing pelts and antlers within her reach. As she set about her task, numerous patched holes were uncovered by her efforts.

What a fucking destroyer; Joe really tore this place up.

Exhausted and covered in dust and molting deer hair, Isabel entered the kitchen to wash her face and hands. She turned on the sink and the faucet violently rattled.

This can't be happening again.

Black sludge spewed from the faucet and into the basin.

"Why is this still happening?" Isabel shouted as she stared at the sludge, turning the bottom of the sink black. As she reached out to turn off the faucet, a black hand emerged from the muck and grabbed her arm. She screamed and pulled away, falling to the floor. The entire sink shook as the sludge slid down the drain.

Isabel.

The voice was not La Llorona calling to out to her, although it was familiar. She had heard that voice calling to her in the river, it was the darkness.

"No!"

Her arm stung where the sludge had grabbed her. Several blisters appeared on her arm as if she had been burned. Catching movement from the corner of her eye, Isabel looked up at the window above the sink. The black shadow figure was standing outside, looking down at her.

"Leave me the fuck alone!" Isabel screamed again, forcefully willing the darkness away with each breath.

The rushing pain of a panic attack reverberated through her broken ribs. She huddled under the kitchen table, struggling to breath. Her heart pounded against her chest as if ready to escape. She was drowning all over again, unable to breath or regain control, she lost consciousness.

Isabel woke up on the floor, her face and ribs still tense from the panic attack. She surveyed the room. There was no sign of the shadow figure or sludge, except for the hand shaped burn mark on her arm. It hurt too much to cry or scream, so she pulled herself from the floor and called Birdie.

Unwilling to tell Birdie the truth, Isabel lied and said she burned herself while trying to heat up a plate of food that Rosa had left for her. Birdie rushed over with medical kit in hand. Isabel sat on the couch as Birdie cleaned her latest injury.

"You shouldn't be up and trying to cook. You have a concussion and need to rest."

"I know. With my eye swollen shut, my depth perception isn't great. I just didn't realize how close my arm was to the pan."

The acid taste of guilt stung Isabel's throat as she lied. Her encounters with ghosts and the darkness were damaging her sense of integrity. She had always considered herself a reasonably honest person. But ghosts, evil sludge, and shadow figures were beyond reason.

"You got yourself pretty good. Geesh, this burn almost looks like it's in the shape of a handprint."

"Huh, that's weird." Isabel said.

Birdie finished bandaging Isabel's arm.

"There we go. Now, lay back and take a nap." Birdie said.

"I can't sleep."

"You need to sleep if you want to properly heal."

"Every time I close my eyes, I see Joe and Debbie. I'm afraid to fall asleep."

205

"They're gone honey and can't hurt you anymore. What if I stay here till Diego gets back? If you look like you are having a nightmare, I'll wake you up."

Doubtful she could sleep, but grateful for the company, Isabel relented, "Okay."

"You'll be alright, Isa; you just need to rest."

Isabel knew that having company twenty-four hours a day would be impossible and eventually she would be left alone again. There had to be some way of getting rid of the shadow figure for good.

"Hey Bird, do you think the brujo can help me?"

"You think you've got the *mala suerte*?"

"Yes, I do."

"I'll give him a call. He can definitely come by and bless this place. Besides you need to get rid of Joe's bad ju-ju if you're planning on living here."

"It's the only thing I can think of that might get rid of all of the darkness that surrounds me."

"Don't mention it; consider it my housewarming gift."

Isabel took a labored breath of relief in knowing that the brujo would soon be there and he might be able to rid her of the dark presence that had been following her since Estella's death. Initially, she attributed the black sludge and shadowy figure to the presence of La Llorona, but now she believed it was a manifestation of the darkness. Safe in the company of her best friend, Isabel fell into an uneasy sleep.

After a few hours, Isabel slowly opened her eyes and saw Diego in the kitchen.

"I've made supper."

"Oh, that's the nicest wake-up call I've had in days."

They ate dinner and watched television. Once their evening had concluded, he helped her up the stairs to the bedroom. Isabel didn't want to talk about her encounter in the kitchen or the circumstances surrounding her latest injury and so she avoided the topic for the entirety of the evening.

Diego worried enough; the truth would only further freak him out.

As they passed, the hall lights flickered.

"One more thing on my list of stuff to get fixed." Isabel said.

"All in good time. Let's get you fixed up first." Diego helped her into bed and said, "Alright, I'll see you tomorrow."

Panic hit Isabel like a punch to the gut. She grabbed hold of his hand, pulling him down beside her and said, "Please don't go. Would you stay up here tonight?"

"Are you afraid to be alone? What's wrong? Are you okay Isa?"

Desperation forced the truth out of Isabel, "No, I'm not okay and I'm sorry I lied about it before, but I didn't injure myself cooking, something else happened.

"What do you mean, what happened?"

"After you left, I started cleaning the house. Everything was fine until I went into the kitchen to wash up. I turned on the faucet and this black sludge formed in the sink. When I reached out to turn off the faucet it grabbed me."

"What do you mean it grabbed you?"

The truth tumbled out of her mouth with surprising speed.

So much for not freaking him out.

Isabel pulled off the bandage to show Diego her arm and said, "Look, it burned me."

"Oh my God. Birdie told me that you burned yourself in the kitchen. She yelled at me for not prepping a microwave meal for you."

"I'm sorry she yelled at you, but I couldn't really tell her the truth."

Diego inspected the blistered flesh of her arm and said, "Holy shit! I thought all the strange stuff you were experiencing was because of La Llorona?"

"That wasn't her. It was something else."

"If it wasn't La Llorona, what was it?"

"Through the kitchen window, I could see a shadow figure staring at me. I think it was the darkness. I think the black sludge was a physical manifestation of it."

"How do you stop darkness? It's one thing if it's a shadow appearing and disappearing to scare you, but it touched you."

"I asked Birdie to call the brujo to get rid of my mala suerte, but maybe he can get rid of the darkness too?"

"That's as good a plan as any, I guess."

"Just please stay here tonight. I don't want to be alone."

Diego laid down beside her and said, "I'm not going anywhere. You're safe with me."

They held hands as Isabel reluctantly closed her eyes.

"It's okay Isa, I'm right here. You're not alone.

***

Rushing black waters and Joe's maniacal laughter forced Isabel awake. She sat up and nearly jumped out of bed, she wiped the salty sweat from her lips and tried to focus. Her heart was racing as she became aware of her surroundings. The room was dark, the soft light of her Glo-Worm illuminated the foot of her bed. She tried to take a deep breath, but her broken ribs would not abide.

It was just a bad dream. Joe's gone.

Isabel could still feel Joe's hands holding her below the surface of the water. She sat down in bed. Diego was snoring softly beside her. Not wanting to wake him, she slowly got out of bed and made her way to the bathroom. The lights flickered as she walked through the hallway. The silence in the house was unsettling and Isabel examined each darkened corner to make sure Joe wasn't waiting for her in the dark.

Stop it, he's gone.

Her anxiety could not be abated, and she shamefully turned on each light. Holding her breath, she stared into the blackness of the bathroom, beyond the hall lights. She flicked the switch and cautiously stepped inside, careful not to look at the clawfoot tub for fear of provoking memories of La Llorona's death vision. Isabel was relieved to find no black sludge in the bathroom sink, or shadow figure in the mirror. Her weary bruised reflection stared back at her.

Not as scary as the darkness but still a disturbing sight.

Isabel accepted her unease and left the lights on as she made her way back to the bedroom. As she opened the door, soft light filled the room. Confusion gave way to panic as the light revealed Diego lying fast asleep, but not alone. Next to him, the bed sheet was unnaturally raised, as if an old-timey sheet-ghost was sitting beside him. The head of the sheet turned toward Isabel. She slid her hand over the light switch.

What the fuck?

Roused by the light of the floor lamp, Diego looked over to the raised sheet and said, "Isa, is that you, what are you doing?"

"No, that's not me!" Isabel yelled as she stood at the foot of the bed and tugged at the edge of the sheet.

Diego jumped out of bed as the sheet pulled away, revealing nothing underneath. Without hesitation, he hoisted Isabel over his shoulder and ran down the stairs.

"We're staying at my place until the brujo gets here!"

A voice called out from the bedroom and said, "Where are you going? We aren't done yet."

Isabel knew the darkness was taunting her.

I didn't give into it. It's angry. If the darkness can't have my soul, then it will try to take my sanity.

She was certain that the darkness was set on driving her insane. She would never find a moments peace or rest until she found a way to ride herself from the grip of the darkness.

Diego hurried down the stairs and through the living room. The jostling was almost unbearable. Isabel demanded, "Put me down."

He gently slid her feet to the floor as they reached the front door. A terrible wailing and rattling erupted from under the kitchen sink. They looked down the hall to the kitchen to see a geyser of black sludge erupt from the sink and spew from the ceiling and onto the floor.

"Let's get the hell out of here." Diego said, as sludge slid down to the floor and snake across the hall.

In a hail of dust and flying rocks, they ran to Diego's truck, and he pulled out of the driveway.

CHAPTER FOURTEEN
Seeing Is Believing

Isabel watched in a trancelike state as the tail of the cat clock swung back and forth against the kitchen wall. Her head slumped as sleep beckoned. With every ounce of her already diminished strength, she forced her tired eyes open. The cat clock smiled back at her mawkishly.

There was nothing to smile about at this hour.

She slumped back in her chair and glared at the cat. Isabel had spent the majority of the night lying beside Diego, but every time she started to fall asleep, nightmares of the black sludge would interrupt her slumber. The black muck would seep into her eyes and mouth, suffocating her. There was no escaping the darkness, sleep only served as a conduit for the continued harassment by an unyielding force.

Unwilling to return to the darkness of her nightmares, Isabel opted to sit in Rosa's kitchen and pound copious amounts of coffee. Exhausted, Isabel longed for sleep, but she feared dreaming of what new horrors the darkness would bring. She gently rubbed her eyes, careful not to touch her bruised and still swollen eyelid. Her vision was fuzzy, but she forced herself to survey the dimly lit kitchen.

The room had been given a modern farmhouse update with a deep sink and granite counter tops. There was a state-of-the-art oven and double wide refrigerator. With the exception of the vintage tchotchkes, Isabel barely recognized the room. She stared at the sink and wondered if the sludge would make an appearance.

Ugh, it would make a hell of a mess of the white tiles and back-splash. Rosa would be so pissed to see her perfect kitchen covered in malevolent sludge.

Her eyes drifted back to the cat clock.

"It's three o'clock, just a few more hours till dawn." Isabel mumbled to herself as she looked down at the stack of notes scattered across the table. Before staring aimlessly around the room, Isabel had attempted to write the outline for La Llorona's story. She jotted down the best of her recollections and made annotations in the margins with additional narrative points. She finally stopped writing when she realized her penmanship had become illegible due to exhaustion.

Isabel took a sip of her coffee and gagged.

"Oh yuck, cold coffee is the worst."

"Let me make a fresh pot," Rosa said as she entered the kitchen.

"Oh shit. You scared me," Isabel said, lurching in her chair.

"I'm sorry *chiquita*."

"Rosa, please excuse me, I didn't mean to swear."

"It's okay. I don't blame you; I would be jumping at every sound if I had been through what you have."

"I feel like I'm one of those cartoon scaredy cats. Every little noise has me jumping to the ceiling."

"Well, I can't sleep either?" Rosa said.

"I'm scared to fall asleep. Every time I close my eyes, I'm right back in the river and Joe is shoving me down beneath the surface. I can't escape him."

"But you did escape him. You survived and I'm sure with time the nightmares will pass."

Not wanting to speak of Joe anymore or the darkness, Isabel stared at her bandaged hand and said, "Do you believe in ghosts?"

"I do," Rosa said as she made her way to the coffee maker.

She had her back turned to Isabel as she went about brewing a fresh pot of coffee. Isabel chewed on her bottom lip waiting for Rosa to continue.

"I haven't had a good night sleep in years. For months after Miguel passed, I could still feel him lying beside me in bed at night. It was the most comforting experience. I would begin to cry and although I couldn't see him, I could feel his arms wrapped around me."

"Do you think his spirit was coming to hold you every night?"

"Yes, I do, but after I cleaned out his closet and donated some of his belongings to help with the grieving process, he stopped visiting me. I no longer felt him at night; it was like he had finally moved onto the other place. I was devastated, it was like losing him all over again and I couldn't sleep."

"So, you haven't had a good night sleep since then?"

Rosa shook her head and said, "The doctor called it insomnia and prescribed sleeping pills. They worked fine for a while, but then one morning I woke up sitting in my car. I was parked in front of the cemetery gates. Apparently, I had driven there in my sleep."

"Oh, my goodness. You drove in your sleep?"

"In very tiny writing on the bottle it says that doing routine tasks while sleeping could be a possible side-effect. I guess I drove to the cemetery because there was part of me that just wanted to be near Miguel, in order to rest."

"That's so scary. What did you do?"

"I stopped taking the sleeping pills and now I just wake up very early and get my day going. I've given up on the dream of peaceful sleep."

"Do you wish he still visited you at night?"

"Sometimes, late at night, I wish his arms would wrap around me one last time. I miss him, but I am happy he has moved on. Spirits deserve to be at rest, not forced to comfort the living who will never stop longing for them."

Rosa placed two cups of coffee on the kitchen table and sat across from Isabel. She looked down at the yellow notepad that rested under Isabel's elbow.

"What's that you've got there?"

Isabel followed Rosa's gaze to the yellow notepad.

"Looks like you've been writing?"

"Yes, I was outlining my account of what happened for my book."

"May I take a look at it?" Rosa said as she reached for the notepad.

Isabel handed it to Rosa and said, "Sure, it's a fictionalized account mind you, so please don't read too much into it. I added the bits about La Llorona to the narrative as an allegory for abuse."

Rosa nodded and retrieved a pair of reading glasses from the pocket of her pink robe. Sliding the frames to the bridge of her nose, Rosa began to read. Isabel took a deep breath and tried to look anywhere but at Rosa. Isabel stared at the old cat clock then her eyes wandered around the kitchen. The white cabinets and brushed brass hardware gave the kitchen an upscale look, but the mid-century kitchen decor alluded to Rosa's love of 1950's kitsch, a trait which she shared with Estella. Isabel recognized the cat clock and hanging ceramic vegetable chain from her youth.

Some things never change, and they shouldn't.

"Didn't Estella have one of those hanging vegetable chains too?"

Without looking up from the notepad Rosa nodded her head and said, "Yes, we bought those together back in the sixties at the County Fair."

"Wow, that's in really good condition for being so old."

"I'm in good condition for being so old too. Now, if you just hold on one moment dear, I'm almost finished."

"Oh, sorry." Isabel said as she stared into her coffee cup.

Rosa read for several more minutes before sliding the notepad across the table to Isabel.

"Your penmanship is terrible, but it looks like you've really got something."

"Thank you, but it's just an outline."

"Is it really? It looks like an eyewitness statement to me."

"Well, there's some facts mixed in, but the story itself will be fiction."

"Doesn't read like fiction. It reads like a memoir. Now be honest, is this what really happened?"

"Why would you say that?"

"Because there is honesty in your writing. It isn't written like a story; it's written like something you witnessed firsthand. I've read all your books and you've never expressed that kind of honesty."

Isabel looked away, trying to summon the nerve to lie.

She knows. There's no point in lying.

Isabel chose to say nothing and chew on the inside of her cheek.

"Did La Llorona really save you?"

"Yes, she did." Isabel was surprised by how good it felt to be honest.

"Have you seen her since that night?"

"No, I even went looking for her. I think she might be gone, but something else has been haunting me, something worse."

Isabel pulled the bandage off her arm and showed Rosa the burn mark left by darkness.

"This thing came out of the sink and grabbed my arm. I think it was part of the darkness."

"What do you mean by darkness?"

"I'm not really sure what it is or where it came from, but it's a kind of malevolent force that encourages the worst parts of humanity. It speaks to us and manipulates people into doing terrible things. I think it's after me because I didn't give in."

217

"What are you going to do? How do you stop such a thing?"

"I don't know, but a brujo is coming to the farmhouse tomorrow and I hope he can help me."

"You know objects carry a lot of power. I think when I cleared away the last of Miguel's clothes, he was free to move on. The symbolism of letting go of something so closely tied to a person, might have shown him that I was ready to let go."

"I haven't slept well in days and I'm a little punchy so I'm not sure I follow what you mean."

"Maybe the darkness is connected to Joe somehow. He was always ruled by his darkest impulses. If you clear out the rest of his belongings, maybe you can be free of the dark presence that haunts you? We removed some pictures and clothes, but there was still quite a bit left behind."

"That's a great Idea. I think I'll head to the farmhouse before the brujo gets here and start clearing out the rest of Joe's crap."

"I hope it helps, at the very least you won't have reminders of Joe in the farmhouse." Rosa said as she raised her cup to Isabel.

Isabel raised her cup, but didn't take a sip, instead she stared out the window toward the direction of the river. The sky was dark, but she could still make out the riverbank in the distance.

"Do you think you'll see La Llorona again?"

"I don't know, but I hope I will. I want to thank her and let her know that I am going to tell the true story of what really happened to her."

"I don't think you should go looking for La Llorona anymore."

"Why?"

"Because if you spend too much time with the dead, you will forget you are among the living. It's best to let the dead rest."

"Speaking of the dead. When I was drowning in the river, I saw this light, and through the light, Estella spoke to me."

"What did she say?"

"She told me to keep fighting and *se fuerte*."

"Then you've gotta take her advice, stay strong and live your life. Enjoy the road ahead and don't get lost in all the darkness."

Isabel considered Rosa's words as she stared out the window watching wisps of ghost-white fog catch the breeze and float across the windowpane. It would be hours before dawn and Isabel had plenty of time to consider the darkness that surrounded her.

CHAPTER FIFTEEN
Clearing out the Dark

After a hearty breakfast and yet another strong pot of coffee, Isabel and Diego drove to the farmhouse to wait for the brujo to arrive and clear out the rest of Joe's belongings. They hoped that by removing his possessions, they would release the negative energy and lessen the dark presence in the farmhouse. Diego had hardly left her side since last night. He stared at Isabel nervously as they walked up the porch. They stood in the doorway waiting for the darkness to appear, but the house was quiet. Diego peered through the windows.

He turned back toward Isabel and said, "No sheet ghosts or shadows."

"That doesn't mean the darkness won't show up later."

"Are you ready to go in?" Diego said.

Isabel shook her head and said, "Nope, but I guess we need to get rid of every last item belonging to Joe. Rosa said it will help and at this point I need all the help I can get."

"Are you sure you don't want to wait until after the brujo blesses the place to go back inside?"

"No, I want to get this over with." Isabel said as she opened the door. She knew by Diego's hesitancy that he wasn't sure about going in either. It was comforting that he was reluctant to enter as well.

No machismo, just honesty.

The door slowly creaked open and smacked against the wall. They watched with bated breath for any sign of movement or black sludge. Isabel looked down to the floor to see if the snake like streaks of black muck had stained the wood flooring. There was no evidence of the sludge. From the safety of the doorway, Isabel tilted her head and peered past the living room into the kitchen. The kitchen was spotless, as if the darkness had never been there.

"Oh my god, it's gone." Diego said as he walked past Isabel and into the farmhouse.

"At least the darkness is self-cleaning."

"That's really not that comforting." Diego said, as he entered the kitchen.

"No, it's not, but at least it's one less thing we have to clean."

Diego's voice echoed from the kitchen as he said, "There's no trace of it in here, nothing in the sink."

The darkness, it won't damage your home, but it will stain your soul.

Isabel entered the living room and glanced at the deer heads and hunting trophies that lined the walls. Even though she had started clearing out his belongings the day before, there were still numerous trophies staring down at her. She approached one of the mounted antlers and tried to pull it down. Her body ached and her ribs tingled as she reached up.

"Jesus Christ, this is really stuck to the wall." Isabel said as she yanked at the hunting trophy.

"What did you say?" Diego said.

Isabel tugged on the antlers, but they wouldn't budge, frustrated, she said, "I think we are going to need tools to get these damn heads off the walls."

"Wow, Joe really stuck those in place." Diego said, as he walked out of the kitchen to watch Isabel's struggle with antlers. An expression of amusement stretched across his face as he watched.

His expression was infuriating. In retort, Isabel said, "I'm happy I'm amusing you."

"Don't take it the wrong way, I don't think I could do any better than you." Diego said.

"Even in death, Joe is making everything difficult. What a giant pain in the ass." Isabel said as she continued to struggle with the antlers.

"Where did they keep the toolbox?" Diego asked as he emerged from the kitchen.

"Estella used to keep them in the garage. I think you'll find them in a big rolling case near the fishing equipment."

"Are you going to be okay if I leave you alone for a minute to get the tools from the garage?"

"I think I'll be fine. I'll just scream if I need you, and if the sludge comes back, you'll find me in the truck."

Diego hesitated before nodding and walked to the garage. Isabel gave up and slumped against the wall. Deflated, she surveyed the living room and set about planning the first of the home improvements. The damaged walls were next on the list. Isabel planned on hiring a carpenter to replace the drywall and remove the last remnants of Joe's destruction. She walked over to a deer head that hung next to the coat rack. She tried to pull it off the wall, but again it didn't budge. Frustrated, Isabel tugged with all her might, pushing her foot against the wall for leverage.

"Oh shit!" Isabel said as she lost her grip and fell to the floor.

"Are you okay?" Diego's voice echoed from the garage.

"I'm okay." Isabel said as she glared up at the deer.

If I were in a Sam Raimi flick, the deer would start laughing right about now.

Slowly, she pulled herself from the floor and waited. Her eyes shifted from the deer to the table lamp. Isabel turned toward the rocking chair to see if it would start rocking on its own.

Stop it, you are being ridiculous.

"This is not *Evil Dead*," Isabel said as she dusted off her pants.

The door opened behind Isabel, and she nearly jumped out of her skin.

"Oh Jesus Christ, Diego you scared the shit out of me!"

"Sorry, I didn't mean to scare you. I got the toolkit, but I have some bad news."

"Oh, awesome, what's the bad news?"

"Joe used the garage as a man-cave and so there's a ton of his shit stockpiled there."

"Ugh."

"If you are okay with it, I'll clean out the garage and you can start clearing out his stuff in here."

"That's fine, I know you'll hear me if I need anything."

Diego dropped the toolbox next to the door and said, "I'll keep the garage doors open just in case but wait on pulling down the stuff that's out of your reach. You don't need to get on a ladder with a concussion, I'll help you with that later."

"We've got quite a job ahead of us."

"I'm always happy to help, Isa. I wasn't lying when I said I was here for you," Diego said as she headed out the front door.

Isabel looked around the room. Her imagination was in overdrive. She stared up at the deer waiting for it to begin yelling, "Dead by dawn!"

She scolded herself for indulging her over stimulated imagination. Isabel pulled the screwdriver from toolbox.

"You're done for." Isabel said as she pulled the trigger of the screwdriver and pointed it at the deer head.

As she approached the trophy, a sense of unnerving stillness came over her. Without Estella's warm presence, the farmhouse seemed bleak and the task of making the home her own seemed daunting. The farmhouse would need considerable repairs to remake it into something resembling home, but it would never be the same. Isabel looked around the living room, the changes the farmhouse would undergo strangely mirrored the internal changes she experienced. Darkness had overtaken the home turning it into a cold place void of love, which was similar to Isabel's emotional state during her estrangement from Estella. She walked around the room considering what the farmhouse and her life would be without the darkness.

Ch-ch ch-changes, turn and face the strange, changes, Isabel hummed.

Isabel began unscrewing the deer head from the walls. The task was surprisingly tiring, she gasped and winced after finally freeing the largest trophy from the wall.

"You poor deer, to think the last thing you saw was Joe's ugly mug standing over you." Isabel said as she placed the head on the floor.

The small hairs on her arms bristled as she realized how close she came to sharing the deer's fate.

I doubt Joe would have mounted my head on the wall-Isabel shook herself and refused to finish the thought.

"Joe's dead; he didn't get the chance to claim a trophy."

Isabel couldn't shake the feeling that she was being watched. Goosebumps erupted on the back of her neck as she considered the unnerving sensation.

"Nope, If I'm going to work in here, I'm going to need some music." Isabel said, trying to refocus.

She walked over to the record collection and slid her finger along the vinyl records.

"Alright, what's the perfect soundtrack for removing the belongings of an evil darkness-driven murderer?"

She almost grabbed the Johnny Cash record but decided she needed something fierce and upbeat. Isabel thumbed through the records until she stopped at the Beatles section of the collection.

"Perfect," Isabel said as she placed the Rubber Soul album on the record player.

She cranked up the volume, hoping that the music would distract her from the low ringing in her ears. Although she couldn't explain the sensation of a voyeur, the ringing had an unfortunate, yet real world explanation.

ɾ. Trujillo said the ringing was the result of head trauma and would eventually stop.

Isabel picked up the screwdriver and said, "Time to get to work."

**

Two hours fell off the clock as Isabel removed Joe's belongings from the living room. Due to her injuries, the work was slow, but she managed to fill two large boxes with mounted deer heads, pictures, magazines and buckskins. She slid the boxes out the front door and onto the porch. Isabel called out to Diego, who was dragging another box filled with Joe's stuff to the side of the garage.

"Hey, how's it going?"

He kicked the side of the box and rubbed sweat from his forehead and said, "I think Joe was a hoarder. How's it going in there? Anything strange happen, yet?"

"Nope, not yet, but I'm almost finished clearing out the living room."

"It might take me a couple of days to clear out the garage."

"Yikes."

"Yeah, that guy was literally the worst," Diego said as he walked back into the garage.

"Yes, he was," Isabel whispered as she closed the door.

Isabel kicked the side of the box and considered what to do with all Joe's stuff. She decided that the hunting trophies would be donated to the Elks' Lodge, but everything else was bound for the dump.

No one wants a collection of beer cans, neon Coors signs, and back issues of Fishing and Tackle magazine.

The music played, filling the room with a joy
as she rummaged around in search of a cardb.
With a loud crack, the record skipped and the song ' ı.
Life" began to play. Isabel peered out from behind tı.
closet door. There were no signs of the shadow figure or
sludge in the hallway.

Nothing to freak out about; old records skip all the
time.

She hoped the record wasn't too badly scratched. It
was one of Estella's favorite albums.

Box in hand, she emerged from the closet and entered
the living room. She stopped dead in her tracks, the empty
box fell from her hand, hitting the floor with a muffled
thud. Letting out a small whimper, Isabel tried to speak but
the words died before they could pass her lips. She stood
frozen in shock as Estella stood by the record player.

Isabel whispered under her breath, "Estella?"

Estella turned away from the record player and said,
"Sorry kiddo, I didn't mean to shock you, I just wanted to
hear that song again."

Estella was radiant, she looked at least twenty years
younger. She was surrounded by a soft glowing aura of
light. Her white dress shifted soundlessly as she
approached Isabel.

"Is this really happening?" Isabel stammered.

Estella smiled and touched the side of Isabel's face;
her hand was cool as it caressed the side of her cheek.
Isabel stood motionless, unable to formulate a follow-up
question. Her mind was going a mile a minute. She had a
million things she wanted to say and an innumerable
number of questions, but they all collided in a confounding
mess. Estella hummed along with the chorus.

"In my life, I loved you most." Estella said, as she sang along with the Beetles.

"It's really you. Aunty, you're really here."

"Yes, I'm here *mija*."

"I'm so sorry. I wish I could have made things right between us. I should have called. I should have told you how much I loved you." Isabel said. The words tumbled out of her mouth with a desperate refrain.

"It's okay, Isa."

"But there's so much I needed to say. I would have taken care of you. I'm so sorry about what Joe did and I'm sorry I left. I should have been there to stop him. I just should have been there." Isabel said as a flood of tears streamed down her cheeks and off the tip of her nose.

"Shh, everything is alright."

"I'm just so sorry, Aunty." Isabel said in a sob.

Apologies and should-haves came out of Isabel in a barrage of remorse. She needed to say everything all at once and she desperately wanted Estella to know.

"I wasn't sure if you'd be able to see me, but I guess you are seeing with more than just your eyes now."

"I'm so happy to see you."

"I regret the way things went between us, but I always knew that you loved me, and I loved you. It was the only thing in life that I was certain of."

"How is this happening?" Isabel said, breathlessly.

"Like I said before, you are seeing with more than just your eyes. Sometimes that happens to people when they come close to death and you were literally knocking on heaven's door."

Shaking her head remorsefully, Estella inspected the bruises and stitches on Isabel's face.

"That swollen eye will open up soon. Don't worry, it will heal. *Por Dios*, they really did a number on you, *mija*, but I'm proud of the way you handled yourself."

"Why didn't you tell me that you were sick? Joe said you didn't think I could handle it. Was that true?"

"No, his words were meant to wound you. Isa, you are stronger than you know. I knew you would have stayed, and I wanted better for you. If I had told you I was sick, you never would have returned to school."

"But if I had stayed, Joe would have left, and you would still be alive."

"There's no point in looking at what could have been. The choices we make shape our path. My choices are behind me now, but you still have a long road ahead of you."

Estella looked at the boxes of Joe's belongings and said, "I like what you've done with the place so far."

"I have plans for the farmhouse, but it won't be the same without you. I'm not sure if it will ever feel like home again."

"Home isn't a place, it's a feeling. If you ever want to know whether you are home, just place your hand on your heart," Estella said as she placed Isabel hand on her chest.

"Every time you feel your heart beating, know that I am with you, because you are a part of me. You are the piece of us that lives on, you are home."

"Piece of us?"

"All of your family that came before. Our lives, our dreams are all realized in you. And we are never really gone, as long as you live. When you feel alone, concentrate, and you will hear my voice or feel my presence."

"I heard you calling me from the tunnel of light. You told me to keep fighting. You said I had an important job to do, what did you mean by that?"

"Isa, I need you to stay focused. I have something important to tell you. You did good by not listening to the darkness, but it's not done with you yet."

"Mom used to talk about the darkness. Was the darkness really talking to her, or was she just crazy?"

"That's a complicated question. Back when we were children, she always saw things and heard voices that no one else did. But she didn't become violent until the darkness started speaking to her. You have to understand, the darkness can twist you and convince you to do things you'd never otherwise think of doing. Your mother and father were victims of the darkness."

"Since I can see you, will I see other spirits?"

"Yes."

A gentle hand rested on Isabel's shoulder. She turned around and was embraced by her mother. She squeezed her tight and said, "You did so good sweetie. You grew up strong and I'm going to need you stay that way."

Isabel looked around the room, fearful that see would see her father next.

"We understand it must be difficult to accept what you are seeing but Estella and I are watching over you."

Tears rolled down Isabel's cheeks. There were too many questions to ask. She started to speak, but no words would form. She trembled as she stared at the spirits of her family. They were luminescent, warm, and appeared to be at peace.

"You came from the light to warn me about the darkness?"

"Yes, we crossed the ether to bring you a message," Estella said, as she stood beside Marisol.

"So how do I stop the darkness?"

"You've looked into the darkness and now the darkness has looked into you. It is a wanting, hungry beast. You managed to refuse it and the darkness doesn't like to be denied., Marisol said.

"It's touched you and left its mark, and that mark will draw creatures and otherworldly machinations might seek you out. You must be on guard. You will be tested and tempted. A storm is coming, and you have a job to do. Fight the dark; hold it back with everything you've got," Estella said.

"I don't understand, what do you mean, I have a job to do?"

"You'll understand everything soon enough. *Sé fuerte* and keep your eyes open. As for your job, do what you do best and write. Tell the story." Estella said.

"Tell what story?"

"The only story that matters, the story of the light holding back the dark." Estella said.

"We love you; Isa and we will always be with you." Marisol said, as he wrapped her arms around Isabel.

"I love you, mom."

"Be strong." Marisol whispered in Isabel's ear.

Estella wrapped her arms around Isabel. For a moment, Isabel was surrounded by the perfect light of peace. The memories of her time with them flowed through her, not in a linear fashion, but a ceaseless wave. The pain and sadness faded away, and there was nothing but the light connecting her to her family and everything in the world beyond. All the love she ever felt surrounded her, intangible, but realer than anything she had ever known.

Her being was intertwined to everything in the light. In that light, all knowledge of the universe was open to her, she felt it live and breathe within her. Isabel was whole and untarnished by the tragedy of her life. In the light there were no questions left unanswered or words unspoken. Every moment touched by love and hope was replayed, flowing as a single stream of consciousness.

This is what heaven must feel like.

The light flared in a blinding spiral. Isabel closed her eyes but could still see the flash from beneath her eyelids. Estella and Marisol vanished, and her arms were outstretched as the last of the light faded away. The detachment from the light was jarring and painful. She longed to be surrounded by it again. As the warmth and connection faded, she was left cold and alone.

The room was emptier and dimmer than before. Isabel's head throbbed, the pain from her injuries came rushing back with startling force. The fading memory of the unification and knowledge of the light seemed almost cruel. By the time she reached the rocking chair, the sensation of the light was little more than a dream, of which she could barely recall. She tried to cling to the tactile sensations of their arms around her and the scent of Estella's perfume, but that soon faded as well.

Isabel wrapped her arms around herself and wept as the chorus of "In My Life" echoed through the room. She stumbled back into the rocking-chair and held her face in her hands.

What am I supposed to do now? This is too much, Estella and Dad crossed through the veil to warn me about the darkness and tell me to fight it. The darkness is coming for me. How the fuck do I hold back the dark?

She sat in the rocking-chair and cried herself to sleep. Sometime later the rhythmic thumping of a hand gently tapping at the front door woke her. She stood up and lethargically walked to the door. Isabel opened the door to find an old man with leathery brown skin and a white cowboy hat waiting patiently.

"Hello, I believe we have an appointment."

Shit, it's the brujo, I forgot he was coming. Before she could acknowledge her guest, Diego emerged from the garage covered in dust.

"You must be the brujo." Diego said as he walked up the front steps and onto the porch.

"Hello, my name is Aurelio Martinez. Your friend Birdie said you were in need of my services."

"Thank God, you're here. The darkness actually hurt her. I've been afraid to leave her alone." Diego said.

"It touched you?" Aurelio said as he turned to Isabel.

"It touched my arm." Isabel said as she pulled up her sleeve to show Aurelio her injury.

The brujo held his hand over her arm. The red blistered flesh looked worse in the light of day.

"Hmm. We need to get to work." Aurelio said.

"You can stop it, right? You can get rid of the darkness?" Diego said.

"Yes, in a way, but we need privacy. You need to leave. Your energy is very protective and might inadvertently hinder the ritual, but don't worry she is safe with me."

"Wait, so you want me to leave?"

"Yes." Aurelio said, as he entered the farmhouse and closed the door in Diego's face.

"What the hell, man?" Diego said.

"Oh, excuse me." Isabel said as she walked around the brujo and opened the door to an affronted Diego.

"We should begin straight away." Aurelio said.

"Yes, but I should say goodbye to Diego first. Pardon me for just a second."

Diego was still standing at the door. His cheeks were red, and he was visibly stunned by the brujo.

"I'll be okay. I will call you once we're done here."

"Are you sure about this guy?"

Isabel turned back to look at Aurelio, there was an aura of light surrounding him that reminded her of the light from the tunnel.

He's connected to the light. He can help.

"I am."

"But-"

"I'll call you later, once the ritual is over." Isabel said as she closed the door.

Isabel turned back to the brujo. Refocusing on her stout houseguest, Isabel realized he was quite short. She towered over him by at least six inches. He had a large potbelly that hung over his belt buckle. Worried he could sense her thoughts, Isabel refrained from internally humming the tune I'm a little teapot. His long white hair and bushy white beard gave him the appearance of a Mexican Santa Clause which only added to his air of wisdom and kindness. He walked with a slight limp and breathed heavily as he shuffled around the living room. A large white satchel, hug from his shoulder. Aurelio looked up and down as if searching of something, then his eyes rested on Isabel. He stepped toward her and placed his hands over hers.

"You've just had a visitation."

"Yes, I did. How did you know?"

He hesitated, not answering her question.

"Now, you see how the world truly is. That's a heavy burden, but I see strength in you. You will come to terms with that knowledge in time and accept that you have a place in the fight against the darkness."

"I don't really understand what I'm supposed to do."

He looked up at her. Isabel could sense that Aurelio was looking beyond her eyes, he was accessing her soul. He didn't blink, or show any expression of judgment, he just looked into her. She wanted to look away, but the blue haze around his brown eyes reminded Isabel of the glow from the tunnel. He was part of the light.

"You must do what they told you to do. *Sé fuerte* and tell your story. You are walking the path, even if you aren't aware of it."

Isabel wilted in his arms, reduced to sobs. He held her and gently rocked back and forth. He smelled of palo santo and sandalwood. She breathed in deeply as she wept.

"*Tranquila*," Aurelio whispered.

After her eyes were dry and there were no more tears left to cry, Isabel composed herself. She wiped away the tears and said, "I'm so sorry for crying all over you."

"It's okay, it happens more than you would think. Now let's get to work. You have more than *mala suerte* to get rid of."

Aurelio opened his satchel and retrieved numerous objects, placing them methodically on the floor. He had several old Cool-Whip containers which held palo santo, shells, roots, a black feather, and lots of candles. He placed the items on the floor, lit the candles and chanted in Nahuatl. Isabel did her best to sit on the sofa and observe the brujo, without making a sound. He pulled himself from the floor, held out his hand, and guided Isabel to the circle of candles.

"I am going to burn the palo santo and say a prayer for your protection. I will then bless the house to remove the negativity of the man who lived here. His violence clings to this place. The darkness has held this place hostage for far too long."

Surrounded by the glow of the candles, Isabel sat in the center. The scent of the burning palo santo was sweet and clean. She closed her eyes as the brujo chanted. His voice echoed through the room, surrounding her. There was magic in his words, the room seemed to pulse and vibrate as he spoke.

He handed Isabel a gnarled root and said, "Once the darkness touches you it leaves a stain, now, imagine that stain seeping out of you and into the root. You have to see it in your mind's eye."

Isabel held the root in her hands and closed her eyes. She tried to imagine the darkness with a physical form, like smoke or ash. She imagined the smoke leaving her body and wafting into the root. She opened one eye to see if it was working. Nothing happened.

Shit, I'm doing it wrong.

"Darkness feeds on your pain, fear, anger, and regret. You have to let go of it to be free."

"I've lived with fear and regret most of my life, if I knew how to let go, I would have done it already."

"You have seen the light; you know what peace feels like. Your sadness and anger are transient. Everything that weighs down your soul falls away in the light."

"But I'm here, I'm not in the light. I'm alone, separated from my family. They are part of the light, but I'm stuck down here, surrounded by darkness."

"You need to try to find the light within yourself."

"That's easier said than done, I've always been able to see the darkness in others and in myself. How am I supposed to find the light when all I see is dark?"

The brujo threw up his hands in frustration and said, "*Ay, por dios.*"

"I'm sorry, I wish I knew how to let go, but I don't. I felt the light in the river and with Estella and Mom. I know that it's real, but I'm not sure I can harness it in myself."

Aurelio knelt down in front of Isabel and placed his hands on the side of her face. He closed his eye and prayed under his breath.

He looked up at Isabel and said, "You're not going to like this part, but it needs to happen."

"What do you mean?"

"You need to confront the source of your pain."

Oh Christ. What's going to happen next?

The candles flickered around them. The door swung open with a gust of wind, Isabel jumped to her feet.

"Don't be afraid." Aurelio said.

"Isabel."

A familiar voice called to her from the doorway. Isabel gasped as her father entered the farmhouse.

"No, I'm not ready to see him."

"You need to confront your greatest fear and source of pain."

"Dad?"

"I understand why you don't want to see me. After what I did, I don't blame you. But you need to let go of your anger, or it will consume you. Rage is an open invitation the darkness."

"I'm not angry at you, I was scared of you. I feared you more than anything, more than drowning, mental illness, and more than death. My whole life I was afraid I was going to hurt those I loved, just like you did. I kept everyone at an arm's length because I knew I was cursed by what you did. I know it was the darkness that caused you to destroy our family, but you listened to it. You were cruel and weak."

"You've heard the darkness and you were able to resist it. You're stronger than I ever was. The darkness didn't just speak to me, it showed me things. I saw its terrible intentions and I broke. But you won't. You don't have to forgive me, but you have to let go of your fear of becoming me. You looked into the void, and you didn't break. Let go of that fear and you will thrive. You are not like me."

Isabel crumpled, falling to the floor into a heap of tears. The fear that had driven her life and work was exposed and seeping out of her.

Who would I become and what would happen if I let it go?

"Let go of the fear and you will be free." Aurelio said.

Aurelio nodded and helped Isabel off the floor. She wiped her cheeks and sat back down in the circle. He placed the root in her hands and stepped back. Alberto turned toward the door and began to walk out, but before he disappeared into the light, Isabel called out to him.

"*Se fuerte, mija,*" Alberto stepped through the doorway, and, in a blur of blinding light and a gust of wind, vanished.

"*Listo?*" Aurelio said as he lit the candles that had been extinguished by Alberto's exit.

"I'm ready." Isabel said.

Having faced her darkest fear, she focused on the root, closed her eyes and imagined the darkness and anger as a mucky sludge that seeped out of her wounds. Isabel opened her eyes.

Did it work?

The patchwork of stitches covering her lacerations burst open. Black sludge oozed out. It was cold as it slithered down her cheeks and arms. She gasped, dropping the root on the floor. Hissing and whispering, the muck swirled and crept into the root, turning it black. Aurelio covered the root with a cloth and put it into his satchel.

Isabel exhaled and placed her arms at her side to steady herself. A crippling weight, she was unaware that she had been carrying, lifted. Breathing easier, she felt exhausted, yet lighter.

Fear and pain are heavier than I thought.

"I will burn this later and tonight. You will say prayers to whatever deity you believe in. I can't remove all of the darkness. It is a part of us all, but the part you fed and held onto is gone."

"I'm not sure what I believe in, but I know that there is a force behind the light."

"Then pray to the light."

Aurelio blew out the candles and helped Isabel to her feet. He handed her a fresh bundle of palo santo.

"The darkness has touched you. Unfortunately, the mark on your arm will leave a scar."

"I think I will end up with quite a few scars from this whole ordeal."

"Remember, the darkness stains. Though it left its mark on you, that doesn't mean it rules over you."

"I'll try to keep that in mind."

"Isabel, take care."

"I think I'll be okay if a nasty scare is all that's left from the darkness."

"Well, I wouldn't say you have nothing else to worry about."

"What do you mean? I thought the ritual means the darkness can't hurt me anymore."

"It no longer has sway over your life, but that doesn't mean it will stop trying. The shadow figure and the sludge are gone, but there may be other agents of the dark that seek you out."

"What do you mean by agents of the darkness?"

"Otherworldly things may be attracted to you now. You must protect yourself. You need to burn a stick of palo santo once every two months during a new moon."

He pulled out a small pouch from his satchel and said, "Reach inside my bag and pick two stones. Don't look inside, just pull out the first two stones that you touch."

Isabel reached inside the bag. Two small river stones rolled between her fingers, she grabbed them and pulled them out. There were small etchings carved into the rocks. She handed the rocks to Aurelio, and he inspected each.

He nodded his head and said, "One rock is fire and the other is a wolf. The fire and the wolf will be your protectors."

"What are they, what do they mean?"

"They are totems, symbols of protection. I will bury them on your property to keep away anything that seeks to harm you. This farmhouse will be your safe haven from the darkness. Nothing and no one with bad intent can cross this property line."

"Thank you so much, Aurelio."

"It was my pleasure to help a fellow child of the light."

Aurelio wiped his brow. The ritual appeared to exhaust him, and Isabel helped him repack his satchel. He rubbed his temples and sat down on the sofa.

"I'm sorry, sometimes the rituals take a lot out of me."

"Are you okay?"

"*No te preocupes*. I'll be fine. Babalu Aye may heal me once I am able to meditate and bring him an offering."

He used an old bandanna to wipe his face. With what seemed like tremendous effort, he scooted off the sofa and stood up.

"Can I get you something? I have coffee, water, or I've got a ton of pies in the fridge, if you're hungry."

"I'll pass; thank you, though. Before I go, I need to bury these totems around your property. Where I bury the totems, darkness cannot pass."

He buried the stone with the wolf etched in front of the steps leading to the porch. For about fifteen minutes he milled around the exterior of the farmhouse, turning the fire stone in his hand. He made his way to the riverbank and buried the stone. He dusted off his hands and stared at the empty clothesline.

"A bride of darkness has been here."

"La Llorona saved me. She's not a monster, she was a victim who was manipulated by the darkness. Is there any way to free a bride of darkness?"

"The only way to liberate a soul from the darkness is to bring that soul peace. La Llorona has been lost in her grief and bound by revenge. I'm not sure she will ever be able to find peace."

"There has to be a way."

"*Fantasmas* can be tricky to liberate, especially one who was corrupted by the darkness. I don't know if there is a way to help her. I don't think you should pursue further action. If you spend too much time with the dead, you may forget you are one of the living."

Isabel didn't have a response to the brujo's words of caution. He was wise and she was a novice in this world. She would consider his advice, but she desperately wanted to help the ghost that had saved her life.

There must be a way to bring the weeping woman peace.

"You and your property are protected. I must go. I have another appointment with another child of light. A young burden eater needs her annual spiritual cleansing. She takes in a lot of nasty burdens and like me, removing darkness wears her down."

"Burden eaters exist?"

"Yes, there are just as many children of light as there are of darkness."

"Could the burden eater be the answer to helping La Llorona find peace? If she can help the living find peace, maybe she could do the same for a heavily burdened spirit?"

"A burden eater can only take the burdens of the living. The dead are beyond their reach, I'm sorry."

"Well shit," Isabel said as she walked Aurelio to his truck. She kissed him on the cheek. "I can't thank you enough."

"No need, I'm happy to help."

Squeezing his massive belly behind the steering wheel, Aurelio cursed under his breath as he shut the creaky truck door.

"I expect to hear from you soon, but it's time for me to go. *Ten cuidado*. Dark days are still ahead, but don't despair, there's light within you."

"Wait, what?"

Without answering, he started up the truck, put it in drive and rumbled down the dirt road. Isabel watched as it disappeared from view. The sky was clear as the sun set, the storm had passed, and the air was crisp and clean. Birds

243

sang in the trees beyond the grass field and crickets began their nightly chorus.

What did he mean by expecting to hear from me soon? And how much darkness was ahead?

The question disappeared from her thoughts as Diego's rumbling truck pulled into the driveway. He slid out of the driver's side as he carefully balanced an arm full of baked goods and another casserole.

Holding a basket of muffins under his chin, Diego said, "I waited for the brujo's truck to pass my place before coming over. The chocolate chip muffins are great, I may have eaten one or two on the way here."

"Thanks for coming back. I'm sorry for kicking you out so abruptly."

"It's okay. Did the ritual work?" Diego asked as he looked past Isabel into the living room.

"It worked, but my soul may be a little worse for wear."

"How do you mean?"

"It was an intense process. I was confronted by the spirit of my father."

"Wow, sounds like you've had an eventful day."

"You have no idea; I'll tell you all about it over dinner. Is that a tuna casserole?" Isabel asked.

Diego nodded, "Yup. So, are you ready for round two of the dreaded tuna casserole tonight?"

"If the darkness doesn't kill me, the tuna casserole might do the trick."

***

Isabel told Diego about her vision of Estella, her Dad, and the brujo's ritual, as he reheated the casserole.

244

Completely spent, she only managed a few bites of her meal. The magnitude of the reunions and revelations weighed heavy.

"You really did have an eventful day. How do you feel?"

"I'm tired, but I feel better, I guess. I watched as the darkness left my body. There was a black sludge that came out of me. It was the same sludge that flowed out the kitchen last night."

"So that stuff that attacked you, was actually inside you?"

"Yes, the darkness is in all of us. It stains you."

"That's one hell of a stain."

"That's putting it mildly."

"Estella told you to write. What are you going to write about?" Diego said.

"I have to write about the light holding back the dark?"

"Well then, I guess you better find some light in all this darkness."

"I don't know where to start."

"Start with finding the light inside yourself and then maybe you can find it in others."

"You're the second person to tell me something like that today. I'm not sure of the light inside myself, but I see the light in you. You're a good man, Diego."

"I see the light in you, even if you can't see it in yourself." Diego said.

"I let go of my darkness today. I feared becoming like Mom. It was the reason I kept everyone at a distance. I'm free of that fear and I don't want to push people away anymore. I don't want to spend my life surrounded by death and darkness. I want to live."

"Then let's start living." Diego said.

"I'm ready. *Se fuerte*."

Dinner and their conversation of otherworldly topics concluded. After washing the dishes, Diego helped her up the stairs and into bed.

"I don't want to be alone. Would you stay with me again tonight?" Isabel said.

"Wow, asking me to sleep with you already. You're moving a little too fast for me Isa." Diego said with a chuckle.

"Ha ha, very funny, but I think we have something here. I mean, I think there is something between us, although, I'm not sure what it is yet."

"Oh Isa, you don't have to worry, I think we need to take this, whatever it is, slowly. Besides, I'm here for you as a friend, and, no offense, but you look like a Romero movie reject. I promise, my intentions are honorable. Don't get me wrong, even black and blue you are still beautiful."

"You're such a bad liar." Isabel said.

"Once you're healed up, if you want, I can sneak through your window. Just like old times, but until then, I'm here for you."

She clutched her cheek as she chuckled and said, "I appreciate that, thanks. Once I'm better, ask me again about sneaking up to my room."

"I will."

He handed Isabel her Glo Worm and laid down beside her. With its soft light cutting through the darkness, she drifted off to sleep in his arms. It was far from the perfect light of the tunnel, but it was close enough. She was safe and content with Diego by her side. Her sleep that night was deep and free of nightmares.

CHAPTER SIXTEEN
The Light

Several weeks had passed since the attack and Isabel settled into her new role taking over operations of Estella's ranch. As she recovered, she became a whirling force of purpose and action. Liberated from the fear and darkness that had gripped her since childhood, she was determined to live the rest of her life surrounded by friends and hope.

She listed her house in California for sale and relocated all her belongings to the farmhouse. With the help of a moving crew, Birdie, and Diego, Isabel managed to combine her home furnishings with Estella's. The farmhouse was a perfect blend of Isabel's mid-century aesthetic and homage to Estella's Southwestern style. Throughout the days, multiple carpenters and electricians repaired the damaged walls and old wiring. No more creepy flickering lights and shadow filled rooms.

During the warmest part of the day, the fresh coat of exterior paint wafted through the open windows, but Isabel didn't mind. The aroma was physical proof of a change for the better. She was sure that Estella would have liked the alterations. In time, the farmhouse felt like home again. Isabel was at ease in her new, yet familiar surroundings.

Her injuries were healing, the black bruise on her face had started to turn yellow and her stitches had been removed. The white of her left eye was still speckled and red, but at least she was able to open it. The scabs and cuts on her back healed, leaving tiny pink impressions in their wake. The scar on her cheek was the most prominent, leaving an angry red line where the stitches had been. White baby hairs sprouted in the spot that had been shaved for surgery. The growth of white hair was a result of the trauma. Isabel didn't particularly mind the streak of white hair or the scar on her cheek. The changes in her appearance were evidence of her survival and she celebrated them, with the exception of the burn mark on her arm. As a reactionary precaution, Isabel started wearing long sleeves to avoid looking at it. She hoped that one day she would come to accept that scar as she had the others.

She had a rather nasty purple and yellow bruise that lingered around her ribs. That bruise bothered her the most, she inspected it nightly in the mirror, hoping to see it fade. The bruise took the shape of a clawed hand, wrapping around her ribs. She decided it was the hand of the darkness, trying to take a hold of her. The thought turned her skin to goose flesh and made her legs buckle at the knees.

As one week flowed into the next, Isabel felt better. Her ribs still ached when she moved too quickly or took a deep breath, but even that pain had become more manageable. Her family's warning continued to perplex her, but she figured the answers would come in time. Isabel focused her attention on healing and writing her new manuscript, which consumed most of her days.

Her emotional scars would take longer to fade. The sound of hammering and roar of the table-saws throughout the day put her on edge. She constantly looked over her shoulder. In still moments, after the carpenters left for the day, Isabel felt as if she were being watched from a distance. She would scan the room for signs of the shadow figure, but it had not reappeared since the brujo's ritual. She had regular visits and conversations with Dr. Duvall and a trauma counselor on a weekly basis. They assured her the anxiety would fade.

Each day was such a flurry of activity that she barely had time to think about Joe or Debbie. The nights, however, were different. The silence of the farmhouse gave way to nightmares and flashbacks. The visions and sleepwalking had ceased, but restful sleep was still elusive.

Most nights, Diego slept at the farmhouse with her, but he hadn't climbed through her window yet. They were taking things slow, and admittedly, Isabel wasn't ready for the next step. Diego had taken her to the Drive-in on Saturday night. They caught the double feature of *Poltergeist* and John Carpenter's *The Fog*. Diego wrapped his arm around her as he munched on popcorn and Red Vines, and for a moment she was a teenager again. Struggling to fight the urge to reach over and kiss Diego, she worried that she still looked like an extra from Night of the Living Dead. Once the claw shaped bruise faded, she would make her move. Diego's company was welcome, and she cherished their growing friendship and the possibility for something more.

Tonight, she was hosting a small get together, in celebration of her official move to the farmhouse. Aside from a couple of unpacked boxes, she was completely settled in. Her guest list included Birdie and her husband James and their children as well as Diego, Rosa, and Deputy Wake.

Isabel and Deputy Wake had developed a friendship over the last few weeks. He introduced her to a trauma survivors' group that met at the bingo hall. The group mainly consisted of veterans and survivors of violent crimes. Although Deputy Wake had told Isabel to call him Severin on numerous occasions, she had to consciously stop herself from referring to him as Deputy. Severin had experienced his fair share of tragedy. His father was a police officer who had been gunned down off-duty, when he attempted to intervene in a robbery. Isabel and Severin bonded over their shared paternal loss. Isabel's expanding circle of friends, gave her a sense of community and family. For the first time in over a decade, she wasn't alone.

Birdie suggested having a housewarming party. She told Isabel that it was time to celebrate the good things in life. Birdie was bringing the barbecue and Isabel was baking a pie. Last Tuesday, during bunco, Norma gave Isabel the recipe for her award-winning pineapple pie. Her only condition was that she name a character from Isabel's next book after her. Isabel tried to follow the recipe to Norma's exact specification, but the consistency of the crust was too crumbly. She hoped that Birdie's barbecued pork-shoulder would be the main event of the evening, and her pie could be a pleasant afterthought.

The housewarming party was six hours from starting. Isabel spent the morning as a thundering force of action. She dusted, vacuumed, and finished unpacking her closet. With the house tidied up and suitable for hosting guests, Isabel had a sufficient amount of time to kill, so she returned to her manuscript.

After three hours of diligent typing, she was close to finishing her final chapter. Fueled by caffeine, Isabel sat at her writing desk. She was writing the story of La Llorona, the weeping woman.

She leaned back in her seat and paused for a moment, "This story doesn't feel finished yet."

She rolled a pen around with her index finger, considering what constituted a happy ending for a ghost. She looked at the book of *Latin American Folktales*, which rested next to her laptop. Isabel opened the book to the chapter on La Llorona.

"I owe her the truth. She deserves a better ending." Isabel said, frustrated.

For the last few weeks, Isabel searched for La Llorona. At the bank of the river, she would call out to the weeping woman, but there was never an answer. Isabel wanted to express her gratitude, but also wished to express that despite not being able to bring her justice or peace, she could at least give truth to her legend.

Isabel took a labored breath, rubbing her aching side. A sharp twinge of pain shot through her side and down her arm. The muscles in her hand twitched, which caused the book to fall to the floor with a thump.

"Shit!" She stared at the fallen book, hoping she could compel it back into her hand via the power of the force.

I'm no Jedi.

"Ouch." Isabel grumbled as her hand hovered over the open book, it had fallen open to the chapter regarding the burden eater. Cautiously, Isabel sat up and started to read the excerpt.

Settling back into her seat, she took a labored breath and continued to read. Isabel was reminded by something Diego had said, "If ghosts exist, what else was out there?"

His question created a pit in her stomach, that had yet to fade. She sat awake at night and wondered, what lurks in the darkness? The only way to ease the spiral of fear was to think back to the advice of the brujo. He said that there were just as many children of the light as there were agents of the darkness. Knowing that there were beings that worked in service of the light, eased her fears.

Burden eaters were real; the brujo confirmed it. He said that burden eaters were children of light. They must hold back the darkness too.

"That's it, that's the story I need to tell next."

Estella had instructed Isabel to write the story of the light, holding back the dark. While writing about La Llorona, Isabel felt as if she was drowning in the darkness of her story. Once she found a satisfying ending to the story of La Llorona, she could stop focusing on the darkness and start telling the story of the light.

She placed the book on the table and retrieved a sticky note. Inspiration rushed through her hand as she scribbled on the notepad, Research burden eaters. Call the brujo and ask to speak with the burden eater he's helping.

She placed the sticky note on her laptop. She snatched up of the book of *Latin American Folktales*. With shaking hands, she flipped through the pages and dogeared the page titled, The Burden Eater.

She leaned back in the chair, "Well at least I've got the subject for my next book figured out. But that doesn't help me with La Llorona's ending."

Excitement for her future writing prospects gave way to sadness as she considered the impending ending of her current manuscript. She wanted the weeping woman to find peace. So many of the women who had influenced, and shaped Isabel's life had met tragic ends. She was unable to help her mother or Estella, but she wanted to help the weeping woman, if she could.

Rubbing the bridge of her nose with her fingers, she leaned back and said, "How am I going to end this story?"

A single stream of smoke escaped the oven and wafted into the den. She sat up quickly, which caused her side to tense and spasm.

"Shit, I forgot about the pie."

She rubbed her waist and forced herself out of the chair. Isabel hurried into the kitchen in order to grab the smoke detector and stop its blaring chirps. She grabbed it, tossed it into the other room and retrieved Estella's chicken shaped oven mitt.

"Please don't be too burned."

Repeating her words like a prayer, she pulled open the oven door. Heat and the sweet scent of hot pineapple pie filled the room. She removed the pie from the oven, placing it on the kitchen window to cool. She examined the outer edges of the crust. Thankfully, it was darkened, but not burnt.

"That's not too bad." Isabel said.

She was sure her guests wouldn't notice the somewhat darker edges of the crust. She flicked away some of the crispy edges and popped them in her mouth. Hot crumbles of crust, burned the tips of her tongue as she inhaled, trying to cool the smoldering bits of crust that rolled around in mouth. The taste of butter, salt and a hint of sugar overpowered any sense that the pie was over cooked. Not too bad at all.

"Eh, they know that cooking isn't my thing."

The scent of hot pineapple caught the cool breeze and the warm sunshine touched her face. She stood in front of the open window and closed her eyes. She enjoyed the quite moment free from shadow figures and looming nightmares. She glanced out the window to the edge of the river.

Where are you La Llorona?

As if summoned by Isabel's will, the spirit appeared at the river's edge. Isabel ran out of the back door as fast as her healing ribs would allow. The weeping woman stood on the sandy bank with an unreadable expression on her face.

"Thank you for saving my life." Isabel said, between gasps.

Rolling spasms reverberated through her broken ribs and for a moment, Isabel thought she might pass-out or vomit. She bent down and breathed through the pain, waiting for the weeping woman to approach.

"I've been looking for you." Isabel said breathlessly.

The weeping woman took a step forward but stopped as if she walked into an invisible barrier. She stared at the spot where the brujo had buried the totem.

"I'm sorry, I can't come any closer. The magic bound to this totem will not allow me cross. I mean you no harm, but, as you know, there is darkness inside me.

"I'm sorry, he did it to keep me safe."

"You don't have to be sorry. I am glad the darkness cannot enter. Given half the chance the darkness would come for you. At least you are safe in your home. There's something else about you that's different. You've found your light."

"I have a light around me. I can't see it; I don't feel any different."

"The light touched you. It gave you a job to do and it looks like you have found your path."

"I guess, I decided to focus on beings of light. I'm going to write about burden eaters, but I have a project that I'm currently working on that still needs an ending."

"Writing about the light is a good idea. You should focus on the light and forget the darkness and all the creatures in it, like me."

"I've been looking for you. Every morning and at dusk, I called out to you. I was worried you had left and that I would never see you again. I wanted to thank you and I want to help you."

"I wanted to give you space. The brujo was right, if you spend too much time with the dead, you will forget you are one of the living. I hoped you would have pushed the memory of me away like you did when you were a child. I hoped that, eventually, I would have been nothing more than a bad dream."

"I don't want to forget you. You saved me and I'm forever grateful. I want to help you. I want to free you from the darkness, but I don't know how to bring you peace."

"I couldn't save my children or Estella. I have failed so many others, but I am glad that I did not fail you. I turned myself into a monster by killing Roberto and Vanessa. I am forever cursed for it but knowing you will live has given me some peace."

Touched by La Llorona's words, Isabel hugged the weeping woman. The weeping woman began to tremble in Isabel's arms.

"What is happening to me?" La Llorona said, as she dropped to her knees.

The weeping woman convulsed as sludge welled from her eyes and dripped down her face. Streaming snakes of muck rolled down her arms and pooled at her legs. The sludge weaved around her legs and tried to take hold of her. Isabel grabbed La Llorona's arms and pulled the weeping woman forward. As her body slid over the buried totem, the darkness hissed and retreated. They watched as tentacles of darkness spiraled into a whirlpool in the sand. La Llorona pulled off her veil and threw it into the pooling muck as it sank beneath the surface. The hiss of the darkness reached a piercing pitch as it vanished into the earth.

Light surrounded Isabel and the weeping woman. Isabel closed her eyes as she held La Llorona. The cold, wet flesh turned warm and soft. As the brilliant light faded, Isabel opened her eyes and released La Llorona. Her pale skin had been changed from deathly white to brown. The electric blue of her eyes faded to their natural color. No longer a bride of darkness, she was transformed. The weeping woman ran her hands over her arms and touched her face.

"I've been a captive of the darkness for so long that I forgot what it felt like to be free." The weeping woman held out her hands to Isabel and said, "Look, I am as I was, before the darkness."

"This is amazing. You're free, but how?"

"It was you. You gave me peace; your kindness and friendship, saved me."

"If you're no longer a bride of darkness and bound to the river, are you free to enter the light?"

She shook her head and said, "I don't know the way to the light, and I am afraid. I don't know what's in the light or if my children are there. What if I can't go where they are?"

Two small voices echoed from the river's edge. The weeping woman clasped her hands over her mouth as she turned around.

"They're here. My babies are here." La Llorona said.

"Mamma, it's time to come home with us!" Jose said.

Jose and Amelia held hands and waved to their mother. The children were surrounded by a glowing aura of light. They reached out to their mother and La Llorona ran to them. She fell to her knees as she wrapped her arms around them. La Llorona trembled as she held her children. She kissed their foreheads as they hugged her tight.

"We were waiting for you Mommy." Amelia said.

"I'm sorry, *mija*, I just got lost in the dark."

"Don't worry Mommy, we found you. We won't let you get lost again; we know the way home."

As she wept, Jose brushed the tears from her face and said, "Mommy you don't have to cry anymore, let's go."

La Llorona smiled, "My children, if I am with you, I will never have the need to shed another tear. I'm ready."

Isabel stood motionless. The redemptive power of peace was the ultimate expression of the light holding back the dark. Reunited with her children, La Llorona would truly know peace. That was a fitting ending to the story of the weeping woman.

The spirit stood up and walked hand in hand with her children. They walked away from the river, passing Isabel. Spindles of lightning erupted from a cloudless sky. Its electric flashes opened a tunnel which awaited La Llorona and her children.

Isabel yelled, "Wait! I want to write your story. I want the world to know the truth about you. What is your real name?"

La Llorona looked back at Isabel and smiled, "My name is Romania."

The three figures turned away from Isabel, continuing to walk toward the tunnel of light. As they reached the entrance, they vanished in a golden flash. The lightning retreated back into the sky and the tunnel disappeared. La Llorona and her children had gone home to the light.

"Thank you, Romania." Isabel said as tears streamed down her cheeks.

The wind blew a warm breeze across her face, brushing away the tears. She turned to look back at the river. It had once encapsulated her deepest fears and carried spirits of loss and darkness. Now it carried a current which brought with it a new sense of hope and redemption. Isabel found the light.

She walked back to the farmhouse and into the den. Sitting at her writing desk, she wrote the perfect ending to Romania's story. What she thought would be her last tale of darkness, turned out to be her first story of light overcoming the dark. The story of the weeping woman was a tale of loss and redemption. Romania was finally free from the dark and so was Isabel.

9 781737 463375